"If this is our nirvana, then I've died happy, Penrose."

The world had turned inside out. She was staring at candles that burned under the water. They were a different kind of fire.

She looked up at Keat. He was a different kind of man. Not a dark twin to Carrick. And what if this really was her brief nirvana? What if this was the only happiness she could grasp? Wouldn't Carrick want it for her? Of course he would. Carrick himself said, "Fire has no choice but grab its moment, whatever moment it's given, and burn."

A different century. A different kind of fire. A different man, one she couldn't help but to burn for. Was this the moment she'd been given? It was. She turned to Keat and said, "Take me to bed now."

"My pleasure," he replied and reached down for her.

HOUSE OF SHADOWS

JEN CHRISTIE

MILLS & BOON

First Published in Great Britain 2016
By Mills & Boon, an imprint of HarperCollins*Publishers*
1 London Bridge Street, London, SE1 9GF

© 2016 Jennifer Grannis

ISBN: 978-0-263-92160-1

89-0116

Jen Christie is a writer who has a passion for reading and writing Gothic romances. Jen lives in St. Augustine, Florida, with her husband and three daughters. She has a love of history and her secret desire is to stop and read every roadside historical marker she drives by.

I dedicate this book to my sister Penny,
who taught me that life is full of second chances,
and they are always worth taking.

Prologue

The grandfather clock tolled, echoing on and on. The sound reverberated in the tunnel until Penrose fell to the floor, covered her ears and buried her head in her skirts. The chimes came from everywhere at once, from all around her and even from within her own mind.

She couldn't think, couldn't move. She could only endure. Dust and plaster rained down and pelted her body. *Please,* she wished, *let it be a dream.* But she knew it wasn't. A dream doesn't hit you with plaster hard enough to hurt. Long, agonizing moments passed. It was as if time ceased.

Quietness returned slowly. The rumbling grew less ferocious until finally the ground was still, and the clock fell silent. Only then did she lift her head and take a breath. Dust filled her nostrils. Coughing, wiping her eyes and face, she called out in a panicked voice, "C.J.?"

He didn't answer. The only sound was a lone splatter of plaster falling to the floor somewhere in the darkness. She must find C.J. and see if he was okay, but it was too dangerous to crawl around without light.

Remembering that there were candles in the hallway, she began inching toward the door. She planned to grab a candle and hopefully find Carrick so that they could hunt for C.J. together. When she reached the door, she fumbled with the latch until it opened. The house was dark and quiet. Still on all fours, she took a deep, shaky breath and called, "C.J.? Carrick, are you here?"

No answer. She crawled out, stood up and brushed herself off, making sure she wasn't injured. Her hands traveled the length of her torso, but the lack of pain did nothing to reassure her that she was all right. She was not all right.

The air in the foyer was cold—too cold for August in Charleston. The house felt different. It smelled odd, of lemons and lavender. Something was wrong. She knew it in her bones.

"C.J.?" Desperation turned her voice harsh. "Carrick? Please! Answer me."

Still nothing.

Her eyes adjusted to the light, and she saw the grandfather clock standing against the wall. Standing. Not toppled over as she'd witnessed moments before. She looked around wildly. The table that normally held the candles wasn't there anymore. The chandelier hung still and straight as if it hadn't even moved, let alone swung wildly while the earth shook.

But what took the breath right from her lungs were the paintings. They were different—with odd, angular images in them. The more she looked around, the more uneasy she became. Yes, something was very, very wrong.

"Carrick?" she called again, taking minute, untrusting steps toward the great room, her hands pressing the air in disbelief. "Carrick! C.J.? Please?" she kept repeating in a whiny, almost begging manner. She held a last bit of hope that the world would right itself, and she'd see the familiar features of Arundell. Her Arundell. Not this twisted imitation.

When she entered the large parlor, she saw moonlight and shadows dancing around the room, revealing a dark doppelgänger of the room she knew and loved. The cold air around her made it scarier and even less familiar.

Yes, the bones of the room were the same. The same lofty ceiling, the same shape of the windows, even the familiar gouges in the doorway that marked the heights of the Arundell boys. But the essence had changed.

Everything had changed. She tried to reconcile the two different versions of her home—one familiar and one not—but she couldn't. It simply wasn't Arundell Manor.

Yet it was.

She went to the window and looked out. The world outside glimmered bright and white beneath the moon.

Bright and white. Snow.

No peaceful pond with a lazy oak tree beside it. No familiar road winding through the Charleston countryside straight to the front doors of her home. Only bare land covered in white stretched all the way to the horizon. Stepping away from the window as if it burned her, she found herself gasping for breath. She wanted to scream, to wail and cry for help, but she had no voice.

She took fast, short steps and went from room to room on the first floor, seeing unbelievable and frightening items everywhere she turned. The house had always been extravagant, but now it seemed garish. Every room was crammed with shiny and bizarre objects, things she didn't understand and was afraid to touch.

A huge mirror hung on the wall by the kitchen and her own shadowy form reflected back at her. Even she looked different. It was as if a ghost stared at her, coated in dust, hair wild and tumbling, the whites of its eyes glowing brightly. She had a horrible thought as she looked at herself. She'd died.

"I'm not dead," she said loudly, voicing that horrible thought. A worse thought sprang up behind it. Perhaps she'd been trapped in a kind of purgatory. A place between life and death.

"No." She shook her head wildly. So did the shadowy figure in the mirror. Leaning forward, she insisted to the image, "I'm alive. Alive." But her image seemed to stare back at her with accusing eyes and Penrose backed away, shaking.

The kitchen was unrecognizable, with silver equipment that had blue flashing lights on the different pieces. She knew it was a kitchen because of the sink, the knives that hung from the wall and the bowl of fresh fruit sitting atop the counter. A piece of paper lay beside the bowl, and by the dim blue light she read:

Dear Keat,
Welcome back to Arundell. Everything should be
in order. The kitchen is stocked. The robots have
been delivered and set up. If you need anything,
just call. Enjoy your time by yourself. Please, try
to relax. Stop worrying. You do your best work
that way.
—V

The note called this home Arundell, but unless the
world had changed overnight, this was not Arundell.
Not the Arundell she knew.

Part One

All in the dark we grope along,
And if we go amiss
We learn at least which path is wrong,
And there is gain in this.

—Ella Wheeler Wilcox

Part One

Chapter 1

Charleston, South Carolina
August 18, 1886

Penrose Heatherton stood at the window, her face lifted to the night sky, hoping for wind. But there was no wind to speak of. The skies were speckled with stars. The moon hung lazy and bright. It was a perfect Charleston summer evening and gave no hint of the troubles that lay ahead of her.

It was hot enough to boil water that night, and she wore her underthings in a futile effort to stay cool. The clothes clung to her damp skin and her black hair hung in sweaty strands. She fanned herself listlessly with the want ads from the newspaper. The effort only made her hotter. It didn't help that she'd just returned from the kitchen downstairs where she'd washed dishes for hours to help reduce the amount of rent she had to pay.

Rent. A knot of worry twisted in her chest and she rested her head against the window frame. Rent was due in the morning, and, even at a reduced rate, she had no way of paying. Renting her room at The Winding Stair Inn & Pub had already taken all of her funds.

She turned her face to the moon, pleading for wind. Tattered clouds sailed across it, scattering silvery light on the ground. None reached her. "Please," she whispered, hoping, waiting, for a gust to come and cool her down.

It seemed that, lately, she was always waiting. For a cool breeze or a hot meal, for a permanent job, for any sliver of relief, no matter how small, that would help fix the mess her life had become. She was tired, so very tired of waiting.

She tossed the want ads out of the window and watched as they fluttered to the ground. Worthless. If she'd learned one thing since her mother died six months earlier, it was that relief didn't come easy. If it came at all. No, she was beginning to understand the bitter truth—that if you wanted relief you had to grab it for yourself.

But you can't grab the wind, so she stood there sweating. Sighing, she went to the cot and lay down. If it got any hotter, even one degree, she would melt into a puddle. But right when she thought that was about to happen, there came a change.

A gust of wind slipped through the window and eddied in the small space. It was a strange wind. Wintery, cool and dry, with a touch of wildness to it. The breeze tossed about the room and swirled around Penrose like a cool promise. She sat up, feeling it slip and slide over her skin, and she had the sense that something, anything could happen.

Right at that exact moment, she heard the sound of boots walking down the hall. The footsteps belonged to Mrs. Capshaw, the landlady of The Winding Stair Inn & Pub. Her walk was distinctive. When it came your way you knew she wanted something, and sure enough, it was coming Penrose's way.

Not a moment later, the door flew open as the landlady swept into the tiny room. There was barely space for her, but she didn't seem to care. Mrs. Capshaw was an ample woman with frizzy red hair and a bosom that sat like a shelf over her stomach. She had sharp, assessing brown eyes, which right then took in the sight of Penrose lounging on the bed. She said in her tough-as-nails voice, "Look sharp, Penny. There's an opportunity for you downstairs."

Instantly, she had Penrose's attention. "What opportunity?"

Mrs. Capshaw was an enterprising woman, always on the lookout for any venture that would be advantageous. Coming from her, an opportunity could mean a million different things, most of them dubious. But opportunities were rare, and Penrose was desperate.

Another cool gust of wind blasted into the room, slamming the door shut. The older woman yanked it open again and held it in her meaty fist. "If you're clever," she said, leaning over Penrose and staring at her hard, "and I know you are, you'll listen carefully."

"I'm listening," said Penrose. She rubbed her arms as she listened. The temperature in the room must have dropped twenty degrees.

Mrs. Capshaw continued, "Right at this moment, there's a woman sitting at a table downstairs. She reminds me of you so very much, young and full of distress. Another sad story, I'm sure. Except unlike you, she's downright foolish. I think you might have a chance to secure a well-paying—" she looked at Penrose meaningfully "—and respectable job."

Penrose jumped up. "Tell me. Is it a teaching position?"

"No. Better." Mrs. Capshaw's sharp brown eyes narrowed and she lowered her voice to a whisper. "The lady is on her way to a post that her agency secured for her. She needs a room while she travels." She smiled, a small twist of the lips. "But she is sitting there downstairs right now, blabbing for all the world to hear about her doubts and fears over the position."

That *was* interesting news. "Go on," said Penrose.

"She's to report the day after tomorrow. Seven a.m. sharp. But, she's reluctant. In fact, she's more than reluctant."

"More than reluctant?"

"She's terrified," Mrs. Capshaw blurted out. "I'm telling you straight off to get it out of the way." She shrugged as if it were of little consequence. "She's heard rumors. It seems her agency was less than forthcoming about the post. Her employer is a troubled individual and the house might be haunted."

For the first time, Penrose felt wary, but just a bit. It was a job, after all. She hedged. "How troubled? And what kind of hauntings? The rumors must be awful for her to reconsider."

"Awful?" Mrs. Capshaw threw her hands into the air. "What can be awful about regular income and a roof over your head?" Her voice lowered an octave as she said, "And wages that would make your eyes pop right out of your head. And, truthfully, do you believe in ghosts?"

"No, I don't." Penrose felt breathy. For decent wages, she'd be blind to a lot of things. Including ghosts. And regular pay? Something she could barely imagine. But she wasn't a babe in the woods. She was twenty-one. Old enough to know a thing or two. Something was wrong. "Still…why such high wages? Something doesn't ring true. Maybe there's truth to the rumors."

Mrs. Capshaw huffed. "'Still' nothing. You've been here six months already. Six months since your mother died and no position to speak of. No prospects, either! I've watched your purse dwindle, your belongings dwindle. You're all boiled down like soup left too long on the stove. Only scrapings left." She wagged her hands in the air. "Penrose Heatherton, you are in debt to me. Not a small amount, either. And if you ask me, that's what awful is." She pursed her lips. "And, yes, the post seems…suspicious. But, if you listen closely, it also sounds like an opportunity." She lifted a pearl comb from the nightstand. "This is the only thing of value you have left, isn't it? And rent's due tomorrow? Do you think I'd take a comb in payment? You're a sweet girl, but you're fooling yourself if you think you'll find work as a schoolteacher. Not in this town. Not with your name."

"But my mother had such a respectable finishing school—"

"No offense, but you are not your mother. She was a Northerner. Sent to the finest schools and from a well-regarded family. She had credentials, Penny. Credentials. The big families in this town adored her because she attended those fine finishing schools. Yes, she fell from grace, there was always that."

"You don't need to remind me that I was her downfall," she snapped. Penrose always had trouble concealing her anger when the subject was brought to her attention.

"I'm not. A baby is a baby to the likes of me. But not to them. Not to those fancy folks. They never minded you as an assistant to her. But an illegitimate child as an assistant is one thing. As a teacher, it's quite another. Plus, your name. Penrose." She sighed. "Your mother did you such a disservice giving you your father's surname as a first name. She thought she was clever giving you that name! Calling him out and exposing him as the father. Those were passionate times, I'll give her that. But she was ignorant. The South doesn't work that way and she was foolish to think she'd change it. Oh, those abolitionists had such grand ideas, didn't they? No bigger name around here. Like a splinter in the eye of the most powerful family. You'll have a tough road around here. Surely my words are no surprise to you."

No, they weren't a surprise. Penrose shook her head. "Just painful."

"The truth hurts, Penny. It hurts." Mrs. Capshaw leaned down and put her hand on the bed. It creaked under her weight. "Just like when that young man stopped calling on you and I told you he wasn't coming back. I say it plain. You'll never find work on your own here. No education other—"

"My mother educated me." Heat burned her cheeks.

Mrs. Capshaw pushed down on the bed. "Let me finish, girl. I said no education other than from your mother. It may be a fine education, but there's no stamp of a finishing school on your papers. In fact, you have no papers. Even worse, you're now living in a pub by the wharf. Your stock is dropping by the minute…what's left for a girl like you? Hmm?" She loomed over Penrose, her shadow falling across her.

Penrose stared out of the window. A sliver of the moon was visible and she focused on that. Her chest felt tight, as if a belt were strapped around it and someone was tugging. Was it anxiety? Or something more? She remembered the strange breeze from earlier and felt the odd, prickly sensation spread over her once again. Change was in the air. Perhaps she should welcome it. "I deserve a break, don't I?" Her words came hot and fast. "Don't I?" She looked at Mrs. Capshaw with a pleading, angry gaze.

"You said it, Penny. Right from your own mouth. You deserve a break. But if you think a break is going to waltz in here and lay itself in your lap, you're mistaken." She shook her head, her frizzy hair barely moving on her head. "Listen, some girls are tough to their bones. Others are soft. Those are the ones that wilt. Still others, and I think you're one of these—are malleable, able to bend and sway. Adapt to changing conditions. You need to adapt. And I'm giving you an opportunity to do just that. What better than to work for a man who doesn't give two shakes what society thinks?"

Mrs. Capshaw was right. Penrose nodded.

"Get off that bed. Stand up and listen to me. Listen to what the post entails and then make your choice." She lifted her hand and stood straight.

Penrose slid from the bed and stood beside her landlady. "I'm listening."

Mrs. Capshaw seemed to soften then. She blinked and nodded, and gave a halfhearted attempt at a smile. "I'm sorry, dear. Life did you wrong. But I'm not a charity. You have to act fast."

"The post," Penrose reminded her. "I need more details."

"It's a single man, a bachelor, and he needs someone to help him in his scientific studies. Someone who can write, who has a bright intellect and one who doesn't mind…"

Everything sounded fine until Penrose heard those words. "Doesn't mind what?"

Mrs. Capshaw spoke in a rush. "Working nights. He works at night, from sunset to sunrise. Though don't worry, because it's respectable. The little miss downstairs told me that the three ladies that walked off before her have never accused him of wrongdoing. He has an affliction, she says. It makes him unsightly, very unsightly, and causes trouble with his eyesight. The sun hurts his eyes and the night is the only time he can see untroubled. But it's the strange rumors of the manor that scare her so. The hauntings. They whisper that he does odd things. Practices dark arts." Then she added pointedly. "But those wages…" She named the sum, a figure so high that Penrose coughed.

No, she choked. An amount like that, well, it seemed almost sinful. Penrose floated in an odd place, willing to be tempted, letting her mind imagine the riches of such a sum but knowing that she should be suspicious. *Those wages, though.* Finally, she said. "Very well, I'm interested. Not committing, but interested. What is your plan?"

"Smart of you to consider it. Just hear me out. I al-

ways say don't let the future toss you about. Sometimes you have to grab it." She smoothed her frizzy
hair down, a useless habit because it just popped right
back up again. "My idea is that we'll help the girl, make
the decision easy for her. You'll steal her post." She
watched Penrose.

"Steal it? Are you serious?"

Mrs. Capshaw nodded. "The girl doesn't want the
job. One look at her face and I knew the truth of it. She
let the name of the manor slip…" Her voice trailed off
in an odd way.

"I can't steal her post!"

"Now you think to be ethical? Right now, when your
whole future is blank—a black hole—and your present
is nothing but hunger. Yes, life did you wrong. But you
don't even have money for the rent! I'll have to move
your room again, to the porch this time. And after that,
who knows?" The threat hung in the room.

It would be easier to stand up and grab a future than
to sit around The Winding Stair wallowing in the slim
pickings that came her way. "I'll do it." She didn't feel
entirely convinced, but somehow the words came out
sure and strong.

"Very well," said the landlady. "The plan is simple
enough. You only have to show up a day early. Let them
know the agency sent you instead of her. Plead pru-
dence on your early arrival. Better to be early than late.
I'll let the young lady downstairs know the bad news.
Let her down easy, let her know it was for the best. By
arriving early, there's no mistaking the job is yours.
I'll break the news to the young lady." Mrs. Capshaw
looked away as she spoke.

"Ah, I get it now. I wondered why you were so generous with an opportunity," Penrose said spitefully. "And once you tell the poor girl she's been wronged, you'll give her the good news that you have a room to rent her. That, strangely, one was just vacated…"

The woman laughed, short and bitter, and her belly heaved. "You're a smart one, aren't you? Yes, I've seen her purse, and it's heavier than yours. Don't judge me. I have to survive. Just like you."

The tight feeling in Penrose's chest constricted even further. It became hard to breathe. "Mrs. Capshaw, I don't know… It seems like such a scheme."

"Well, you only have to listen to the girl to know I'm right. She's downstairs right now, blabbing away to Charlie, telling my husband all her woes." She plucked the heavy black gown from the peg on the wall and tossed it in Penrose's direction. It sailed across the room like a dark ghost and covered Penrose in an embrace.

Mrs. Capshaw continued, "At the very least, come and hear her for yourself."

The dress hung limply over Penrose. She felt small and uncertain all of a sudden.

"Don't dally," said Mrs. Capshaw, coming over and grabbing the dress, then holding open the bodice so that Penrose could step into it. "Here. Time's wasting, always wasting. We have to hurry."

Penrose stepped into the dress. The gown swallowed her. She had always been petite, but now she was thin—too thin.

Mrs. Capshaw didn't seem to notice and she stood back, admiring Penrose. "That's more like it. You'll see. It will all work out. Turn around, dear," she said.

Penrose turned, and the woman drew the gown tight and began buttoning it up. "This is your only dress?"

she asked with concern. "The one you wore to your mother's funeral?"

"I'm sorry. It's all I have." The rich black fabric had faded to gray at the elbows and the hem had turned to fringe. "I sold the others," she whispered, hating the need to confess the small, shameful adjustments she'd had to make in the past few months.

Mrs. Capshaw sighed. "It's so morose. I can only hope a somber look will work in your favor." She tightened the final button and cinched the ribbon into a bow. "Now, where's your bonnet?"

"I'll get it. It's at the window. I need to comb my hair, too." In her heart she was still reluctant, her decision not yet made. But she went through the motions, fighting the comb through her inky hair. While she wrestled her hair into a tight bun, Mrs. Capshaw explained what she was to do.

"Charlie can drive you to the manor," she said, referring to her husband and bartender. Even though Charlie was married to Mrs. Capshaw, he was no Mr. Capshaw. Simply Charlie. She continued, "You'll have to sleep the night outside. We can't risk you leaving tomorrow. She might catch on in the light of day. Anyhow, it shouldn't be too hard. The gentleman's name is Mr. Carrick Arundell. Remember, seven sharp. Very specific about that. Don't worry about the little miss here, it's all for the best." She took Penrose by the hand. "Come now, let's go down the stairs."

When they reached the landing, Mrs. Capshaw put a hand on her shoulder. "Hold it," she said. "Hmm. Can't do to arrive without any belongings. It will make you look wanting. Needful." She twisted her lips as she thought and then lifted a finger. "I've got it. Just a moment." She left Penrose on the stairs.

Penrose heard her then. A breathy, feminine voice wafting up the stairwell. She couldn't help herself and crept lower, down the winding staircase until she could see her—with the benefit of a wall that partially hid Penrose from view. The woman sat at the corner table. Even though the late crowd had begun to arrive, Penrose could still see her clearly.

No, this woman hadn't sunk to the level that she had. Oh, certainly she oozed that refined look of genteel suffering, a bit worn at the edges. No doubt, there was even a small, graciously suffering smile on her lips. The kind of smile that Penrose couldn't quite muster anymore.

The little blond head bobbed as she spoke. "It might not be worth the fear, the fright of living with such a man," she drawled.

What could be so frightening about a mere man? Nothing, that's what. But to make matters worse she continued, "I'm not so hungry that I will endure fright and intimidation. Not me. I can always stay with my sister. Perhaps another might endure such a thing, but I'm hesitant. Are things so bad that I must suffer for employment?"

Penrose's eyes burned, and her fingers itched with the urge to strike out. *Yes, they are, you silly woman. Yes, they are.*

"But what about those wages?" Charlie asked.

The woman named the amount of pay, and a small choking noise escaped from Penrose's lips. Both the woman and Charlie turned in her direction and she slunk back into the shadows.

"They say," the woman continued in a grave voice,

"that he must pay such a wild sum because of all the awful things that go on in that house. I've heard he's wicked. I've heard he's…dark."

"The men talk, you know. I've heard the same." Charlie stood leaning over the counter and wiping a whiskey glass with his rag. "And worse, too. Still, those wages. Any man would be proud to earn such a sum for a year's labor."

"Oh, that's not a year of wages. That's for a month."

The shrill clink of the glass slipping from Charlie's hand and hitting the counter rang out. Or maybe it was the sound of her conscience turning to ice. But whatever decency was left inside her hungry soul fled when she heard that sum. Right then and there, her mind turned rock-solid certain. The risks be damned. Dark arts meant nothing to her. That job would be hers. All she needed was one paycheck, just one, and she could recover. She could start again in a new city. She could open her own school with a new identity.

Distinctive footfalls came down the stairs. Penrose turned and saw Mrs. Capshaw standing on the rise above her. "Well?" she asked in a hearty whisper. "Heard enough?"

Penrose nodded. "Have you the bag?" she asked pointedly.

"Of course." Mrs. Capshaw held it out. "I stuffed it with newspapers to look full."

"It's perfect," said Penrose, taking the bag. It was dusty black and light as air. "I'll go and wait outside for Charlie."

"Of course. I'll let him know." The woman grabbed Penrose by the arm. "Penrose, you won't regret this. Trust me."

Trust was not a word she associated with Mrs. Capshaw, but the woman seemed sincere, and she nodded in reply. They descended the rest of the stairs together. Once on the ground floor, Penrose moved through the pub area swiftly, Mrs. Capshaw right behind her. Charlie looked up and smiled from behind the bar, but before he could say a single word to her, Penrose opened the door and stepped outside. Not once did she look at the woman. She couldn't bear to. She didn't want to risk developing a conscience and changing her mind.

Outside, she leaned against the wall of the inn and took deep breaths. What exactly was she doing? Mrs. Capshaw stood stoically beside her.

Penrose breathed a sigh of relief when Charlie emerged from the pub. "Are you okay, Penny?" he asked, taking a long look at her before turning to his wife. "What's going on? Why did you pull me outside?"

"I need you to ready the buggy. There's something you need to do."

"Oh, no," he said with a sigh. "What are you up to?" He shook his head. "I should've known—you had that look about you." Turning to Penrose, he said, "Has she pulled you into some plan?"

"Well…" began Penrose.

Mrs. Capshaw practically pounced on the man. "Charlie," she muttered, "leave be and don't intrude. This is for the best. You'll see. Don't say another word of protest. Go and ready that buggy. Take Penny to the river road that leads to the mansions. Drop her off and come right back. She's lucky enough to have a position waiting."

He looked dubious, his white, bushy eyebrows drawing together. "All of a sudden like this?" Suddenly he leaned toward his wife and his voice grew accusing. "This wouldn't have anything to do with our new guest, would it?"

A little huff of anger escaped the woman. "Of course it does. It has everything to do with our guest. But don't say a word, Charlie. Not a word. My plans will work out this time." Mrs. Capshaw spoke with authority. "You drive her to the river and return to me. Straightaway."

"Answer me this first, wife. Where's her position?"

"Arundell Manor."

It was the first time Penrose heard the name. Arundell Manor. The words hung in the air like an echo from a bell. It pleased Penrose and a strange sense of calmness swelled within her.

Charlie did not have the same reaction, however. "Arundell Manor! You're snatching that woman's job! That's no coup! Are you cruel? You're sending her there?"

"Charlie," said Mrs. Capshaw in something close to a growl.

"Arundell Manor? You must be three sheets to the wind! That man will kill her as surely as we stand here now. There's something very wrong with that man, and all of Charleston knows it. He's dangerous and wicked… and downright frightening. The stories I hear about that…that monster."

Beneath the lamplight, Mrs. Capshaw looked at Charlie with a gaze of iron. "Charlie Capshaw, you will keep your mouth shut if you know what's good for you."

"I can't in good conscience—" he sputtered.

"Stop," said Penrose. She was strangely settled in her mind with the decision. The name of the manor struck a chord inside her as if fate had been summoned and there was no stopping it. She put her hand on Charlie's arm. "Charlie, I've already accepted it, whatever may come," she said with resolve.

Charlie looked at her a moment before shaking his head. "You don't understand, child. I hear things in the pub. He's trying to create a man. Think on that. It's said that no woman will ever go near him. Ever. Some have even whispered dark magic is afoot in that house."

"Charles Edgar Capshaw. There you go again! I've told you before..." Her voice trailed away to nothing. Mrs. Capshaw had never spoken quite so harshly before and they all turned quiet. She looked to Penrose. "Don't listen, dear. Go, go to the position and see for yourself." Then she turned to Charlie. "Get the buggy! And be quick about it!"

He backed away in small steps, shaking his head. "Mark my words," he said in a low voice before turning and stomping off into the darkness.

"Don't let Charlie scare you."

"He doesn't," she replied, which was the truth. A future with no income scared her more than men's tales when they were deep in their cups.

Charlie returned with the buggy and, after she was settled, he drove her through Charleston, past the harbor with its ships bobbing in the water and the fat moon flying high above them. Penrose smelled the sweet perfume of gladiolas heavy in the air. She felt oddly happy. Dark magic or no, the pay would take care of everything. She laughed.

"I wouldn't take it so lightly," said Charlie, glancing over at her, flicking the whip above the head of the horse. They passed through the gates of Charleston and traveled through the thick woods before reaching the stone gates of the manor. The iron gates were thrown wide open, heedless of any intruders. Charlie slowed the carriage to a stop, then turned to look at her. "Penny," he said, patting her on the shoulder, "promise me you'll be careful."

"I will. I promise. Everything will be fine, don't worry."

"I always worry when Mrs. Capshaw is scheming."

She picked up the valise and climbed down. "This time, it will work out grand. You'll see."

"I hope so, dear. I hope so," he said, snapping the whip in the air. With a neigh, the horse came to life and the carriage pulled away. It had gone a few paces when he called out to her. "Remember, Penny, you can always come back and start again if you'd like. Don't think you're trapped. You're never trapped."

"Thank you, Charlie," she said, and watched as the carriage rode out of sight.

She set off down the manor road with nervous steps, unsure exactly what she had gotten herself into. Only one thing was certain. The choice had been her own, so she deserved whatever the future held for her.

Oak trees lined the bone-white road like sentinels, and she walked beneath them until the road spilled out onto a wide clearing of land. Some distance away, the house floated, eerie and ghostly white under the moonlight. She settled under one of the large oaks at the end of the path, her eyes trained on the ghostly house. Two windows were illuminated. They glowed like orange eyes and she saw the dark figure of a man cross in front of them. Her heart beat wildly. Was that him? Was that Carrick Arundell?

Once more the figure passed by the window, except this time he stopped and stood in front of it. Her skin pulled tight in gooseflesh. It seemed that he stared through the darkness and looked right at her. Her heart beat wildly, and her thoughts ran unchecked. Perhaps right now he was practicing his dark magic. *Stop it*, she chided herself. He was only a man. He couldn't be that bad.

The light of day would bring answers. Tomorrow she would know everything. Tomorrow her future would become the present. In the meantime, she must sleep. But she couldn't stop herself from watching the dark figure pace back and forth in the window. Back and forth, again and again. Endlessly.

Chapter 2

Penrose opened her eyes, her body stiff, the dew from the evening before settled on her skin and hair. Arundell Manor stood before her, no longer ghostly, but regal, and she couldn't stop staring at the sight. The early sun poured pink rays of light over the white stone walls. The windows—and there were dozens of them—all glistened in a gold sheen. The rich green grasses that stretched before her were silvered in morning dew. A pond, invisible to her in the night, lay under a blanket of mist. The home slept in quiet splendor.

Her gown was damp. She stood, brushing away the pine needles and drops of dew before straightening her hair and bonnet and pinching her cheeks for color. Lifting the valise, she walked along the bone-white gravel path, each step of her boots a loud crunch in the still morning air. There were forty-four steps leading to the massive front doors, she thought as she climbed and counted each one. She was aware of every move as if someone was already watching her from behind the glittering windows. Penrose couldn't shake the sensation.

Standing in front of the brass knocker, she took a deep, steadying breath. *You can do this*, she told herself. The rising sun warmed her backside and seemed almost to agree. Lifting the heavy knocker, she let it fall and listened as the hammer strike echoed on and on behind the door. She waited, then waited some more, but there was no answer, so she tried again.

Finally, there came a fumbling noise; a latch turned and the door swung open. Sunlight streamed past her and into the house, striking a crystal chandelier that hung low in the foyer. Glass orbs and shards grabbed the light and tossed about a brilliant rainbow of colors, blinding her. She flinched and stepped backward, her boot heel catching on the fabric of her skirt. Down she went, limbs akimbo, the piazza floor rising up fast to greet her. But as she fell, she caught a glimpse of a man—a dark outline of his tall frame. His features were invisible against the white stone of the house.

Then the ground slapped her hard enough to rattle her teeth. So much for a good first impression. The sunlight poured relentlessly on her. She shielded her eyes and looked up.

"You find me that offensive?" His voice was low and sleep-filled, tainted with anger. No, she realized, the voice wasn't tainted with mere anger—it was laced with something close to rage. Or worse.

From beneath her hand, her eyes darted left and right, searching for the man who spoke with such venom. "I can't see you," she said, feeling foolish.

A face swung into view, inches from her own. "I'm easy to miss," he said. Eyes the color of a thousand sunsets swept over her face in a harsh gaze. Reds and purples and blues shifted and swirled within the irises. She shrank from him and sucked air into her lungs like a dying woman. Her hand fell away from her brow, revealing the man in his entirety. Stupidly, she sat there, blinking, trying to fathom exactly what she was seeing.

He stood there in the bright sunlight, white as snow, clad in black sleeping trousers and a robe that lay open to his waist. His skin was powder white—white beyond fathoming—as if milk had been added to an already pale skin tone, bringing forth an unnatural brightness. To look at him was to look upon the facets of a diamond; it hurt the eye to take him in. His muscles were etched into hard lines on his torso and he had a winter's blaze of white hair that crowned a youthful, vigorous-looking face. All that white hair and he couldn't be more than thirty-five. She stared, openmouthed.

"At least have the courtesy to shut your mouth while you stare at me," he said, each word scraping out exactly as her boots had on the walkway moments before. He held out a hand.

She hesitated, swallowed hard and then finally slipped her hand into his. His hand was warm and she couldn't help but be surprised by this. She had half expected his touch to have the cold chill of death on it. He pulled her to her feet, yanked her right up, and she stood in his shadow—for he was very tall, indeed—panting, trying to collect her thoughts.

"Well?" he said, a sneer twisting his features. Was he handsome?

"I'm sorry," she said, her brain scrambling for words.

"The agency sent me, sir. I'm here for the position." She chanced one more look—she couldn't help it. His face was too young, too beautiful and too strong for that white hair. And those eyes. God help her, those eyes.

He said nothing, merely watched her as she watched him. He seemed determined to shock her, unconcerned as he was with his half-dressed state. "Have you seen enough?" he finally asked. A touch of sleep lingered in the drawl of his voice, giving him an almost casual arrogance.

"I apologize," she said, busying herself by leaning down to pick up her valise. "I was surprised, and all the lights startled me."

He sniffed and shook his head. "The agency sent you? And who exactly are you and why did you come to my door at this ungodly hour?"

"Heatherton." She extended her hand. "Penrose Heatherton."

He didn't take it. His eyes held hers. She thought of the crystal rainbow from the chandelier; the colors shifting, changing. Finally, he said, "Tell me, Miss Heatherton—"

"Yes?" She held her hand extended for another moment, a bit too long, before pulling it back and wringing both hands together awkwardly.

"Miss Heatherton," he repeated, his Southern drawl low and conspiratorial. "Why in the world are you knocking on my door at the break of dawn?"

"The agency told me to arrive at seven a.m." This wasn't going well, she realized. Not at all as she had imagined it. For a lot of different reasons.

"P.M.," he said harshly. *"Post meridiem.* Or generally speaking…in the evening. I told the agency specifically that I needed the applicant to show up at seven p.m."

"Oh," she said foolishly, feeling the blush rise in her cheeks.

His gaze skipped over hers, lowered to her lips and returned once again to her eyes. "That's right—p.m.," he said slowly. "So, not only are you a full day early, you reported at the wrong time. I was asleep, and now you've woken me."

"I'm so sorry." The blush in her cheeks must be red as fire, because her face burned.

"I'm certain you've noticed my affliction. I am cursed with paleness. A lack of pigment. Albinism." His chin jutted into the air defiantly. "It does not lend itself to sunlight. I keep night hours, and I'm very protective of them." He sighed, and those unapologetic eyes didn't look away from her. "But you're here. Though I specifically requested someone who wasn't attractive. Makes it easier." Those eyes still rested on her. The heat on her face grew to volcanic levels. "I take it you can read and write?"

"Of course."

"How's your eyesight?"

"Perfect."

He nodded. "And your hands? Can you can handle fine tools and small mechanical parts? Smaller than a fingernail?

"I'm very sure-handed."

"You can work the night through? Adjust to my schedule?"

"Certainly."

"Good. It's what I value most. That, and discretion." He stepped aside the slightest bit to make room for her, forcing her to brush against him as she entered. "Come in."

She took in the interior of the house with a few quick glances: white marble floors, a high ceiling—two floors high—stairs that curled in an elegant arc to the second floor, archways that led to other rooms. A huge grandfather clock began to chime. Sheets covered the furniture and paintings as if the house were bedded down while its owners were away. Splatters of rainbow light still spun over everything.

He shut the door and the blinding rainbows disappeared. When she turned around, he was beside her, almost too close. Shocked at his willingness to invade her independent space, she pulled away from him. Her reaction was an odd mix of aversion and excitement. He seemed dangerous.

He stilled. "Forgive me. My eyesight is very poor, and I am used to stepping close in order to see something." Then, with a lingering glance, he turned around, and she knew that a moment where they might have established a cordialness between them was lost. When he spoke, it was with a firm and cold voice. "I won't give you a tour as you've already interrupted my sleep. I'm heading to bed. You will start tonight." He turned and began to climb the stairs.

She followed, taking small, anxious steps. "I'm to work your hours, then?"

"How else do you expect to be my assistant?" His voice boomed in the open space. The stairs creaked under his weight as he climbed, his black robe swirling in the air behind him.

"Of course, Mr. Arundell."

Without turning around, he waved his hand angrily. "Don't call me Mr. Arundell. My father was Mr. Arundell, and he's dead now. Call me Carrick. You'll be ready to work at dusk and you'll be with me until dawn. The work is intense, requires a steady hand and a sharp mind. Are you certain that you're up for the task?"

"I am." She peered down the hall. "Is there anything you want me to accomplish before we start tonight?"

"The day is yours, Miss. Heatherton. But if I were you, I would sleep, for the night will be a long one."

"Yes. Of course."

"You have the run of the house, except for the doors in the kitchen that lead down to the cellar. That is my workroom, and you only enter with me. The house has no staff. You'll have to see to your own needs." He was standing on the landing by then. "I'm sure your agency has warned you of my...disposition."

"Yes. I've been warned." Not enough, though, not enough, she thought. Or perhaps she should have listened to Charlie more closely. But, still, the pay would be worth it. She hoped.

"Good. Then I can dispense with pleasantries. You'll find a small stairway in the second-floor hall that leads straight up to your room."

"Fine, yes, then I'll see you tonight."

"Yes. Tonight." As he walked away, she was unable to tear her eyes away from his retreating form.

Then he was gone, and she stood alone in the entry hall. Or so she thought.

It was a testament to Penrose's desperation that she stayed the day in that strange mansion. Forty-one rooms and she had walked through fourteen of them before her fear got the better of her and she went and sat in the front parlor, which was so large it was more of a great room. Not a person or servant had shown themselves, and yet the house looked well maintained and orderly. One thing drove her crazy—no matter where she went in the mansion, she could hear the grandfather clock ticking.

The front parlor had a large picture window that looked out over the front lawn. The view was like a fancy oil painting, with a serene pond and a large oak tree standing watch over it. It was easy to imagine a family gathering in this very room every evening, playing games and enjoying the twilight hours. But the eerie quiet of the house belied that image. It was a tomb. And even though the house was dead quiet, save for the clock, something else unsettled her even more. She was standing, staring out of the window and wondering exactly what it was, when the realization hit her.

It felt as if someone was watching her.

The sensation was similar to what she'd felt when she first arrived. But it didn't seem like nonsense this time. It was very real, and she spun around, eyes darting left and right, skimming the room. What did she expect to find? This was silly. She had the sudden urge to be free of the house, to stand outside in the sun, where everything made sense. There was nothing scary with the wind in your hair and the sunshine on your cheeks.

Her mind was made up. She would go outside. As she walked from the room, she glanced at the door frame and something caught her eye. A growth chart had been carved into the frame. Names and dates were scratched into the wood, noting the heights of children as they grew. All the scratchings were muted and dulled with age.

The tallest carving was dated 1865 and inscribed with the name Carrick. Twenty-one years ago; the same year she was born. She guessed Carrick's age at thirty-seven or so. Penrose ran her finger over the mark. He would have been too young to head off to war. She noticed other names, Carville and Sampson, that were almost as high as Carrick's. Older brothers, she reasoned, though the last dates etched for them were 1861 and 1862.

Penrose almost missed the last marking. It was so very low on the frame. She had started to walk away when her gaze caught the raw color of the newly scratched wood. There was no date, but the scar was so fresh that it had to be recent. Only the initials *C.J.* were visible, carved crudely, angular and far too large.

On the other side of the door frame, there were other odd markings. Tally marks—single lines gouged in the wood, with a slash running diagonally through them. Someone was counting in blocks of five, and there were dozens and dozens of blocks. She didn't know what to make of it and ran her fingers over the gouges, wondering.

She went outside the double doors at the rear of the house. There was a small flight of stairs that ended on a gravel path. Pecan trees dotted the rear lawn before they gave way to marshy grasses. The Ashley River flowed in the distance, dark as mud and slow as honey. Immediately, she felt better, walking along with the sweet aromas of the summer flowers perfuming the air. Honeybees flew lazy arcs around her head. She walked until the heat got the better of her.

It was getting late. She wanted to be well rested for work. When she turned around to head back inside the manor, what she saw stopped her cold. There was a stone cellar beneath the house, and in the window she saw two figures bent over as if working at a desk. For a long time, she stood there, hand on her hip, staring at the window.

They didn't move. She walked forward, slow as molasses in winter, her eyes trained on the window. She was half expecting one of them to jump up and scare her silly just for their own amusement. But, no, they were dark and still shadows in the dull shine of the windows. Standing and staring at them, she almost wished they would jump out and scare her. At least she'd know they were real people, then.

They definitely weren't real, or if they were, they were fantastic at posing perfectly still. There wasn't anything human about them. The way their bodies slumped looked awkward, a position that no one could hold for very long. Resting her hand on the wall of the house, she bent over the railing and tried to get a better look.

She had to lean out quite a ways before the shine on the window disappeared and she saw them clearly. They were faceless and formless wooden beings, slumped over in their chairs. The wood was perfectly cut and shaped to form odd, rounded limbs, hands like paddles and oval-shaped heads. They had no features on their faces, only smooth, dark wood.

Much as she tried to muffle her thoughts, Charlie's words about Carrick and voodoo spells kept popping up. What kind of man was he?

After backing away from the window, she turned and ran back into the house. She may have been desperate and the pay might have been high, but it might not be high enough to make her stay here.

She went to find her room, her skirts sweeping the

floor as she walked. She climbed the stairs to the second floor, gripping the balustrade with one hand and her air-light valise in the other. A stretch of red carpet covered the hallway. Dust bunnies gathered at the edges of the baseboards.

There were so many doors. Which one was his? She slowed, listening at each door, goose bumps on her skin, afraid he would somehow know and yank open the door. But all was quiet. Finally, she found the small stairwell at the end of the hall. Grim narrow steps rose in a tight spiral, and she had to focus on her feet as she climbed. A single door welcomed her at the landing and she stepped inside a large and airy attic that had been converted into a room. Though sparsely appointed, it pleased her.

Certainly it was a huge improvement over the storage closet she'd slept in for the past six months. A bed and dresser were tucked in a corner and there was a closet against one wall. A circular window, the biggest she'd ever seen, looked out across the front lawn. She ran her hands over the sill. The ledge was big enough that she could crawl up onto the sill, curl up and survey at the grounds.

She undressed and stretched out on the bed, relaxing against the pillow. But that creeping sensation returned again, the feeling that someone was watching her. She crawled under the covers and pulled them to her chin. It helped a little bit. Dimly, she heard the grandfather clock toll eleven mellow chimes. It was still morning. It felt like a lifetime since she'd first arrived at the manor. The lids of her eyes felt heavy. She gave in to the urge and closed them.

A few moments later, a strange shuffling noise grabbed her attention. It was an odd, sliding, shifting sound, like a cotton sack being dragged along a floor. Rising and wiping the sleep from her eyes, she went to the door and looked down the stairs. They were empty. But the sound persisted. She went completely still to pay attention.

The walls. The sound was coming from within the walls. A tight wave of icy fear swept her body as she listened. What a fool she'd been to race over here and hop on the easy-money bandwagon. That scraping, swooshing noise just wouldn't stop.

Penrose sighed. Better to know. It was always better to know.

In her white cotton underthings and with her dark hair spilled around her shoulders, she tiptoed to the wall. She pressed her ear to the wooden panels. Silence. But something or someone was there. Taking shallow breaths, she walked along slowly, swallowing often to keep the bile from her throat. Again. A scratching. Scraping. Following the noise, she traced her finger over the plaster, drawing closer to the source. When the sound increased suddenly, she knew she'd located it. The sound was low to the ground. Dropping to her knees, she pressed her head to the wall and closed her eyes. The noise was quite distinct and just on the other side.

"Who's there?" she whispered, surprised by the sharpness in her voice.

Complete silence. Then, distantly, the sound dimmed, more scratching. Still as stone, she stood, her whole being focused on the sound as it drifted farther away until there was only the sharp, quick hiss of her own breathing. She returned to her bed shaken, convinced she'd never sleep again, let alone take an afternoon nap. But she was wrong and fell quickly asleep.

* * *

Carrick Arundell parted the thick curtains and looked out at the unfamiliar sight of the afternoon sun. He hated the day, hated that aching yellow ball inching its way across the sky. It did nothing but bruise his eyes and burn his skin. It was the night he lived for—for the long, dark hours when the world was asleep and he emerged to create his inventions.

On most mornings, the rising sun was easy to ignore. Except for today. He'd twisted and turned in bed, reluctantly watching a streak of sunlight stretch across the floor. Finally, he'd given in. There would be no sleep today.

It didn't sit well with him. He needed his energy. A thousand small setbacks plagued his project, and every single one had to fall into place before the mechanical man took his first step.

Now he could add one more setback. An image that he couldn't get out of his mind. His new assistant standing in the doorway, pure midnight from head to toe. Black dress, black bonnet, black hair and a winter-white face peering out at the world. Any man would be tempted. But he wasn't any man. He couldn't afford to be.

No, it was more than that. It wasn't just the project. It was the sight of her stepping back, her lips curling in disdain. The poor girl could barely talk. Dropping the curtain, he went to his wardrobe and began to dress for the evening.

Maintaining focus was crucial. Every day, his eyesight grew even weaker.

There was no choice but to control his thoughts about her. It wasn't that he didn't like women. Quite the opposite. It was that women didn't like him. They stepped away, turned away, or looked down at their shoes when he approached. The only companionship he'd ever known, he'd paid for. Even then, the women turned their faces away from him.

Penrose had turned away, as well, but not before he caught a glimpse of her expression in the bright flash of the lightning. She'd looked up at him in a mixture of fear and horror. He'd grown immune to such looks. But coming from her it angered him.

Long ago, his heart had turned to iron. If he had his way, he would shun everyone. Keep the whole damn world out. But he needed the help of a steady hand and a good pair of eyes. Pretty blue eyes, a voice inside him added.

He went and looked for her, and when she couldn't be found, he went up the small flight of stairs to the servant's bedroom. The door to her room was ajar a few inches and he peered in and saw her sleeping on the bed. Toeing the door open, he stepped inside. Maybe he should have just knocked, but it happened before he knew his foot was moving, and then he was inside the room.

He watched her sleep. It seemed wicked, an indulgence more sinful than the women he paid to lift their skirts for him. Here he was, a man of thirty-six, and he'd never once seen the serene, soft expression of a woman lost in her dreams. Her features were soft now, not guarded like when he'd first met her.

The attic was warm that afternoon. She had two high spots of color on her cheeks. Her beauty was unusual, angular even. A sharp prettiness. The kind that could cut a man. But those two spots of color flaming away against all that tumbling black hair softened her looks. She sighed, and flung an arm out, revealing bare skin all the way to the strap of her undergarment. It was damn tempting.

He heard the clock chime the half hour. A half hour of prime working time lost just watching her sleep. Like a fool.

When he reached out to wake her, he shook her much harder than he intended to. Her eyes snapped open and met his gaze. For a brief second, she looked at him openly, her expression unafraid. He wanted to stop time, to linger in that tiny moment. But then the moment was gone.

Penrose's eyes widened and her hands clutched at the covers, instinctively pulling them higher. She was like all the rest, he realized, as he felt the shutters on his heart slam shut.

Chapter 3

Penrose came to alertness from sleep in an odd rush, as if rising from a fog. Images still swirled in her brain— of Carrick looming above her, the chandelier spinning and spinning out of control, and the glittery windows of the manor watching her with their golden gaze. She knew if she opened her eyes, it would all prove true. So she lingered, stubbornly refusing to be roused. The grip turned harder still and shook her shoulders just firmly enough that she couldn't ignore it anymore. Finally, she looked up and right into the kaleidoscope eyes of her new employer.

"You overslept." It sounded like an accusation coming from him. The shadowy light of the afternoon made him appear deathly pale. Anger or some other emotion etched his face in a deep scowl.

"I'm sorry," she said, voice heavy with sleep. She

was disoriented, staring hard at him before rubbing her eyes. It was difficult to know if she still slept and he was just a dream. "I must have been very tired," she managed to say.

He nodded. "Well, then, I'll leave you to get dressed. Meet me downstairs in the cellar."

"Fine. I'll hurry."

He left. She jumped up and dressed quickly, blood pounding in her veins. She wasn't sure if it was fear of him or guilt at oversleeping, but she ignored it and moved quickly. She went to the kitchen to take the stairs that led down to the cellar and was surprised to see Carrick standing at the counter, eating.

"Come. Eat," he said, barely turning to look at her. She went and stood next to him. He held out a steaming cup of coffee for her and she grabbed it greedily and took a sip. He was eating johnnycakes. She lifted one from the basket, smeared it with butter and took a bite. It was warm and buttery.

"Tell me, Miss Heatherton," he said, between bites, "how it is you came to the agency?"

Her stomach dropped when he mentioned the agency and she spoke quickly, trying to change the subject. "Please, my name is Penrose. But everyone calls me Penny. If you want me to call you Carrick, I'd like the same."

"Penny it is, then," he said, and took a swig of his coffee. "Penrose. A prominent name around here. How did you come by that as a given name?"

She froze, johnnycake in midair. She wanted to lie. It was right at the tip of her tongue, yet when she opened her mouth, the truth came tumbling out. "My father was a Penrose."

"I see. Skeletons in the proverbial closet, then? Since the family name is your first name and not your last, I'll ask how come he tossed over your mother?"

For some reason, his harsh tone didn't bother her. Nobody spoke plainly about this subject. It was a refreshing change and she found that more truths came forward. "My mother was an abolitionist."

He made a strange noise and spit coffee out of his mouth. He laughed, hunched over next to the counter. Finally he regained his composure. "A Penrose and an abolitionist? Now that's funny. They are the most painfully backward family on God's good planet Earth. So, was your mother able to sway him to her point of view?"

"No. Then he died in battle right before the end of the Civil War. Just before I was born."

"Hearts and beliefs are the two hardest things to change. You were born at an interesting time. You were born before or after the Civil War ended?"

"More than that, I was born on the very last day of the war. At midnight, in fact. My mother said that they had to choose what day to pick as my birthday. Obviously, my mother chose after the war."

He went completely still. "My, my, my. A midnight baby, and on the last day of the war? The very last minute? You're doubly cursed, Penny. Can't you see it? One foot on the bright side of freedom and one foot in the shameful past. A suspicious mind might say you're destined to live two lives."

There was something sinister about him standing there—easy as you please—talking about curses. "I wouldn't dare believe in such nonsense. I'm a practical sort." But her words sounded forced, a bit too high.

"Are you, now?"

She nodded and took a bite of the corn bread. Silence fell over the room.

A few minutes later, he spoke up. "Ready to work?"

They walked down the stairs. This house had so many stairways, she thought to herself. The foyer. The attic. The kitchen. It was as if the house intended for people to get lost in it. Cool air rising from the cellar swirled around her as she followed him the last few steps into the workshop, looked around and struggled to keep her chin from dropping to the floor.

She couldn't take even one more step. Not one. The room was simply too much to absorb. She could only stand and stare dumbly. It wasn't so much the space. Oh, it was impressive—cavernous, cool and dark, with high ceilings and a fireplace big enough to stand it. It was more the feel of the room. Expectation hung in the air, with the sharp smells of woodsmoke and oil. Every inch of the floor was crammed with odds and ends, books, piles of gleaming metal bits, cords, tubes, wires and tools. She felt as though she'd entered a deep and secret mine where magical things could be wrenched free.

Her entire life had been orderly. Downtrodden, perhaps, but orderly. Their little home had been converted to a humble finishing school, the kind the middle-class folks sent their daughters to. She grew up amid books that were neatly shelved and papers that were always stacked neatly. There was the feeling of possibility in the school, too—and it felt wonderfully familiar. But the school had provided an orderly process of discoveries. This room was chaos. She wasn't sure what to make of it.

"It used to be the kitchen," Carrick said, walking to the fireplace and tossing a handful of tinder into it. He struck a match and threw it onto the wood. A flame blazed to life. He fanned it, sending a hiss and spray of sparks into the air. "When my project outgrew the library, I moved the kitchen upstairs and took over this room." He gathered some logs and fed them to the growing blaze. Even though it was high summer, the cellar was chilly, so she welcomed the heat.

Carrick walked about the room lighting lamps and candles. He handed a candle to Penrose, and she helped him with the rest. He continued, "The problem with this room is the lack of light. I have lamps on all the walls, but the large open space where I do my work needs even more light."

A schematic of the human body hung on one wall. Another had a large calendar. And then she saw what had scared her silly earlier—the wooden beings slumped in their chairs. Her heart stopped, she swore it did, and she brought her hand to her chest to feel its beat before relaxing a bit. What did he do with them?

"Are you coming?" he asked.

"Of course."

He continued, "Though lamplight is fine, the direct brightness affects my eyes. I prefer candles close by. You'll be making candles for me. I require special ones."

"I see," she said, making a mental note to arrive early and have the workroom lit and ready for him.

He gestured toward the center of the room, where a huge work area made up of many tables pushed together formed a half circle. In the center of the tables, something large bulged from underneath a blanket. Whatever it was, it was larger than a man and twice as wide.

Approaching, she held the candle in the air. "What is it?" she asked, unable to hide the wonder in her voice.

Carrick stood behind her. She neither heard his approach nor felt his presence, so when he spoke, it startled her. He stood inches away. "That is the future. A mechanical man." He held up his candle. "Go ahead, pull the blanket off."

She bent down, yanked the blanket away, and the mechanical man stood before her. She blinked and looked up. He was tall, taller than Carrick, taller than any man she'd ever seen. He had a barrel chest, a boxy head and two small lanterns that served as eyes. Wide shoulders sat atop his torso and rivets ran up and down his body like buttons. He resembled a metallic boxer, stout and strong, his skin glistening silver-orange in the firelight.

"What does he do?" she asked in awe. "Can he even move?"

"Anything you want," Carrick said with pride. "Within reason, of course."

He seemed to burst with life. He seemed solid. Dependable. But there was something threatening about a heap of metal sculpted into the shape of a human. Some inner part of her recoiled. Not a big part, but enough of a part to steal her words for a few moments as she took in the sight of him. *Him.* Funny that she thought of it in such familiar terms already.

"Just like in those paperback novels," she said. She'd once read a scary story about a man who built a steam-powered person and then attached him to a buggy. The man walked across the entire country step by step. When they reached Kansas, the steam-powered man went haywire and killed the man who had created him. That was fiction. She now stood before the real thing, and she wasn't sure if that made her feel better or worse about it.

"Yes. Just like in those fanciful stories. Except this one is real." She'd almost forgotten about Carrick. Almost. But the he stood close enough behind her that when he spoke she could feel the air from his breath on the back of her neck.

"How do you give him life?" she asked. "How do you do that?" It was the thousand-dollar question in her mind. She whispered the next word. "Magic?"

He laughed harshly. "Is that what you heard?"

"Perhaps."

"And what do you think of the things you've heard?"

"You're not paying me to think about what I've heard." She turned, forcing her eyes to meet his and hold his gaze. "That's what I think."

"You're either very clever or very hungry."

"Or both."

"Are you as prim and proper as you look?" The tone of his voice changed in that instant. It grew deep and mellow, almost dreamy. But not soothing. Not by a Georgia mile.

She stood stiff, aware of the length of his body right behind hers. He didn't touch her. He didn't need to. She could feel the heat from his body as surely as she could from the fire in front of her. "Now, you tell me. Do you like to be judged by the way you look?"

"Touché, Miss Heatherton."

"Penny. Call me Penny."

His lips graced the tender spot behind her ear. "Penny," he whispered, saying the name so low that it came not as a sound but as a rumble against her skin. Then he was gone, the hard strike of his boots ringing out on the stone. She was left with a wave of cool air.

He strode in front of her to the mechanical man. "Does he scare you?"

"Yes. He makes me nervous. It's a feeling I can't describe. But I'm drawn to him," she answered, unsure if she was referring to the mechanical man or to him.

He was quiet. "Some quake in their shoes when they see him," he finally said.

"What's his name?"

"Name?" He laughed, a mellow, rolling, velvety sound. "He doesn't have one, of course."

"But he has to have a name. How can you create something that looks so, well, humanlike—and not give it a name?"

"You can name him. It makes no difference to me."

"Harris." The name came to her instantly and once she spoke it, it fit nicely. "We'll call him Harris."

"Harris," he said thoughtfully, walking to Harris and running a finger along his steely arm. "That sounds fine. And yes, to answer your question, he can move. When he's functioning. But that's part of the problem. Somewhere inside of him, a gear is tooled wrong. The timing is off, so he can't walk. I've altered the design a million times. It seems there's always a fatal flaw, and I always discover the flaw too late to correct it. Then I'm forced to destroy my creation and start again. I'm hoping that I've discovered the flaw in time."

She looked up. "How do you know that all flaws are fatal? Perhaps you shouldn't design them with one goal in mind but rather an open idea of their potential."

He turned. "You're sharper than I gave you credit for, Penny."

"Thank you." She felt a rush of pleasure at his compliment.

The heat from the fire filled the room, making sweat break out on her forehead.

"You grasp the fundamental concept. One that I'm aware of. The earlier types I created were simply too crude. It's been an agony just to get to this most basic creation. And even though I love doing it, I rue the day I first got the idea." He sighed and went to the windows, opening them first before going to the doors and propping them open, too.

"My apologies. I get too wrapped up in it." Sweet night air filled the room. A pleasant, earthy smell filled the room, carried up from the river by the wind.

He walked over to a wall where a poster of the human anatomy hung. Pencil marks and notes covered the simple drawing of the human being. "I have a question for you. What do you think is more important, form or function?"

Penrose thought for a moment about whether beauty or purpose should be held in higher regard. "Well, I think the function should be the guiding principle."

"Agreed."

"Whenever possible, the form should be pleasing, as well."

His eyes moved from the picture to Penrose. "Very good. I'm pleased. Ideally there would be a balance between the two."

He went to the wall and placed his hand over the image of the human hand. He was a big man, tall, and his hands eclipsed the one on the diagram. "The real key to designing a mechanical man is to decide where form and function join. Where they come together."

"I don't understand."

"I need to reduce form to its barest minimum. Man

will never be able to reproduce the complexity of the human body. It's up to me to decide what's essential and what I can leave out to save on engineering costs and time." He looked back to the poster. "What is the most basic element of being human? If you can answer that, then my instinct says you'll also have perfect form."

He saw the confused look on her face and approached her. "Here, I'll show you. Hold out your arm."

She lifted her arm and held it straight out to the side. He put one hand on her waist. "May I?" he asked.

Nodding, she felt strangely giddy.

He lifted his other hand to her shoulder. Using two fingers, he traced a path down her extended arm. Fire followed his touch. She wrenched her lips closed to contain a gasp.

He whispered, "I need to decide what part of this arm is inconsequential. Of course, it's all perfect in the flesh, but I eliminate what's not necessary, and decide what is essential."

His hand stretched out to grasp hers. He lifted her arm high above her head and stepped closer, bringing the scent of pinewood shavings with him. "The question is, what is it that allows you to raise your arm like this?"

"Muscles," she replied in a whisper.

"Of course. And tendons, too. The delicate interplay between them, when to pull and when to push, that's what matters most. That's what fascinates me." He leaned forward and looked into her eyes. "The real question, the one we're not asking, is what gives the signal to these muscles, what tells them to move?"

He let go of her arm and tapped her temple. "This does. Right in here. That is something we'll never, ever be able to replicate. But I want to."

He was so close she could count his eyelashes. He kept speaking, but she heard nothing save for the pounding in her heart. Her nipples tightened, and the sensation unnerved her. Her cheeks burned, and she tried to step back to gather her wits. She felt fear and excitement, a potent combination. He was unlike any man she'd ever known and she wasn't sure what to say.

He pulled away, a cold look settling over his features. "Did the agency tell you what your duties would be?"

"A little bit," she said, turning away, trying to hide the flash of shame because there was no agency. Mrs. Capshaw would be the end of her, she just knew it.

He pointed out a simple desk, off to the side. "Part of the time, you'll work there. Taking notes. Sketching for me. The rest of your time will be spent helping me tool the components. I struggle to see those small details, which is what caused the problem I have to begin with."

"That sounds fine," she said. She looked again at the wooden figures, remembering how mysterious and life-like they looked from outside the window. There was no life in them now. They looked defeated, slumped. Ropes bound them to the chairs and held them upright. They had no faces, no features. The wood had been whittled and etched away to reveal the essence of a human body. Arms, legs, hands.

Yet they were beautiful. It was as if whittling them down hadn't made them less—it made them more. It brought out their essence. She walked toward them and gingerly touched one on the shoulder, half expecting it to turn and look at her. "What are they?" she asked in a hushed tone, afraid of his answer, knowing full well how silly she was being. But there was definitely something curious about this man.

"Mannequins. My earliest attempts. I keep them because I have a fondness for them. They remind me that progress is possible. Why? Did you think I used them for another purpose?"

"I wasn't sure."

It was too hot. Carrick stood at the door, lingering and scraping his boot absentmindedly back and forth over the gravel. Her hands didn't flutter. That was the first thing he noticed. Some of the others that came here stood trembling, their hands fluttering like trapped butterflies as they stared up at the mechanical man— Harris. Hell, even he thought of him as Harris now.

But her? He saw it. Interest. She looked afraid, yes. But for one brief instant, he saw the spark of wonder. Plus, she named him. That had to be a good sign. She might be the one to help him for the long, hard haul that he knew lay ahead.

Her gasp when she first saw the mechanical man was the single most heavenly sound he'd ever heard. They both saw the same thing in his invention—potential— he knew it in his bones. Of course, he'd become too excited, got too close and scared her. Scared her. Scaring people was something he was far too good at.

Even with that painful disappointment, his spirits were still riding high because she just might work out. Her intellect was apparent. Other assistants worked methodically but without vigor, and he felt the burden of constantly explaining task after task to someone who didn't care to learn the concepts or take leaps of initiative. He held out hope that she might work out just fine.

"How long have you been designing the mechanical man?" she asked, turning to look at him with those blue, blue eyes, and he found himself struggling to pay attention to her words.

"Six years."

"Six years?" Her perfect lips made an O of surprise. "That's a long time to remain committed to something that still hasn't born results."

"The results? The end?" He laughed. "What's that? Every morning when I go to bed, I have to restrain my mind from dwelling on my project. I would think of it all day, every single moment, if I could."

Penrose returned to her desk and began working again, but the uneasy, flighty feeling in her chest lingered. The feeling was strange, excitement and fear mingled together. He was exciting to be around, but he was a volatile person. And mysterious. Her stomach twisted at the memory of his hand on her shoulder.

He paced the room while he spoke. She took notes. Scribbling furiously, she did her best to keep up with him. His ideas were explosions of brilliance, and as he spoke, she slipped into a kind of trance, channeling his words directly onto the paper.

He spoke of the function of the mechanical man, of ways to solve the dilemma with the gears, of the possible need to retool some of them and the supreme need for flexibility of design.

It was revealing to hear his thoughts aloud and easy to take measure of his mind. He had an organized way of thinking, linear and clear. His ideas were concise and simple to understand, and her pen flew across the paper. At times, he paced the floor or hesitated before speaking. She waited, pen in the air, and as soon as his words began to flow once again her scratchings on the paper renewed.

He came and stood behind her. After discussing the particularly difficult redesign of a gear, he put his hand on her shoulder and asked, "Did that make sense? I think if we change the ratio, the output will be stronger."

A twist of nervousness tightened within her. She looked up at him, her eyes wide. The sight of him—tall and regal, with his white hair framing his handsome face—affected her, making her breath heavy.

"Yes," she said, nodding as if she understood perfectly. But the only thing she understood was his hand and those long elegant fingers resting on her shoulder.

She couldn't breathe. More than anything she wanted to rest her cheek on that hand, to feel it caress her skin. Never before had she reacted in such a way. Something strange was happening.

Somehow, her pen kept moving, danced across the paper and finished the last sentence. The realization that she wanted more of that touch made her hand shake and her script wobbly.

He had such passion. A singular-minded obsession. She wondered what it would it be like if he lavished that passion on her.

The thought flamed her cheeks, and she pulled away from him, turning her head. Instantly, his hand disappeared from her shoulder. She wanted to face him and say something, but what could she say? Nothing at all.

Stepping away, he continued speaking, pacing the

floor. And she continued writing as if nothing had passed between them.

She wrote so much her fingers hurt, and the tips of them became stained with ink. It felt like an instant later the grandfather clock tolled the midnight hour. Time seemed to speed up when she was with him.

She stretched her tired, achy fingers, waiting for the chimes to stop and Carrick to start lecturing again. But as soon as the clock fell silent, another sound rang out.

It was the sound of crashing noises coming from outside, and the second she heard them, a terrible sense of foreboding settled over her.

As soon as Carrick heard the crashing sounds coming from outside the workshop he was up and out the door. He didn't know what he was expecting—C.J. maybe, up to some antics—but when he went outside only the summer breeze greeted him. He looked around. Nothing.

He heard the faint sound of a woman's gasp. It was light and breathy with an air of surprise and something else, something he couldn't name.

He looked in the direction of the sound and saw a woman standing just outside the circle of light that came from the window. She wore all white and had a sheen of yellow hair that trailed just below her shoulders.

An angel. That was his first thought. She floated out there in the darkness, hovering with a strange look of fear and longing on her face. Such longing.

She couldn't be a ghost. No such thing. "Hey," said Carrick sharply. "What are you doing out here?"

Instead of replying, she shook her head slowly and began to back away.

"Hey!" he called again, louder now.

The woman began backing away, the shadows swallowing her. "Stop!" he said, "Don't go. Tell me who you are."

Penrose came and stood right behind him, her body pressed against his.

"What is it?" she asked, craning to see outside. "No!" she shouted, surprising him so much that he startled. "Go away!" The tone of her voice was frightened. More than frightened.

"Do you know that woman?" Carrick asked.

The woman turned to Penrose, and something passed between them. He felt it like a bolt of lightning.

The woman outside looked angry, beyond angry. Her posture was rigid. She lifted her hand and pointed at Penrose. For a moment, it looked as if the blonde were about to speak, but she shook her head again and, in a swirl of white skirts, turned and fled.

Some primal instinct flared inside of him, and he took off running after her. No one should be on the property. He didn't know what she was up to, but he fully intended to find out.

"No, Carrick!" screamed Penrose. "Don't follow her!"

He paid Penrose no attention. "Stop!" he shouted to the woman. It was dark. He had trouble enough seeing at night, let alone running through the trees.

He heard her crashing through the woods, and this made her easier to follow. He loped along behind her, his long legs closing the distance between them. Her crashing sounds were getting louder by the second. Once he caught her, he would get to the bottom of this little mystery.

* * *

A heavy, oppressive feeling settled in Penrose's chest. As soon as she saw the woman, she knew her ruse was up. Her breath died in her chest at that moment. So did the little feeling of hope that finally she had started to feel. She should've known the scheme would end badly.

Anytime she tried to get ahead, something came along and set her back. Now Carrick was out there, chasing that woman, that beautiful, perfect woman who by all rights should be standing right where Penrose stood.

Now alone in the quiet workshop, feeling numb, Penrose looked around her. The budding hope that had begun to grow inside of her was already dying. She looked around, trying to memorize everything in the room because she knew she would be leaving. Carrick would show up any minute, yell at her and kick her out. She'd never see the workshop or Harris again. Or Carrick. Her reaction surprised her.

In one quick fix, she had thought she could solve her problems. But she'd only made them worse.

She noticed that her fingers were stained with ink, and she went to the table, picked up a rag and began wiping the stains away. Minutes dragged by, and when the clock gonged again—one in the morning—the door swung open.

Carrick filled the doorway. He looked wild. His white hair stood on edge.

Penrose's hands stilled and fell to her side. The rag dropped to the floor.

He stared at her long and hard, his shoulders squared, and he took great, heaving breaths.

She wasn't sure how to react. She was too afraid to say anything, to reveal anything at all. Perhaps he hadn't caught up with her.

But one look at his face told her he had, indeed. More than caught up with her, she realized, noticing the angry set of his lips. He'd spoken with her.

In three strides, he crossed the room. She barely had time to gather her breath before he loomed over her, his beautiful, angry features hovering right above her face. "What trickery are you up to, Penny?"

He knew. It was over. A horrid wrenching twisted in her gut, but something else was there, too, some wild, fluttery, panicked sensation. A painful feeling of loss and shame. She didn't want him to think badly of her. "I'm sorry," she blurted out. "I'm sorry," she repeated. "I never intended…"

He shook his head slowly. "The conversation I just had with that woman," he said, walking around her. "And the things I've learned about you." He stopped, leaned forward and took her chin in his hand, forcing her to look into his strange eyes. Angry eyes that seemed to swirl with dark colors. "It seems you weren't honest with me, were you?"

"No," she whispered, too flustered to come to any self-defense of her behavior. She felt the hole that she'd dug widening beneath her feet, and the blackness threatening to swallow her up. If only she could look away from his eyes, but his hand at her chin was no longer gentle. It held her tight.

"What game you play, I don't know," he said. "But you will not win it. This I guarantee you—you will not win it. You came and looked me in the eyes, and deceived me." He leaned close. She smelled the woods on him and the scent of summer blooms. "I know your secret. And I wager there are even more to find out, and, trust me, I'll find every single one."

Penrose knew what he was talking about. He was talking about her. About the blonde. "Please, you're scaring me," she said. Her words came out too soft, too weak. "Where did she go?" she asked him.

His chest pressed against hers, and he made no accommodation for her at all. She was forced to hold her breath. He said, "Do you care where she went? Do you really care as long as she's not here?" He stepped even closer, forcing her tighter against the table. "And why is she here, Penny? Do you know that?"

"I needed a job," she whispered her confession. Her eyes met his, imploring him to have sympathy. "I was hungry. I didn't know..." Her voice trailed off.

"She gave me the impression you knew a great many things, Penny. And that you weren't so innocent, that you committed a crime against her, and now she suffers for it," he said. "Her words, not mine."

His demeanor was decidedly very, very different, and she didn't know what to make of it. Mrs. Capshaw be damned to hell. "I'll leave," she whispered.

He chuckled, and the threat behind it gave her shivers. "You'll do no such thing. You made your bed—now you'll lie in it." Lifting her chin higher, he leaned closer until his lips touched her ear. "Or you can lie in mine, if you prefer," he said. "In fact, she mentioned something of the sort."

Not one word came to her lips. Not one. She could only breathe, but even that was a struggle—little gasps that caused her breasts to push against his chest. "I'm sorry," she finally whispered.

"Are you?" With his other hand, he traced up the side of her torso. Higher and higher, skimming over her breast, her shoulders, until his long fingers caressed the back of her neck and edged into her upswept hair.

Yes, his demeanor had changed so very much. Whatever the woman had said, she unleashed a new man in Carrick.

Penrose closed her eyes, unsure if this was even real. But her body told her it was real, very real, for it throbbed with life and feeling.

With his other hand, he traced a thumb over her lips, and she whimpered.

"Perhaps she wasn't lying." His voice, now at her ear, smooth and cajoling, seemed to be speaking right into her soul. "Are you afraid of me?" His voice was so, so low.

With his thumb on her lips, she couldn't speak. She shook her head no. But she was trapped and could only stand there, enduring the feel of him.

He removed his thumb. "Let me repeat my question. Are you afraid?"

She couldn't keep lying to him. Oh, she wanted to, but her pounding heart wouldn't let her think of an excuse. "Yes," she said, nodding. It was everything about him. His sharp, strange beauty. His odd ways. The way he frightened her.

But it was too late to say anything. His fingers guided her to look at him and then his mouth descended onto hers, deceptively soft.

She stilled, hardly believing what was happening. But it was happening.

He drew her closer, enveloping her, holding her

against him. His kiss turned hard and demanding. Anger lurked underneath. She knew it from the way his lips slashed, hot and accusing, over hers.

It wasn't merely anger. It was more than that. Something almost dangerous. Seductive.

Sinking, melting, she surrendered to the feeling. He tugged at her lips, coaxing her mouth to open and then his tongue thrust inside, claiming her. Triumphant.

Heat spread between her legs. An odd sound escaped her mouth, and a shiver swept over her. Her whole body shook from it, surprising her.

Her reaction seemed to inflame Carrick. A rumble came from his throat, and his kiss grew bolder, hungrier. All night long, his touch had been measured and precise. Incremental. Now it turned wild. Uncontrolled. His hands swept up her skirt hungrily, grabbing fistfuls of fabric, digging for her body beneath. When he found it, he growled and pressed against her, and she felt his hardness through the folds of her skirt. It made a pulse of pleasure beat between her legs.

From deep inside, an unrestrained, breathy shudder swept over her body. She whimpered and pressed farther into his kiss, overwhelmed with wanting him.

He stilled. Through her dress, she felt his hands clench angrily. "Dammit," he said harshly. "I can't do this." He stepped away from her. "I'm sorry," he said, avoiding her gaze, already turning away from her. "It's too damned complicated. More than that. God, it's so much more than that."

Reaching out and putting a hand on his chest, she leaned up and tried to kiss him. "Please." She didn't want it to stop.

"You are young and foolish," he said in a measured voice.

Taken aback, she stared at him hard before she said, "And you have no heart."

"Now you know the truth of it. My real affliction. Let's get back to work and forget this ever happened."

Chapter 4

Penrose went to bed agitated, filled with thoughts of his touch. Her lips were still numb from his kiss. Her body still betrayed her attraction to him. She lay on the bed, certain that she wouldn't be able to sleep and that images and memories of Carrick would haunt her. She snuggled deep under the covers, trying to block out the sun.

She had finally settled in and let out a long sigh, when a sound came from behind the walls. The noise continued for a moment, and then it stilled, too, almost as if whoever or whatever made the noise realized she was listening.

A sharp zing of terror shot up her spine. She held her breath, not breathing, waiting for the sound to begin again. It did. Slow, halting little noises. Self-aware noises, as if the need to be quiet was paramount. No.

This wouldn't do. She simply had to find out what caused the sounds.

She sighed in an exaggerated manner and made rustling noises from the bed. She slipped quietly from the bed, her feet hitting the floor softer than a mouse's, and then she padded with delicate footsteps to the wall. Leaning close, she pressed her ear to the wall. And that was when she saw it.

The morning sun slanted just right over the wood, illuminating all the imperfections and she saw a minute gap between two of the boards. Tracing her eyes along the gap, she saw hinges that were hidden so well in the pattern of the wood that she'd never have seen them if she weren't looking for them. They were painted white to match. Once she found the hinges, the outline of the secret door was easy to spot.

She dug her fingernails into the gap and pulled. Nothing. Following a hunch, she placed her palms on the wood, and pressed quick and hard. She was rewarded with the sound of a click, and the door sprung open.

The pale face of a child appeared. Violet eyes, big as dinner plates, stared into her very soul. She careened backward, struck by a shock stronger than lightning. Down she went, landing in an awkward, crab-like position, gasping, staring into the wide and shocked amethyst eyes of a child.

Three or four breaths passed before the child broke her gaze, spun around and began to scurry into the tunnel.

Her heart pounded so hard that she should have fainted, but anger rose up hard. Swiftly, she dived forward, plunged her arm into the hold and grabbed the child by the ear. A yowl came from the tunnel, and she pulled with all her might until the body of the child—a boy—came tumbling out and lay on the floor. Wide eyes—he looked just as shocked as she felt—stared into hers. The boy lay panting. Eight years old, she guessed. Pale like Carrick, white hair and bright skin.

"Who are you?" She sounded possessed, her words strangled.

No answer. She twisted her grip on his ear. "Tell me, child."

"C.J.," he spit out. His little face twisted in anger. "Now leave off."

"No. I'll not leave off." She said. "Who? What?" Her thoughts were tumbling as she struggled to understand exactly what she was seeing. "What in God's name are you doing crawling around in the walls?"

"I live in there." He threw the words out. Almost boastfully. "It's where I belong."

"No one belongs hidden in the walls. No one." She let go of his ear. Her hands were shaking. "Who are you?"

"I told you my name is C.J. For Carrick, Junior. Son of the great inventor." His tone was biting. "Only I'm not his son. No matter what my ma said."

"Don't be so hateful," she hissed. "And what do you mean by your ma said?"

"I mean when she was alive. That's what I mean. She died. Last summer. That's why I came here to live."

"I'm sorry she died. But this is madness! A child living in the walls!"

He looked away and slid his foot from side to side across the floor. "It happens. Life isn't all roses."

She agreed with him on that point. "No, C.J., it's not. But how come..." She struggled for words. "Why aren't you in a bedroom? In the house?" A horrible thought came to her. "Does he make you stay there?"

He laughed bitterly, a sound no child should ever make. "He didn't make me go in there. But he sure doesn't mind."

"You shouldn't be so hateful toward your father," she said. "Surely he must care for you." But she doubted her words even as she said them.

"That's what you think."

"Hey, now," she said, trying to be friendly. She put her hand on his shoulder, and she noticed with some relief that it had finally stopped shaking.

"Stop!" He pushed her hand away, his entire body curling from her touch.

"Okay, okay," she replied. "I'm sorry. Listen, it's strange to crawl about in the walls. Maybe I should talk to Carrick. You need to be out of the walls. For your safety."

His look turned sly and challenging. "Go right ahead. *Miss Penny*. Yes, I know your name." His chest puffed up. "I'm none of his concern. I'm no one's concern but my own. Least of all yours." He darted away, quicker than a rifle shot, diving right back into the tunnel.

Though the thought of entering the dark space made her shudder, she dropped to her knees and raced behind him through the little door. Light shone from behind her and lit the way ahead. Once she crawled in, the space opened up, and she was able to stand, though just barely. The walls were tight at her shoulders. The space unnerved her, and she considered turning around but didn't. "C.J?" she called out. "Come back. Please. I can help." She wasn't quite sure how, but she'd at least try. She crept forward until she saw a wall ahead, and just before the wall, the floor opened up into a hole.

Here she stopped, looked over and saw a wooden ladder fastened to the wall. Rough ridges were gouged into the floor. Markings, she realized, so that in the dark the child would know where the hole was, and he wouldn't fall through it. Peering down the hole, she was afraid and yet mesmerized by it. She wouldn't dare descend into those depths. Ever.

C.J. made rustling noises as he scooted around in the darkness.

"I'll know if you come up here again!" she called to him. The movements stopped, and she took it to mean that he was listening. "The next time you come to my room, announce yourself by knocking." She added, in a kinder tone, "And I'll invite you in. I could use a friend, you know!" Her voice echoed in the hollow space before dying away.

She made her way back through the tunnel and crawled from the hole. Then she climbed into bed and lay, panting and coated in dust, staring at the ceiling, thinking of the bizarre events of the day until, finally, she slept.

Penrose slept all day. In the late afternoon, a shaft of sunlight bathed her bed and woke her. She stood, went to the window and looked outside. Charleston was glorious. It always was in the summertime, but there was something special about the light in the last days of summer. The colors were bright and rich, almost dreamlike. But she barely enjoyed the sight because she was so very angry at Carrick. A child in the walls. Sickening.

The grandfather clock began to chime, a distant, dim

sound. It was time for work. Penrose tidied herself and went downstairs, her mind stewing.

He was waiting for her beneath the chandelier. The second she saw him, she flew down the stairs, rushed right up to him. "How come you didn't tell me you had a son?" she asked, and then her voice turned shrill and accusing. "A son who lives in the walls? The walls!"

"I didn't tell you because you didn't ask." His eyes were a maddening swirl of colors as a sneer cracked his lips apart. "You said it yourself. You're not paid to wonder or worry. So don't. It's none of your concern."

"None of my concern!" Her hands flew up in the air. "He's a child! Who is caring for him? He's lost his mother. He needs parenting. If you're letting him run loose in the walls, who feeds and clothes him? And why doesn't he go to school?"

"He cares for himself. And if you spend some time with him, you'll see that the last thing C.J. needs is schooling." He looked at her sharply.

"He's eight!"

"He's ten. And raising myself worked out just fine for me. I spent countless years in those walls. I survived, so I imagine he'll survive."

"You lived in the walls?" She couldn't hide the shock in her voice. "Why?"

His back grew rigid. "Sometimes it's easier not to be seen. Even in your own family." The last words came in almost a whisper. "Especially in your own family."

She kept thinking of the little boy's eyes. Those eyes that looked right into her soul. "But he's your son!" she said passionately, following him through the hallway.

"I don't even know if he's my child. One day, right out of the blue, he just showed up. I found him inside the house. In the hallway. He told me the sheriff dropped him off and left him because he was my son." A muscle by his eye twitched. "Clara—his mother and a...a woman of the evening—died of consumption. Because of his coloring they assumed he was mine."

He turned suddenly and began to walk away, heading toward the kitchen. She followed hot on his heels as he sped through the kitchen, lit a candle and then disappeared into the stairwell that led to the workshop. "I don't even know if these things are passed father to son. My father certainly didn't have my coloring. And my mother sure as hell wouldn't lie with a man who had even a single flaw, let alone a grand one like mine.

"Let's go start our work, shall we?" He began descending the tight spiral staircase, holding the candle for light.

Her steps were quick and fervent as she followed him. "Why didn't you just deny it?"

He stopped. She bumped into his back.

Slowly, he turned around. They were mere inches apart. Even though he stood a step beneath her, he still towered over her. His gaze roamed freely over her face. "Because I couldn't deny it," he said. "But I couldn't confirm it, either."

It took a moment for the implication to sink in. She sucked in her breath. "Oh."

"Yes," he said, "Oh. Take a good look at me, Penrose. It'll be no shock to you that upstanding women don't seek out my company."

There was some truth in his words. She was ashamed to admit it, but before today, she might have felt the same. She looked at him with fresh eyes—the uncertainty over his coloring and features was welling up once more. She still feared him. But there was no denying his strong features and wide shoulders. Or that intense, driven gaze. There was something else, too. Something she couldn't quite name. Even now, she wanted to reach out and touch him. But her fear of him held her back.

But all she could do was say quietly, "Just because you were raised like that doesn't mean he has to be. I wager that you are his father. He favors you in more than coloring and looks. He favors you in attitude, and that is not exactly a compliment. Now he'll walk in your footsteps for sure and learn to squirrel himself away from the world." She didn't mean for her last words to sound sharp, but they did, and there was no taking it back. Trying to make it better, she said, "You're merely pale. It's no reason to hide."

"No," he said in a steely voice. His gaze swept over her face before announcing, "*You* are 'merely pale.' *I* am colorless." His face contorted in anger. "You would have me teach him the world is a kind place for people like us? You want me to send him out there?" He jabbed his finger in the direction of Charleston and ground out the next words. "I've been out there. And even if he weren't my son, I wouldn't torture the child like that." He shook his head, turned around and kept moving down the stairs. Over his shoulder, he said, "You can't understand what it's like to not fit in. To stick out in a painful manner. We do okay by ourselves." His sigh echoed in the stairwell. "Now, are you planning on working or not?"

"Of course," she said, immediately chastised and regretting her boldness. She needed this job. She'd better learn to keep her mouth shut. "I'm sorry if I spoke out of place."

He didn't answer her. The moment was gone, the discussion over.

Even though Carrick lit a fire in the workshop, the room remained cold. He was cold, too, like ice to her. He sat at his desk and spoke to her in a dispassionate, monotone voice, issuing orders without ever looking up from his task.

Penrose followed his directions almost as if she were a mechanical woman, but inside her a tempest of very human emotion roiled. Fear, anger, awe. Was there no end to the wild emotions this man caused in her?

The night dragged on and when dawn finally came, she was relieved to slip away and try to get some sleep. She said good-night to him and began walking up the stairs. When she was halfway up, she heard his low voice echo in the space. "Wait. Penny, wait."

She stopped. She felt every strike of his boots on the stairs somewhere deep in her soul, and she trembled, wanting but at the same time afraid of what might be coming. What she hoped was coming. He came into view like a ghost floating up toward her. Then he was right there, just in front of her, and she could feel the maleness of him like a potent force.

He looked like no man she'd ever seen. He was so wild looking as he towered over her, staring at her with an angry, set expression. "Penny," he said in a rough voice.

"Yes?" She was breathing hard, her chest rising to within a hairbreadth of his.

He kissed her, his hands swooping behind her back as his body pressed against hers, propelling them upward and forcing her to climb the stairs until she felt the wall at her back. Then his body came down hard, and his lips harder still. She felt his erection pushing against her, and she moaned.

"The fault is my own." He pulled away. "Christ Almighty, you make me break every promise to myself." He said. "You should stay away from me. I'm no good for you."

Angry, she wiped her mouth. "I agree completely," she said, then spun around and ran up the stairs.

Chapter 5

It was midafternoon when Penrose woke up, still angry at Carrick. He was so unpredictable. She dressed, yanking on her clothes and dragging the comb through her hair. A knock came at the little door that led to the tunnel. "Just a minute," she called out, finishing up and then pressing on the secret spot that opened the door. It opened, and there stood C.J. with a candle in his hand, backing up as if he'd changed his mind. He retreated even farther, almost disappearing, the flame of his candle flickering in the darkness.

"Don't go," she said, dropping to her knees and holding out a hand to him. "Please. I need a friend. You do, too."

There was only silence. She couldn't see him in the darkness but thought he was still nearby. She didn't want to enter the tunnel again. Not if she could help it. "I'm too afraid to follow after you, and I could use your help today."

"With what?" he asked in a small voice.

She smiled. "I need someone to show me around. To show me where the food is kept and the supplies, too. I need a washtub. I have a list of things I'd like to accomplish before work starts this evening. I don't want to bother Carrick."

Finally, there were shuffling noises, and the tow-headed child popped out of the opening. Penrose scooted back to allow him to exit, and out he came, shyly until they both sat on the floor facing each other. She took his hand and held it in her own.

His hand was cold, and he didn't return her grip, but he didn't pull away, either.

"Thank you for agreeing to help me," she said.

He nodded.

They stood up and went down the stairs together, and she had her first real tour of the home. C.J. showed her the washroom, the new indoor bathroom that Carrick had installed. Then he took her to the kitchen and showed her a sideboard full of food, prepared and stored well. There was salted ham and pickled onions, breads and jams, and even a few jars of honey. C.J. sat at the kitchen table, and Penrose looked for something to eat.

"Who made these? Not Carrick." She knew him well enough already to know he didn't care about food. The man was too skinny by far.

"No. Twice a week Mr. and Mrs. Algood come. They help us around here. They bring provisions, and Mrs. Algood does the washing. Some cleaning, too, but Carrick gets grouchy if she stays in the house too much."

"Who keeps the grounds?" She dug around in the pantry, lifting items and reading the tin cans. She settled on a couple of biscuits and some jam and sat down next to C.J.

"Mr. Algood. He brings goats and cows to eat the grass when it gets too high. The rest of the time, we are on our own."

Penrose looked at him pointedly and playfully pushed his shoulder. "You mean you are on your own."

C.J. shrugged. "It's fine. I like it this way. It's better than going to an orphanage."

"No school?"

"I don't need it."

"You can read?"

"Yes. Arithmetic, too. I'm smart. I don't need school. I'm through with that."

She raised her eyebrows at the ferocity of his words. "You haven't been to school for a whole year?" She opened the container and pulled out a biscuit, which she split, smeared with jam and then handed half of it to him.

He looked surprised but took the biscuit from her. Biting it, he said between chews, "No, ma'am. I haven't. I can show you that I don't need it. I'll be right back." He jumped down from the stool he sat on and ran toward the foyer of the house. He was gone a few minutes, and when he returned he carried a stack of papers in his hands. Spreading them on the counter, he said, "Have a look."

She leaned over the papers and saw that numbers, equations and drawings of body parts lined the sheets. They were so advanced that there was no possible way a child had created them. "You did this?" she asked.

"Yes."

She held the stiff papers close, trying to take in the

sketchings and mathematical equations, but the meanings of them eluded her. The concepts were, quite simply, above her. "What are they?"

"When I first came here, I saw Carrick working. I've been thinking about his projects ever since. These are some of my ideas."

The sharp mind behind them was clearly evident. "Have you shown these to Carrick?" she asked, peering at him over a paper she held.

"Never." He was emphatic.

"Hmm," she said reflectively. Penrose had better sense than to press the issue. "Come on, let's finish eating."

After they had eaten, C.J. showed her around the grounds and took her to the river. The path led straight from the rear doors of the home, past the gardens, down the lawn and to the marshy banks of the water. The brown water ran slowly, obstinately, and the mayflies danced readily on the surface. The sun was beginning to arc downward.

It was a struggle to keep her mind away from Carrick, and she had such confusing thoughts, too. Anger and lust braided together. Sometimes it was hard to tell the two feelings apart. Well, there was nothing to be done about it, she reasoned.

Although it was still afternoon, Penrose wanted to open up the workroom before Carrick. "I have to go to work now," she said as they walked back to the house together, "but I hope we can spend more time together."

"Me, too," he said.

Penrose walked into the workshop early, as intended, while the space was still and quiet. She felt better, calmer, but still confused by Carrick. She watched the dying sun stream faint orange light into the dark room, lighting the dust motes that floated as fiery colors in the air. The wooden mechanical men stared expressionless out of the window.

The room was inert without Carrick. Whatever she thought of his personality, there was no denying his force in the workroom. She started the fire and lit the lamps and candles. The room still seemed empty. When Carrick was there, he brought motion and excitement, and something more...a wild possibility that at any moment a discovery might happen. She walked over to his workbench and ran her fingers over the many papers that covered it, taking in all the rushed drawings, evidence of a bright mind that was always thinking.

A noise came from behind her, and she turned to see C.J. standing by the mechanical man, looking up at it. "You know he's doing it wrong," he said with assurance and certainty. He was so young to possess such a confident intellect.

"How do you know he's doing it wrong?" she challenged him.

"He lacks vision. He has a purpose but no vision." The boy threw down the words as if they were laws. "This design is too heavy to work well. He's ignoring a better one."

She almost choked trying to hold back a laugh, not because what he said was funny, but because it was so succinct, so prescient, that it shocked her to hear it coming from a ten-year-old. She didn't doubt the truth of his words, because he was so very driven. Like his father.

"Well, you must be quite the inventor to have such knowledge."

"I am," he said proudly. "I already have mechanical things. Beings and such." He spoke in an offhand, boastful way. "You can come see it if you like." His purple eyes looked at her questioningly.

"I'm afraid I should stay here and wait for your father," she said, eyeing the door. "But how about tomorrow? And where is it? Is it upstairs in your room?" Penrose asked.

"No. I have to take you somewhere special." He lowered his voice and said, "Into the walls."

"C.J." She wasn't quite sure what to say to him, the thought horrified her so. "I can't go in there."

"You have to," he said. "It's the only way I can show you my experiment." He added, "You did promise, you know." Then he brightened. "Plus, you've already been inside of the tunnel. It's not very scary. My secret room is on the bottom floor, and it isn't near so scary down there."

How could she say no to such an eager request? "All right, I'll do it. But it'll have to be tomorrow. Your father will be here any second, and I need to work. I'll wake up early tomorrow, and you can show me everything then."

His eyes lit up. "Really?"

"Really," she said. "You better run along for now."

"Okay. Thanks, Penny," he said, his white hair bobbing up and down as he nodded. He turned and ran up the stairs.

Penrose tidied and cleaned the room, and then sat at her desk rereading her notes while she waited for Carrick.

"See something you like?" Carrick's voice surprised her, and she jumped.

"I was just..."

"Relax," he said, swooping past her, wearing his dark shirt and pants. "I was teasing." He was putting on a leather apron, tying the strings around his back, and he threw her one, as well. She put it on.

All of a sudden, he became serious. "Penny, I want to apologize," he said. "For my anger, and for making you feel bad." He dragged his fingers through his white hair. "It's just that…"

"Don't worry about it," she said.

He held up a hand, silencing her. "Penny, I'm not someone you want to be with. I can only focus on my project. I don't want complications or distractions, or pity."

"Pity?" she said. "I don't pity you at all."

"Enough. My decision is made, let's let the matter rest." He walked toward Harris, who stood gleaming in the glow of the fireplace. "Now, for tonight I think I'll have you work right beside me," he said. "We are to begin assembling some of the components that I've repaired."

So they began. He put on powerful eyeglasses with lenses thicker than her wrist, and as surgeon and nurse they operated on the mechanical man. One by one, he handed her gears and then gave her instructions on how to install them, peering over her shoulder to oversee.

"Can you check this?" she asked when one troublesome gear wasn't falling into place.

He leaned over her shoulder. "Press that small part. Yes. That one." He guided her hand to the right place.

When he touched her, her body reacted.

Her mind split into two halves. One side followed along with his instructions. The other side of her could feel only his presence. The scent of him—a hint of pine—and his body pressed against hers swamped that side and threatened to swamp the other side, as well. He was too focused to notice anything other than his project, so she indulged her senses and absorbed all that she could.

"Here, now hold this piece," he said, touching a small knob.

She grabbed the piece he was referring to, and Carrick tightened another. The gear slid into place.

"That's it," he said. "This is what vexes me. One tine on a gear and my whole future swings in the balance. One little cog out of place and it can all be ruined."

On and on they worked in tandem, their hands constantly touching, meeting briefly. He was right beside her, and she grew to know his breathing and the catch of his breath before he uttered a curse in frustration when something didn't go the way he expected. His hands were beautiful. Long, tapered fingers that caressed the parts and coaxed stubborn pieces into place. Their bodies brushed against each other. Only once or twice did she lose her composure, but she covered it up and pulled away. Her reactions, no matter how small, seemed to make him angry, so she did her best to control them.

Carrick was lifting a small tool when it clattered down and landed behind the mechanical man.

"I'll get it," she said, and twisted around the mechanical man to pick up the tool. When she tried to rise, she found she was trapped. Threads from her underclothes had become snagged on a sharp weld. If she moved too quickly, she risked toppling the mechanical man, but she couldn't undo the snag herself and stood there with one leg raised into the air.

"I think I'm stuck," she said, trapped in her strange position.

"I'll help," he said, pressing his body against her as he dug into the folds of her skirt. "Your threads have come undone," he said.

"So they have," she answered in a breathy voice. His hands on her body were such an intimate, thrilling sensation that Penrose felt dizzy and worried she'd fall over. She steadied herself by putting a hand on his back, but that made her light-headedness worse.

He tugged on her shift, gently. "Your dress needs mending," he said softly. "All of these loose threads."

"Everything about me needs mending," she said.

"I wouldn't say that," he said, tugging again. "There, you're free," he said when the fabric suddenly came loose.

She stood up, strands of her hair escaping from her bun. Loose wisps floated around her face. "Thank you," she said. A touch of willful impulse filled her. She wanted him to kiss her again, to have his hands on her body. She'd never known anything like the hot and sudden rush of lust that overwhelmed her at his touch. She lingered, willing him to touch her.

He turned around and kept working. It was as if he had no desire to revisit their kiss of the night before. With a mask of indifference on her face, she focused again on the task at hand.

It took all his effort, but Carrick kept his face still as stone as he worked. He was a man, after all. A man in too close proximity to a woman he wanted to kiss. Once again. More than kiss. He shouldn't have touched her. Once was excusable. Twice was unforgivable. But unforgettable, too. Dammit, he had a goal. A singular goal that he'd woken up every day and worked toward for the past six years.

Here he was, almost at the finish line. His libido wasn't going to ruin it for him, not for a woman who didn't want him anyway. When she had shuddered so deliciously under his touch the night before, he wanted to believe.

He stared at the component that he held in his hands, turning it over, fiddling with it but not seeing it. His thoughts kept returning to her. Why was he so cruel, so dismissive of her?

He knew why. Of course he did. He was cruel for the same reason he had hidden in the walls as a child. Better to reject and push away than to be scorned and mocked. That was a pain he didn't care to visit again.

Besides, he had to keep his focus on his goal. His life might be lonely and painful, but he could accomplish this one thing. Leaving a legacy and making a difference was most important, and he needed to steel his desire. The last thing he needed was complications.

No, the last thing he needed was to put his heart, his tin heart into the hands of another person. He swore that would never happen and, so far, he'd kept his word. Christ, she tempted a man. Beyond reason and sanity. The boy liked her, too. It would be so simple to let her in.

Simple, yes, but impossible. Easy lives didn't come to tortured souls, and he damn well knew he was a damaged person. If he fooled himself into thinking that he could have an easy life, fate would laugh at him.

A part of him wanted to fire her and send her away. God knew, he had a good reason. But the glisten in her eye when she looked at his creations… She believed in him. The rest he could forgo. He could suffer through an erection. He could endure the soft feel of her skin when she touched him.

In just one day, he'd already become wickedly attached to her presence in the workshop. The way her whole body lit up from the most minor successes, something as simple as finding a screw that fit perfectly. Every other assistant that he'd hired either refused to enter the house or sat next to him every night and uttered sharp expressions of disdain. He was so linear, his thoughts mapped out and his daily routine planned. She was as wild as the summer wind. He'd been cold for so long. So very long.

After his mother died and he was finally able to live all alone, he'd rejoiced. *Forget the world*, he thought. He didn't need the hassle of lingering looks and snide remarks. No. Gladly he'd spent year after year squirreled away in his mansion. He was fine with it. Only now, he couldn't imagine being without her in the workshop, let alone the house. Or his bed. That scared him. Scared him more than anything.

He would keep his head down. And try like hell to keep everything under control.

Chapter 6

It was close to dawn, but Penrose was still bent over her desk cleaning the tines of a gear with a miniature wire brush. The past few days had sped by in a rush. She had worked hard, hard enough to be stressed. But the repetitive motion of the work at hand soothed her. There was a change in the air. Instead of the cool, unmoving chill of night, a breeze blew and played with the stray hairs that fell across her temples. Shades of sunrise would begin at any moment.

She looked up from her work and watched him as he hovered over a piece of metal. He wore his thick glasses and, with his wild white hair, one would think he'd look like an old man. Nothing was further from the truth. He looked vital and fierce and completely obsessed with the object he was holding. Over and over he ran his fingers along the surface, following the curve of the metal.

He closed his eyes as his fingers danced along it, as if he was listening to it. His eyesight may have been very poor, but his hands saw more than enough. She realized that Carrick was an artist as much as an inventor, coaxing life from the objects he created.

Those hands. She envied the metal. She wanted to know what those fingers would feel like running along her thighs, her stomach, her breasts. To see that concentrated look in his face as he listened to her body with his touch. The things she would say to him…without ever muttering a word. She sighed.

Carrick looked up at her, smiled and said, "Don't worry, Penny, we're almost done for the evening."

"I've cleaned the gear," she said, shaking the thoughts from her head. "The edges are sharp again. I think it will work now." She put down the magnifier glass and rubbed her hands together. Her fingertips hurt from using the small tools.

He gave her a nod, a simple thing. But, in the workshop, any approval from Carrick was hard fought and won, and she took it with great pride. It was, for him, a compliment. The quiet coo of mourning doves sounded through the windows.

Carrick said half-dreamily, "For countless generations my family has sat right here and listened to the mourning doves. It's a timeless sound."

She closed her eyes. He was right. It could be any time in history.

"Sometimes it bothers me to think I'm just a link in the chain," he said.

She looked up then and saw him blowing away dust that had collected in his workspace. He continued, "And sometimes it soothes me to be part of something bigger than myself."

His words and the wistful quality of the morning coaxed a small confession from her. "I wish I had a place that I belonged to. A home. I feel like a leaf in the wind, tossed about."

He said nothing. Only the sound of the doves filled the air. She'd revealed too much. She felt his eyes on her, but she didn't want to look up and meet his gaze. No, she didn't want him to see into her soul. Busying herself, she gathered the tools to put them away. Partly to change the subject, she said, "Carrick? Can you tell me about the tunnels in the house? They're so strange. Where did they come from?"

He stood up and stretched his arms high into the air, then wound them around in circles, loosening his muscles, and said, "The manor was built before the Revolutionary War. The rumor is that the tunnels served as a storage area for ammunition and to hide troops. My father once said that eighty men lived in the walls for a whole month once." He removed the thick glasses he'd been wearing, rubbed his eyes and laughed. "I'd hate to think of the smell that created. The mansion means a lot to my family. It's always been in the Arundell family. For good or bad, we are the manor, and it is us. We'd do anything to protect it."

Penrose brought him the piece she had been working on. "Here you are." Their fingers touched as he took it from her.

"That makes me curious," she said. "How is it that the manor survived the war? How did you save it from Sherman when every other plantation was razed to the ground?"

She should've noticed the bristle in his words. The pain. But she hadn't and pressed on. "What did you have to do?"

His eyes flicked in her direction, angrily, as if they were conceding something. Holding her gaze, he nodded. "All right, I'll tell you." Turning away, he walked toward a shelf and began to fiddle with the tools. "Sherman came through when I was about twelve or so. At the time, my gangliness as a young boy only added to my strange looks. Worst of all, I had embraced rebellion. I couldn't enlist like my pa and brothers. I was too young, and my affliction made it impossible. The slaves were all gone by then. I had a part in that, too, but that's a different story. Anyway, one of my brothers was already dead. We didn't know it, but at that moment, my pa was dying of fever in a camp. It was only my mother and I. We heard that Sherman was close, and my mother, clever woman that she was, came up with a solution that kept him far away from here." He snorted softly. "I must tip my hat to her because it worked."

It seemed that only a moment had passed, and yet the day was noticeably brighter. He was so complicated. Intense. She didn't so much fear the darkness in him anymore, but rather the depths of him. Or rather the depths of his pain.

They were both quiet, like a lull before a storm, and then he continued. "I was the solution. She put a sign about my neck, mussed my hair up fierce and then put faint streaks of mud beneath my eyes. On down the road, she put up another sign that read Warning, Yellow Fever. Then she brought me down to the gate along with the Persian carpet from the drawing room. She had me lay on the carpet and then rolled it up around my body, leaving my head and the sign exposed. I had to lie there, pretending to be dead for the entire day while the troops marched by. She made it clear, abundantly clear, that the entire future of the manor rested on my back."

It was so awful that she couldn't think of a word to say because anything she uttered would be an insult to him, so she walked over and put her hand on his arm. He pulled away sharply, almost meanly. But her touch seemed to trigger something deep within him because he began to speak so fast she could hardly follow his words.

"For more than an hour, I heard that army coming. You could hear the footfalls from miles away. A rumbling thunder headed straight toward me. I lay there with my eyes open, watching the birds flit about in the trees. When the troops drew close, I stilled and closed my eyes. When the harmonious thunder of an entire battalion's boots echoed loud and clear, I knew that they were just down the road. All of those soldiers walking in lock step." He shook his head. "They were a machine. The ground shook. I never looked. I didn't dare. Boot after boot stomped by my head and I lay there like a talisman warning them away."

He took a breath and continued on, "It was the officers that I hated most—those foulmouthed righteous men that called me the devil and many more names I won't say to you. I'm certain that if their troops weren't there, if they didn't have to keep up impressions, they would've abused my body just for sport. Though I was grateful they gave orders to pass by, I was more grateful that my mother was smart enough to keep my arms wrapped up tight because if I'd been able, I'd have smashed their faces to pulp."

A soft purr came from the doves outside. After his horrible story, she was surprised to hear that the doves still cooed. His festering wound of a memory had been lanced, the poison drained. In the lull after such an admission, she could see him stiffening, contorting his body the way he did when he was full of hate. When he spoke, it had a false brightness to it. A barely concealed bravado. "Well, Penny, now you know just how important Arundell Manor is to our family."

She was going to speak, and he must have sensed it, for he moved abruptly, nodding his head toward the stairs as he walked away. "Come on. The sun is up. It's time to quit."

C.J. woke her later that afternoon. "Are you ready?" he asked.

She rubbed the sleep from her eyes and leaned up from the pillow on one elbow. He was looking at her with a hopeful expression and an infectious smile, holding a lantern in his hand.

"Why do you have a lantern in the afternoon?" she asked, still confused by tendrils of sleep.

"Did you forget? We're going into the tunnel. So you can see my workshop. I have one, too, you know."

She had forgotten, and she was still exhausted. Another hour of sleep sounded wonderful. But how could she disappoint him? Forcing a smile on her face, she told a little white lie. "How could I forget?"

"Where we're going it's pitch-black. Don't worry, you won't be scared. You'll have me."

"Okay, let me get dressed first. But, C.J., I don't want to climb down that ladder."

"You don't have to. You can take the other entrance, the one right next to the grandfather clock."

"Okay, I'll meet you downstairs, then."

After he had shut the door, she dressed and readied herself for the day. She wished she had another gown instead of her dour black one. Perhaps after she'd been paid, she'd go to town and buy fabric to make one. By the time she made her way downstairs, she felt more awake and greeted him with a smile. He waited for her by the grandfather clock, a small, pale child next to the mammoth timekeeper. Looking at the clock, she was surprised to realize that she'd grown so used to it that she rarely noticed the chimes anymore.

"Are you ready?" he asked. "Hold this for a moment, will you?" he said, handing her the lantern.

She took it from him, and he went to the wall by the stairs. He pointed to the perfectly concealed doorway and pushed on the wood. It snapped open quickly, revealing a three-foot-high door. He crawled inside. Penrose dropped to her knees and handed him the light.

"Aren't you coming?" he asked.

Her stomach shouted a thousand protests, but her mouth said, "I'm coming. I promised you, so I'm coming in." It was hard to crawl with a skirt on. She was forced to push up the fabric so that her knees had purchase on the ground. With the hiss of her skirts scraping against the floor, she crawled into the space.

His angelic face was illuminated by the light, and she focused on that, ignoring the darkness that framed the boy. Darkness that seemed never-ending.

"You did great, Penny!" he said. His cheery voice echoing inside the tunnel sounded macabre.

"Thank you, C.J.," she said. "But we're still right at the entrance. Let's hope my courage holds out."

"It's not much farther, just a little bit and then the space opens up to a little room. My own workshop," he said with more than a touch of pride in his voice.

She crawled along a small stretch of tunnel. All of a sudden the space opened up and lamplight filled the emptiness, revealing a small room. A pile of blankets lay in one corner, and a few plates with crumbs on them sat beside it. In another corner stood a makeshift worktable piled with tools, candles and wood scraps.

Able to stand now, she walked over to the rough table made of wood scraps. She lifted a tool. "You stole this from your father?" she asked.

His chin went up. "He doesn't miss 'em."

Setting the tool down, she said, "No, I imagine he doesn't." She ran her touch over a box of candles and matches. Then something at the end of the table caught her eye. It was a strange box made of metal with wires protruding from the top of it. The wires ran to the floor into two containers that held some kind of liquid. She reached down to one of the containers.

"Don't touch it!" He ran over to her. "It's an acid compound made of zinc and carbon. It could burn you. It's called a battery. It provides power to my creation. Here, let me show you how it works."

From underneath the table, he pulled out another box. "Here," he said, holding it up to her. "You can open it."

He held the lantern while she bent over and lifted the lid. Yellow light spilled into the box and revealed a wooden bird. It was roughly hewn, its body still covered with chisel marks. The beak and eyes were merely suggested, not finely etched. Delicate wings made of paper unrolled in her hands. They'd been cut to shape, glued to the bird's body, and were decorated with pencil-drawn feathers. Two strings ran from the edge of the wings. "It's beautiful," she said. It was beautiful. Childlike, yes. But she couldn't help recalling his words from the other night—purpose and vision both. "You made this?" she asked.

C.J. unspooled the string as he spoke. "I did," he said proudly. "I carved it myself. Had to cut the block in two, scoop out the insides and then glue the two halves together. It's lighter with the insides scooped out." His shot her a look. "Weight is important, you know. Crucial." He threaded the string to a contraption that sat right next to the battery. It had gears and two loops that he tied the string to.

He pulled a wire from the battery and touched it to the contraption. The two prongs clicked to life and rotated. The strings drew taught, and the tension stretched to the bird. The wings lifted, and then as the prongs on the device swung in a circle, the string went slack, and the bird's wings dropped down again.

The motion was so simple… Slow, yes, but beautiful. The motions were repetitive, harmonious and fluid. It was like watching a primitive bird. One that couldn't yet take flight but was determined it would.

"It's amazing," she said to C.J. And it truly was. The child had a brilliant connection of ideas in his mind to bring about such a complex creation. The design was simple yet beautiful.

"Look," he said. He held the bird up in the air and mimicked flight. "One day…" he said meaningfully. "One day. I think the real trick of such movement is a simpler source of power. That and the external rope that mimics muscle movement." He no longer sounded like a child when speaking of his invention; he sounded focused and single-minded. C.J. looked up. "Well, to have true, free range of movement you need an almost portable power source. Think of the mechanical man. He's practically a locomotive with all the steam he requires in order to run."

"Does your father know what you're doing in here? He should if he doesn't."

"He won't care."

"I assure you, he will care, C.J. He needs to know how smart you are. You and he are so much alike. I know you could help him. More than I can." She had no doubt about that. How had Carrick missed the boy's genius up until this point? It seemed an impossibility. Carrick must be so far into his own world that he was blind to what was right in front of him.

C.J. huffed. "I don't care if he does know. He could care less about me, and I care even less about him."

She put her hand on his arm. "I'm sorry. You don't have to live in the tunnels, you know. There's nothing to be afraid of out there."

He yanked away and looked up at her with anger. "I love it in here," he said passionately. "Everything about it. And even more, I can travel the length of the tunnel. It's safer for me in here, rather than out there. I feel... I don't need to be afraid in here."

"You don't need to be afraid out there, either. You belong here. It's your home."

He shook his head somberly. "No. You don't understand. It's his home. This—" he looked around "—this is my home."

Standing next to the peculiar child, and buried in

the dark, dank place as they were, she wondered what her place was in the whole bizarre situation. A beautiful but frightening house, a beautiful but frightening man, a ghost of a child, and more secrets and mysteries than she knew what to do with.

Suddenly chilled, she rubbed her arms for warmth. "Come on, C.J.," she said in a hollow sounding voice that echoed around them. "Let's get out of here."

Chapter 7

August drew to a close. Penrose felt herself unwinding, settling in and growing roots. She adored everything about Arundell Manor, from the peaceful pond and the graceful oaks to the crickets that sang outside the windows every evening. Sometimes she wondered if the house had a soul. It was a strange thought, even to her, but it was as if the house welcomed her, made room for her and enjoyed her presence. Every afternoon, summer storms rolled in, and after waking to the sounds of thunder, she went downstairs to sit on the veranda and watch the spears of lightning in the growing clouds, waiting for the pelting rain to begin. Her mother had always told her that with rainstorms came invitations for second chances, and it seemed she was right.

More often than not, C.J. came and sat beside her. Twice he brought his marbles, and they used chalk to sketch a wide circle onto the floor. While the persistent rain fell, they played marbles with Penrose on her knees, analyzing each shot and trying desperately to win. To no avail. C.J. was a tough player and both times trounced her soundly.

Work on the mechanical man progressed, though Carrick still seemed unsettled. He regarded her with a frozen indifference—always polite and encouraging, but never more than that. Their two, brief encounters seemed more like a dream than a memory. She ached to feel his touch again though she hid it as best she could.

Just after a thunderstorm ended late one afternoon, Penrose and C.J. were shooting marbles when they heard Carrick coming down the stairs. C.J. made himself scarce, running down the steps of the veranda and across the lawn. "C.J.!" Penrose shouted. "Please stay!" But the boy was long gone, and when she turned around, Carrick stood in the doorway. His expression was like stone. Lately, it was always like stone. "Are you ready to work?" he asked.

She nodded but felt far from ready. Had they really kissed? She'd thought of it so many times, yet it seemed like a thousand years ago. But her skin still burned with the memory of his touch. Her body felt alive when she looked at him.

She pressed her lips together and tried to maintain composure. She wanted that bliss…the sweet bliss that carried her away when he touched her.

On that night, all of her propriety had slid away so quickly, so easily, and she would gladly forgo it again. With his stern looks and cold coloring, he was so visually arresting. She'd seen the essence of him, his heart of fire.

The look he gave her burned right through her. She stood up, smoothed her skirts, blushed and stammered, "I'm...ready."

"Is everything okay?"

"It's fine," she insisted. "Let's go."

Carrick stepped aside, and she squeezed past him. In the center of the foyer, she looked at the family portrait that hung in such a place of prominence. "Are you in that picture?" she asked.

He stood behind her, not touching her, but his presence was a wall of strength at her back. "What do you see in that picture?"

Ignoring the surge of butterflies that fluttered in her stomach, she answered, "I'm looking at a perfect family picture." It was idyllic, three young Arundell boys were frolicking on the grass while their parents sat on a blanket looking over the scene. Arundell Manor appeared behind them, looking serene and stately on the hill. The oak by the pond was there, though younger and with less stately branches.

"Look closer. It's far from perfect," he whispered in her ear. From behind her, he reached over and traced a finger along the canvas until he reached a brown-haired boy, younger than the others, with cherub cheeks and a wild look to him. The boy was running down a hill, laughing, with his brothers in pursuit. His finger tapping the boy, Carrick said in a low, harsh tone, "That's me."

"How can that possibly be you?" Confused, she turned and looked at him.

"It is me." His jaw clenched. "Or I should say, it's the me my parents wished for. The one they pretended they had."

She looked at the child in the picture once more. If he was anything like he was now, it was cruel to paint him so carefree and happy. Crueler still to erase his coloration. He'd been completely eradicated and a fictional character painted in his place. She put her hand on his arm.

He pulled away. Ignoring that, she continued. "It's a shame they did that to you. I'm sure you were a beautiful child. It must have hurt."

"Hurt?" he said with a laugh. "It didn't hurt me." His next words pierced her soul. "It destroyed me. Now, for all time, whichever Arundell descendant looks at this picture will think me to be that child. A happy little boy living a happy life. When I was someone else entirely."

He pointed to the parents. "Look at them. Look. The perfect couple. One would never know that they made their child hide in the tunnels whenever they threw a ball or guests visited. You'd never know that man…my father…looked me in the face and told me I should have died rather than bear the Arundell name."

Carrick was right. It was such an injustice. If Penrose were the artist, she would have painted him off in the distance, always in the distance, beautiful but cold, like an icy angel. "They did you an injustice," she said. Anger flared in her. "Now you do it to your own son."

"You're mocking me," he said.

"It's the truth and you know it." She reached out to him again, but he shook her off. "Please."

"It's not all bad. I wouldn't have the mechanical man if they hadn't treated me with such disdain."

"Why is that?"

"I hate pity," he said simply. "I don't want people to think of me with pity. I have plans. I want to change the world. So don't pity me. God, the irony. My family fought to keep their slaves, and all died in the effort. They told me that a person's dark skin color made them inferior. Yet, every single one of them treated me as if I was the most inferior of all." His words tumbled out fast and harsh. "Me! Me. I'm the palest of them all, and yet I should hide? They're all hypocrites! Every single one of them. Every man on earth. I reject them all."

"There are many who wouldn't judge you…" Her words faded as she spoke them because she doubted the truth of them. No, he would be judged, and harshly. The world was cruel. It judged a woman for being poor. It judged a man for being dark, and it judged a child for being too pale. People had such a narrow idea of perfection.

He took a deep breath and said, "Now that we've belabored a part of my life I'd rather skip over, would you care to work?"

"Of course, I would. Let's get the mechanical man up and running right away. We're so close." She followed him down the stairs and into the workshop. Right away, Penrose noticed the empty chairs by the window. The wooden mannequins were missing.

It was shameful, but immediately her mind went right to C.J. She looked at Carrick. His attention was focused on the mechanical man, and he didn't notice the chairs were empty. She had the urge to ask him about it, but she also knew that if it was C.J. who had stolen them, he would be in serious trouble, and she wanted to talk to him first.

Penrose went to her desk and busied herself, and soon enough Carrick was hard at work on the mechanical man. As he moved about, he muttered under his breath.

A few hours later, he said, "Penny, come take a look at this."

Carrick stood next to Harris, who towered over him. Carrick turned and looked at her with barely contained excitement. "I think we're there. I think it's a go. Every dowel, every rod, every gear fits perfectly. Let's fire him up."

His excitement overtook her. She wanted to hug him, and the urge was so strong she gave in to it. She threw her arms around him, pulling him tight and kissing him on the cheek. "Let's do it!" she cried.

Stepping back, he thoughtfully rubbed his cheek where her lips had been. But he didn't look upset. Not at all. "Yes," he said. "Let's do it." He stoked the fire and pulled the vats into the enormous fireplace, and while the water heated, he paced the room excitedly.

"I'll be right back," she said. C.J. should be with them to watch Harris brought to life.

Carrick paid her no mind. He was too busy preparing the mechanical man.

She grabbed a candle and ran up the stairs to check C.J.'s bedroom, but, of course, the boy wasn't there. There was one other place the child could be. In the walls. Gathering up her courage, she went to the little door by the staircase, opened it and peered into the dark tunnel.

"C.J.!" she called out. She heard a rustling noise and held up the candle. "C.J., wake up! Something exciting is about to happen! Carrick is about to fire up Harris. The mechanical man!"

"What?" he said in a sleepy voice that echoed down the tunnel to her. "He's going to start him?"

"He is! Come on...hurry!" she urged. Penrose backed out and waited for him in the hall. At that moment, the grandfather clock began to toll. Twelve mellow strokes of the bell rang out. "Perfect," she said to the empty hall. "A new day. A new beginning."

The boy emerged from the tunnel with sleepy eyes and mussed clothes. Day clothes. The child should be on a schedule, she thought. He needed tending to—and badly.

She hoped that once Harris fired up, the excitement would spill over between father and son and that they would bond. A fragile hope, but still there. If nothing else, they had the love of inventing in common. It would be something to build on. She dared not voice her secret hope. It was such a silly hope that she was even reluctant to wish for it, but she couldn't help it. The child needed his father, and the father needed his son. He was just blind to it.

She held C.J.'s hand and led him down the cellar stairs and into the workroom.

The room crackled with excitement. In the fireplace, the flame burned brightly as the sun and threw an orange gloss over Harris. The vats steamed and the vapor billowed out and filled the room with a thick haze. The mechanical man stood stout and proud, his tin skin shining bright, and his lantern eyes already lit and glowing with excitement. It was as if Harris knew something terrific was about to happen to him.

Wild-eyed with excitement, Carrick looked up at them as they approached. "It's all set up. We need to wait for the steam to build up enough pressure to bring him to life."

"Do you think it will work?" asked C.J. He had the same bright look of expectation on his face that his father did. If Penrose needed any further proof that they were father and son, it was right there.

"I think it will work," she announced confidently. C.J. and Penrose stood side by side and waited.

Suddenly, the tubes that fed the steam into Harris stiffened. A grinding noise and a series of rattles came from deep in the belly of the mechanical man. C.J. squeezed Penrose's hand, and she squeezed his back. Carrick came and stood next to them, completely still. Everyone waited.

With a puff of steam from the top of his boxy head, Harris came to life. His eyes burned bright, and his massive body shivered and clattered with the sounds of metal against metal, followed by a whirring noise, and with aching slowness and a loud clacking noise, the mechanical man lifted his arm.

Goose bumps crawled over her skin. "He's saying hello," she said in a breathy voice.

"Just wait," said Carrick. "He'll take a step." He stood eagerly, leaning forward, eyes riveted on the mechanical man.

With a series of rapid clicks, the mechanical man lifted his leg, cranked it higher, then higher still. With a sudden finality, the leg came down and he lurched forward.

They all shouted at once and threw their arms in the air. Everyone hugged. Penrose felt such joy. Of course, Harris was no different than a train or an engine, but somehow to her, he was so much more. He was the extension of their hopes and dreams and with this step, he gave them what they desperately needed.

"It's the second step that's always the problem," said Carrick in a worried voice.

More clicking noises came from Harris. He cranked forward on his foot, settling his weight on it, and then his other foot began to wind, to lift higher, and as the leg moved, a whiny squeal came from him. He began to lean, just a fraction at first. "Please," said Carrick with a voice bordering on desperate.

They waited with their breath held, watching that metal foot move higher and then swing forward.

With a loud groan, the mechanical man heaved forward, held itself upright for a moment, tottered, and then collapsed. Right to the ground in a riotous heap. His lantern eyes shattered. His limbs came apart. Tubes sprang from his backside and whipped wildly around the room, hissing and spewing steam. Harris crashed loudly as he broke apart and the pieces skidded across the floor.

Penrose gasped. C.J. screamed.

Carrick stood stock-still, staring straight ahead, his arms limp at his side.

Thinking fast, Penrose went and pulled the tubes from the kettles. The hissing and whipping lines slowed and then came to rest. The corpse of the mechanical man lay in pieces with steam rising from his broken body. He looked like a fallen soldier. A dead dream. It was the very worst thing that could ever happen. Ever.

Without saying a word, Carrick went to a chair, sat down, slumped over and rested his head in his hands.

C.J. looked shocked, crestfallen and scared, too. She took the child by the hand and reassured him. "It's okay," she said, wiping the sweat from her brow with her sleeve. "We'll try again. Maybe tomorrow," she said though in her heart she doubted the truth of her words. Harris was just too broken. "Why don't you run to bed and let me talk to your father?"

The boy nodded. All of the excitement had left his face, and he looked much as he had before. Sullen. Angry. "I knew it wouldn't work anyway," he said in a defiant tone.

"Go on back to bed now," she said, and turned him toward the stairs. "Go on."

He raced up the stairs without looking back.

Penrose walked over to Carrick. With the steam hanging in the air, she could barely see him.

"I can't get it to work," he said, not looking at her, not lifting his head from his hands. "No matter what I do, I can't get it to work."

At his feet lay an iron rod that had broken apart from Harris. Carrick reached down and picked it up, studying the piece. When he spoke, his voice was deathly quiet. "God, I can design a clock. I can design a mechanism to specifications so miniature that it boggles the mind. But I can't take this damn project to completion." He looked up at her with an anguished expression. "It vexes me. I've tried wires, but they catch on the internal mechanisms and corners. I've moved the central housing. Nothing has worked." He clenched his fingers. "Steam is too damn problematic. The components are a nightmare."

His eyes met hers and her heart broke to see their flat, dark color. "I've failed." He shook his head. "Ruined. Ruined before anyone even knows my name. Why did I think I could make a difference? That the world would even care?" He sighed, the most defeated sound Penrose had ever heard. "I'm just another fool with a dream."

Penrose went and knelt beside Carrick. Steam curled around them. "You can't give up," she said. The conviction resounded within her. "We're not giving up," she said, placing a hand on his leg. "I'm not."

"It's easy for you to say. You can walk right out that door and get yourself a new life. I don't have that luxury." He dragged his hands through his hair. "I wanted the world to know my name. To remember me." Carrick lifted the heavy rod and bounced it in his palm a few times. He drew a quick, sharp breath, lifted his arm and threw the rod across the room. It crashed into the wall and clanged onto the floor. "Is that too much to ask?" he shouted.

She tried to calm him. "It's not too much to ask, Carrick. You just haven't asked the question enough times. Let's try again."

"I'm done."

She scrambled for the right words, the exact right thing to say that would lift his spirits and renew him. "Even a misstep is a step forward," she said, knowing that those words were wrong. Any words would be wrong just then. But she had to try. She took his hand into hers. Heat flooded her skin.

Full force, the memory of their kiss swept over her. The way his lips had claimed hers, the sensation of his entire body pressed against hers. On impulse, she brought his hand to her lips and then ran it tenderly along the line of her jaw. "No effort is ever wasted," she whispered.

Carrick slumped forward, resting his forehead

against hers. He took fierce breaths. His hands wound into her bun, needy and demanding. He pressed his lips against her forehead and leaned onto her. He was heavy, but she held his weight. Still taking those angry breaths, he dragged his fingers deeper into her hair, loosening it from the bun. It spilled around her in a midnight fall of curls.

He moaned when her hair sprang free and grabbed handfuls of it, pulling forward and draping it around the two of them so that the whole world was distant. Her hair was a black river against the white ice of his skin.

When he spoke, his words were angry and biting. "Look at you. All soft and pliable. Soothing me." His grip was a vise holding her against him. "You think to lure me into revealing a tender heart beating in this chest? Well, you'll be disappointed, Penny, because I'm as empty as the mechanical man."

He wrenched her face upward, and she stared at him, inches from him. His nostrils flared, and his eyes glistened with unshed tears. She wanted to wipe them away, but she couldn't move. Suddenly, his lips came down fiercely on hers, revealing an anguished part of himself that knew no words, only pain.

She clung to him and kissed him back, desperately, achingly, her hands grabbing at him, trying to convey what words couldn't. He kissed her with a volatile mix of passion and need. Penrose, who for so long had focused on how little she had in life, realized how much she had to give.

She pulled away from him, but her hands had somehow wound into his hair, and she gripped him tightly. "Carrick Arundell," she said. "You will change the world. Mark my words. Mark my words." She began to stand, pulling him up from the chair as she did.

"What?" he asked her, "Do you have plans for me? Are you going to fix me and bring me to life like the mechanical man?"

"No, Carrick." She took his hand, kissed it and then ran it over her breasts, past her waist, before pushing it deep between the folds of her skirt. "I'm going to bring you to life in an entirely different manner." The boldness of her actions surprised her.

A low, guttural sound came from his throat. His hands wrapped around her, pulled her tight against him, and through her skirt she felt his hardness.

"Is that what you want?" he asked, still a trace of anger in his voice.

She didn't answer right away, simply stared up at his troubled eyes. Finally, she spoke. "Yes. That's what I want. And more."

"God, you drive me crazy," he said in a hoarse voice.

Kissing, bodies entwined, they moved across the room, with Carrick guiding her toward a table. With one fell swoop, he wiped the table clean, sending parts and pieces clattering to the floor. He pushed her against the table, his hands at her back as he unbuttoned her gown. Jerking the dress down, he shoved it impatiently to the floor.

She wore her shift, and it stuck to her damp skin, revealing every contour and shadow. The air chilled her skin. Her nipples tightened, and she saw his gaze move to her chest. It made her hotter for him, and her chest rose and fell as her breath grew fast.

He slipped a finger under the fabric and peeled it away from her skin. He unwrapped her body slowly, dragging the cotton down her body. When he bent to lower the shift past her waist, she gasped, knowing that he was right there, right next to the spot that ached for his touch. He tossed aside the clothing. She stood nude before him.

Stepping back, his gaze traveled the length of her body. "I promised myself I wouldn't do this," he said. "And every day I struggled to keep my promise. But dammit, looking at you now, I was a complete fool to do so. You are mine, Penny. Remember that."

"I am yours." The words had come out before she realized what she said. But they felt right to say and, listening to them, they felt right to hear.

She stepped forward and began to unbutton his shirt, and when it was off, she ran her fingers over the ridges of his muscles. Goose bumps rose on his skin as she touched him. There was so much power underneath his skin, but that's not what drew her to him. No, what drew her to him was his mind. His fierce passion for creating. But those muscles under her fingertips were heaven.

He placed his hand on her chest and gently pushed her down until she sat on the table, legs dangling. He nestled between her legs. The feel of him, right there, shocked her. It was so intimate, almost a promise of what was to come.

He kissed her, leaning forward, forcing her to lie back on the table, and she peered up at him, nervous. He towered above her and ran his hands along the length of her legs. She closed her eyes, shutting out every sensation except for his touch, which left a trail of heat along her skin.

"You are perfection," he said.

She opened her eyes. "You are, too," she whispered.

And he *was* perfection. But he looked dangerous just then, almost feral, his eyes darkened by an intensity she'd never seen before. They were gray streaked with purple, the color of early night. She squirmed against him. "Please," she begged, not certain what she was begging him for.

He stilled. "Please what?" he said, lifting his hands from her body, a wicked tilt to his lips. "What exactly do you want?"

Her hips bumped against him. She tried to speak with her body, but his hands didn't respond, remaining a fingertip above her skin.

"No." He shook his head. "No. Please, what? Tell me, my little Penny. I want to hear you ask for it. I need to hear it."

She whimpered, reluctant to say the words. Unsure of what she even wanted.

But he was insistent. "Say it," he ordered her.

"Please," she whispered in a low voice. "Touch me."

"Louder." He spoke fiercely, as if hearing her words were the most important thing to him.

She spoke full and loud, but her words came out in a rush. "Please, please, Carrick. Touch me. Take me. Please."

He made a deep growling sound and raked his hands across her body, over her breasts, fanning out over her stomach before pausing above the cleft between her legs. "So beautiful," he said, feathering a touch over the center of her. "Black as night." His hand dipped between her legs, and with two fingers he spread her lips, looked down, and then he hissed. "Hiding a pink rose."

She cried out as he touched her. With his fingers on her body, he became an artist once again, tracing over her most secret part, exploring her, bringing breathy whimpers from her lips. Instinctively, she spread her legs wider, wanting more. Needing more. "Please, Carrick," she said again, no longer whispering.

"Not yet," he replied. She saw his pale skin lit by the firelight, his large shoulders throwing her into shadow. He unbuttoned his pants, and she heard them fall to the floor. She closed her eyes again, waiting.

But then she felt his breath between her legs and then his hot tongue slid between her folds. She made a choking noise and lifted herself up, leaning on her elbows. She took in the sight of his head buried between her legs.

His eyes were closed. His hands held her buttocks, and his mouth was wild. Demanding.

She cared about nothing except that tongue—hot and private, and so wicked. She began thrusting against him, lifting one hand and lacing her fingers through his hair. Directing him.

She began to moan his name over and over again and fell back against the table. Suddenly, his mouth was gone.

He stood above her. "I need you right now," he said.

Climbing onto the table, he covered her. Their bodies were slick with sweat and slid against each other. She opened her legs wide and felt his hardness pressing against her center, sliding up and down against her wetness but never entering her. It was torture.

And it was really happening.

"Please," she said.

In response, he kissed her deeply, and she tasted the tang of her own arousal. He pressed against her opening and then pushed. She cried out from the sharpness of the pain and dug her fingers into his back.

He froze. "Are you okay?" he whispered into her ear.

Nodding, she said, "Just move. Please, just move."

He did, but gently, in a long, slow thrust that opened her farther. Every sensation faded away, and she was aware of a sharp feeling of fullness. An exquisite ache. He pushed even deeper, so slowly that she cried out in frustration.

"I'm holding back," he said with his mouth against.

"Don't hold back. Go." She needed him.

"You don't know what you're asking for."

"Maybe I don't. But I want to find out."

"You drive me wild," he said, sliding his hands beneath her shoulders, lifting her torso and pressing her breasts against his chest. He began to move.

She felt herself yielding, opening up to him. The pain was completely gone, replaced by a delicious, tingling numbness. Lost to the feeling, she grabbed him, urging him on. That feeling ruled her. It was all she could focus on.

The tingling spread, deepened and turned to hot little pulses of pleasure every time he buried himself deep inside her. She lived for that moment, that brief collision of their bodies. Every thrust pushed her higher, and soon she found herself whimpering and crying out in time to his movements.

The feeling gathered force and built inside of her, and Carrick was insistent, plunging into her, forcing her closer and closer to an abyss that she didn't understand. She teetered on the edge, resisting until the very last moment when she couldn't fight it anymore.

She gave in to it completely, to the rush of pleasure

that exploded inside her. It felt as if she were flying and falling at the same time, and she called his name over and over again. Almost from a distance she was aware of his cries, his hands at her as he found his own ecstasy.

And there, in the steamy workshop, amidst the wreckage of his dreams, they clung to each other until the world slowly returned.

He sat up, and she wanted to cry out from the loss of his body next to hers. "Come to bed," he said. "My bed." Taking her hand, they walked up the stairs together.

Chapter 8

It was not yet dawn, and Penrose sat upright in Carrick's bed, her knees tucked beneath her chin as she studied Carrick. He lay dead to the world, sprawled out and tangled in the covers, his hand possessively thrown over her hip.

In sleep, the mask he showed the world was removed and his features had smoothed out to reveal a classically handsome face with lips that looked as if they might curl into a smile at any moment.

She had a confusing mix of emotions. Her body felt chafed and raw and alive. Her were lips swollen, her heart full. But worry plagued her. He couldn't give up on his dream.

She couldn't sleep. It was useless. She closed her eyes for a moment, just to rest them. When she opened them, a pink aura glowed on the horizon. Dawn had arrived.

Energy coursed through her body as soon as the thought came to her. She wouldn't give up. Very carefully, she disentangled herself from his hand, slipped from the bed, and began to dress herself. If she cleaned the workroom and restored order, if she organized the parts of the mechanical man, that might clear the slate for Carrick. It might inspire him again. Winding her hair into a tight bun, she vowed to herself that she wouldn't let him walk away from his dream. Not if she had anything to say about it. Especially not if she enlisted his brilliant son.

Her plan set, her hopes renewed, she flew down the stairs and went to the hidden door to the tunnel. With a quick knock, she pushed open the door and poked her head in. "C.J.?" she called out. Looking down the passageway, she saw his little room ablaze with light. He appeared, first his feet, but then he ducked down, and she saw his face. "Hi," he said to her. "How come you're not sleeping?"

"Because I need your help," she replied. "Can I come in?"

The darkness of the tunnel closed around her as she crawled along it. C.J. waited, holding up the lantern for her to see. When she emerged into the little room, she was surprised by the sight of the wooden couple sitting on his desk. She'd forgotten about them. She said in a sharp voice, "You did take them!"

"What of it?" he replied defiantly.

It made her so angry. Hadn't Carrick endured enough? She was about to chastise him—and harshly, too—when she noticed something. One of the mannequins was propped up into a sitting position. His wooden skin had fresh scrapings on it. He had wires running from his limbs. Wires that extended to the alkaline battery on the floor. "C.J.! What did you do?"

He shrugged. "I fixed him. Or I'm in the process of it. Watch." He went to the alkaline battery and started it, and as Penrose watched, the wooden man began to move. Only his arm. The man lifted it easily and gracefully if not a little slowly. Yet there was a simple beauty in the movement that spoke of a real step forward in design. "I hollowed out the limbs," he said. "Scraped all of the wood out. The shavings are in the corner. That eased the burden on the battery. It works like a charm." He scratched his temple. "It's still limited. I have to reconfigure the whole mannequin, but it's a start."

"C.J. Do you know what you just did?"

"Yes. I'm redesigning the mechanical man the correct way."

She laughed at his childish boldness, nodding through the film of tears that gathered in her eyes. "I knew it! I was coming here to talk to you, and look! Look what you've done!" She pulled him into her arms and hugged him. "C.J." All she could manage to say was, "Please, explain it to me."

He did, telling her about his plans for the wooden mannequins. Based on his explanations, Penrose knew in her heart that the boy spent a lot of time in his workroom while his father slept. By the time he finished explaining, she couldn't contain her smile, which stretched from ear to ear. "We have to tell Carrick!" she said.

C.J.'s face twisted in anger. "No!"

"Why not?"

"I hate him. That's why not."

"You don't hate him. You're mad at him, and you're

scared, too. You have a right to be, but you don't hate him." Her words were matter-of-fact.

His whole demeanor changed, and his body stiffened. "I don't care what you call it. I still don't want to share it with him."

Penrose knelt and took his small hands into hers. "Will you do it for me? Please? I have this feeling in my heart that it might change everything."

His teeth gnashed together.

Clearly it was not an easy decision for him, but she waited, hoping that he would agree to her plan.

"Oh, I suppose so," he said, letting out a big, dramatic sigh. A look of pride flitted across his eyes.

"Thank you!" she said, "I'm going to the workshop to tidy it up a bit. Can you gather up all of this safely and bring it to me? After we set up, we'll have a grand reveal to Carrick."

"I can do that," he said. "But do you promise I won't get in trouble for stealing the mannequins?"

"I promise," she said, tousling his hair, leaning down and giving him a kiss. "Thank you, C.J."

He pushed her away, but halfheartedly, and a smile tugged at his lips.

The workshop looked as if a crime had been committed there. Penrose supposed that, in a way, one had. Harris resembled a murder victim who'd been cruelly dismembered. Fragments of tin and iron lay everywhere and she busied herself stacking the broken parts of the mechanical man in an orderly fashion. She swept the floors and arranged the tables so that the room recovered some of its organized look.

"I'm here," said C.J. He carried two boxes, one in each arm. "But I'm not sure what you want me to do."

She smiled at him. "Just set it up, and then we'll go and wake Carrick. Do you need any help?"

"A little," he said.

After clearing a table, she helped C.J. unpack the boxes and position the mechanical man. He went and retrieved the battery, walking stiffly down the stairs so as not to spill any acid. "I'm going to have to enclose this acid," he said, thinking aloud to himself. "It'll be safer and more portable that way."

Listening to the child, Penrose felt like singing. "You'll have to explain it to your father."

"I'm not sure he'll be happy." He looked very doubtful all at this thought.

"Well, there's one way to find out, isn't there?" she said. "Let's go upstairs and wake him up."

Penrose barged into Carrick's bedroom, full of ideas and hope, but as soon as she entered the room she stopped in her tracks. The room was dark, with only a tiny ray of sunshine sneaking under the drapes. The ray of light fell on the bed and illuminated Carrick's half-naked torso. Hot memories flooded her, but she put them aside. There was no time for that now.

"Carrick?" she said.

He stirred in bed but didn't wake.

Her resolve notched back a few rungs, and her excitement turned to a flighty nervousness. What if he got mad or didn't like the idea? But C.J. looked at her so hopefully that she couldn't back out.

Coughing first, she said, "Carrick." Her voice was far too quiet for the task of waking a sleeping man.

C.J. tugged on her hand and said, "Louder."

Carrick stirred. "Who's there?"

"Us," she replied.

He lifted his head at the sound of her voice. He twisted around and squinted his eyes. "What do you want?"

Her stomach tightened to hear his husky, sleep-laden voice. Her own voice sounded too high, too excited as she said, "Get up! Something big has happened."

He popped straight up in bed. "Is there a fire?" he asked. The sheets had slipped farther, revealing a fine trail of hair sliding down from his navel.

"No, nothing like that." She rested her hand on C.J.'s shoulder. "C.J. has made a breakthrough for the mechanical man."

Carrick made a face. "C.J.?" He sounded incredulous.

She inwardly cringed at the tone of his voice. Next to Penrose, C.J. shifted his weight from foot to foot. "Yes, C.J." Her voice was sharp with rebuke. "Is it so inconceivable that your son would have ideas just like you did? That he'd be as smart as you." Oh, he made her angry. "Or even smarter than you?"

The more she spoke, the angrier she became. She tossed her arms in the air and almost yelled, "We're going downstairs to wait for you. Get dressed and meet us down there." She took a few steps, saw C.J. lingering and went back to take him by the shoulders. "Trust me, Carrick. It's worth it."

He rolled to the edge of the bed and rubbed his eyes. "Let's do it, then."

Penny and C.J. waited for Carrick in the workshop. He sailed into the room, dressed haphazardly, his white hair tangled from sleep, and greeted them with a nod.

"C.J., go on and show him," she said, urging the boy toward Carrick.

C.J. shifted from foot to foot nervously. He began to speak, "Well...I got the idea from this toy I made." He picked up the bird and held it out. "I made it all by myself."

Carrick looked at Penrose briefly, his eyes accusing her of wasting his time.

"Carrick," she warned him.

The boy continued, "Sometimes during the day I come in here and look around." He looked very sheepish.

Carrick said, "Go on."

C.J. said, "You have a few good ideas."

Carrick raised an eyebrow but remained quiet.

"Well, anyway. I programmed the toy to move."

Carrick held it in his hand, turning it from side to side. He lifted the paper wings, ran his fingers along the strings. "How did you do that?" he asked.

"I made a battery."

"Humph." Carrick's expression was unreadable. He was still analyzing the bird. "So, it's a decent design, but I don't know if it was worth getting out of bed for."

"Wait." Penrose held up her hand. "Just listen. C.J., tell him about the mannequins."

The boy said excitedly, "I thought to myself, if we hook up a mannequin to the battery, I can make it move, too."

Carrick stilled for a moment. "Say that again."

"If we hook the mannequin up to the battery, I can make him move, too. With some work. He's too heavy right now. But I got his arm moving, at least."

Carrick turned and looked at the mannequin, which

was propped up on the table. He took a breath as if he was planning on speaking, but then he closed his mouth and stared again at the mannequin.

Penrose saw his brain fire to life. Now he was looking at the bird. He pulled on the wing and it went up and down. His fingers danced over the bird as if absorbing some essence from it. Then his eyes darted to the mannequin.

"C.J.," she said, "go start the battery."

C.J. sprang up, ran over to the battery and then, a moment later, the wooden man lifted his arm in a graceful salute. There was no steam, no clanking noises. Only a simple movement by a simple wooden creature. And it was marvelous to see. The arm kept moving in a circle, and C.J. excitedly explained all that had gone into the design. How he'd hollowed out the wood and adjusted the gears in the box to program that one simple movement.

Carrick watched all of this silently and then said in a near whisper, "Penrose."

Penrose shook her head. "No. Not me. C.J. Your son."

"C.J.," he said.

The boy stopped talking. He looked at the ground, his cheeks reds.

"Come here," he said gruffly.

C.J. went and stood next to his father, and Carrick did the most surprising thing of all. He leaned down and gave C.J. a hug. The hug was awkward, as if neither of them knew quite what to do, but then Carrick said, "I'm proud of you. Proud. God Almighty, you just changed everything."

Penrose smiled, and C.J. beamed.

Chapter 9

The next day, even though the sun came up hot and fast, Carrick never returned to his bedroom. Rather, he and C.J. stayed in the workshop, side by side, each talking quickly, eager to share their ideas. Within a few hours, the mechanical man had a new life and a new vision. C.J. proudly announced that the man would be called Harris prototype number two, which made Penrose happy.

The morning passed in a blur with Penrose bringing them food while they toiled, heads bent over sketches, arguing over the merits of this or that feature. Whatever happened from here, whether the mechanical man failed or succeeded, at least there was a connection between father and son. A smile lingered on her lips, and she had a quiet happiness within her.

It would have been impossible to sleep, so she

stayed up and kept busy working around the house. She brought in more firewood for the workshop, tidied the kitchen and made beeswax candles. They were wide, so they'd burn longer and Carrick could use them without a candleholder. As the day came to a close, she thought to herself that she felt truly at home and, additionally, that there was so much promise in the air.

She went downstairs. The workshop seemed brighter than before. Perhaps it was the fresh candles she lit and arranged around the room, but it seemed just as likely that C.J.'s enthusiasm and ideas lifted everyone's spirits.

Penrose approached Carrick and C.J. They were huddled around their project and she cleared her throat. When they turned around, she saw what they'd accomplished. A new mechanical man had risen from the ashes of the previous one. He was a mixture of wood and metal, with thin, spindly limbs and a stout metal torso. His gas-lamp eyes were enormous on his new wooden head. He looked otherworldly with his spindly limbs and futuristic body.

"What do you think?" asked Carrick with an excited expression. "It's good, isn't it?"

"I can't believe it!" she said. "Look at him! I never would've thought to blend the two men together." She wanted to remember this moment forever.

Carrick had taken C.J.'s suggestion of the alkaline battery as a source of power, and C.J. had listened to Carrick's belief that metal was necessary for the design. But perhaps the biggest breakthrough was that C.J. had talked Carrick out of making the robot walk. Instead, they had used the wooden legs and put rollers on the bottom. Carrick explained to her, "It's simpler. Such a simple solution that I couldn't see it. But there it was right in plain sight." The joy of discovery seemed to outweigh the pain of previous disappointments.

"You should see it work. It's not finished yet. Only the two arms are functioning, but when we attach the gears to the rollers in the feet, it'll be in operation. What gears we put in the power box will dictate his movements. Everything is falling right into place." He smiled. "As if it was meant to be."

C.J. tugged at her sleeve. "We put the entire housing of the gearbox inside the tin torso. It's perfect. I knew it would be. I just knew it."

"You did know it," said Carrick approvingly.

At his words, C.J. looked down awkwardly and shuffled his feet, but the corners of his mouth tilted up in a smile.

Penrose helped them until ten o'clock, when C.J. started to nod off.

"Off to bed with you," she said to him and walked him down the hall. When they reached the tunnel entrance, she said to C.J., "Are you sure you don't want to sleep upstairs in a real bedroom?"

Shaking his head, he said, "No, I still feel safest in the wall. Maybe one day..." His voice trailed off. He looked up at her. "Would you mind tucking me in?"

"Sure," she answered, a bit reluctantly.

They crawled into the tunnel together, C.J. in the lead holding the candle. He crawled into his little bed on the floor and she sat beside him.

"Today was the best day ever," he said.

"It was a great day," she agreed. "But I have a feeling there are many more to come."

"I hope so, Penny," he said.

She kissed him good-night and crawled out of the

tunnel. When she emerged, the front doors were wide open, and she saw Carrick by the pond. He stood there, his hair brilliant in the moonlight. A blanket lay spread out on the ground behind him, surrounded by a dozen lit candles, all twinkling like stars. He looked like the king of midnight holding court, made to rule the darkness.

He motioned to her, and she stepped outside.

A mellow moon hung in the sky. Fireflies swirled in lazy arcs above the lawn. Carrick held a candle in his hand and stood staring out at the water as she approached.

Without turning, he spoke. His voice was low. "Have you ever wanted something so badly that it was all you lived for?" he said, handing her a candle. Their fingers touched.

"I don't have those kinds of passions. I wish I did." Penrose looked at the flame. She'd never burned bright for anything.

"No, you don't. It's a desperate feeling. A compulsion. Sometimes you don't know why you're doing it, you just can't stop." He sighed, and it was a lonely sound.

They'd worked so hard and still he wasn't pleased. She walked closer to the water's edge, leaned down and placed her candle in the water. It bobbed but remained lit and began to move away from the shore, directed by some unseen current. It seemed a hopeful omen.

She turned around and was surprised by Carrick's expression as he looked at her. In all her days, she would never forget the sight of that look. It was a look of pain but also one of surprise. His eyes were wide and almost appeared shocked. His mouth was drawn down at the corners. "What's the matter?" she asked.

"I just realized something." He seemed faraway and lost in thought as he spoke. "We are like that candle floating on the water. We have one brief moment to shine before we're doomed to the dark mercy of the fate. One little moment. Think on that, Penny." He shook his head. "And I was chasing the wrong thing the entire time."

She went and put her hands over his. "No, you weren't. Of course, you weren't."

Almost as if the universe disagreed with her, the candle on the water bobbed and, with a hiss, the flame disappeared.

A cynical, half laugh came from Carrick. "Penny," he said. "Fire has no choice but to grab its moment, whatever moment it's given, and burn. I know this now, and I burn for the wrong thing, don't I?" He bent down and picked up another candle and went to the water.

"Don't," she said, suddenly afraid of another flame disappearing. Suddenly it seemed so hopeless.

He turned away from her, leaned down and placed the candle on the water. "Even if its fate is doomed, it still has to burn. It can't miss its moment. Even if it's the wrong one."

The night sky seemed big and vast and dark above them. It frightened her. Her voice was too sharp when she spoke. "It's not dark mercy, Carrick. It's indifference. The water doesn't care if the candle sinks."

Turning around, he looked at her and said, "Whatever we call it, the truth is that we have such a short amount of time." His brows drew together, his eyes dark. "It's so easy to get lost."

She stepped closer to him, and he wrapped his arms around her. His touch soothed her. Looking at him, she asked, "So this moment right here, you think this could be our one chance at happiness?"

He placed a finger beneath her chin and lifted her gaze to his. "I hope there are many more. But let's treat it as it is. As if this is all we have." He took her hand. "Come, lie on the blanket with me. Let's look at the sky."

They went to the blanket and lay down. Carrick propped himself up on one elbow, and she lay beside him, tilting her head back to look at him. He was so handsome in the moonlight. Behind him stretched the night sky, dotted with stars, petulant and flickering.

She bit her lip and looked at him, knowing what was coming but nervous just the same.

Leaning forward, his lips came down, gentle but insistent.

She lifted up, meeting his kiss eagerly.

He responded by kissing her harder, guiding her to the blanket and pushing her down upon it. Never in her whole life would she tire of the feel or the smell of him. He stole the thoughts from her mind, and she was left with only reactions. Reactions to his touch and the need for more.

Then he hugged her and whispered in her ear, "If there were only one day left and this were it...if this were all I had, I would be a happy man, because this..." His lips touched hers. "This is heaven."

With a will of their own, her hands crossed his chest as she pushed the shirt from his shoulders. Running her hands over his warm skin, she drank in the feel of all that strength bound beneath his skin. How could his skin look so fragile and his body be so strong? He was like lightning, beautiful and bright. And scary.

A wild need overwhelmed her. She wanted the lightning. She wanted all of him, everywhere at once. Lifting her skirt, she tried to shove his hand beneath it, but it got tangled in the fabric.

"Here," he said, lifting her to sitting. She faced away from him while he traced a finger along the row of buttons that ran down her back. "Patience," he murmured. "If this is our one night, let's linger."

Unlike the night before, he moved with aching slowness unbuttoning her dress. His fingers trailed from button to button, his lips kissing each section of exposed flesh. Finally, he shrugged the dress and undershirt from her shoulders. Night air swept over her bare skin, and she turned cool, with only his hot touch to anchor her.

Those hands, hot as sin, slipped around her waist to her breasts and traced rings of fire around her nipples. Her whimper sounded out into the night and turned the crickets silent.

He took a sharp breath and his fingers dug into her flesh. Roughly, he rubbed his palms back and forth over her nipples before cupping each breast fully and squeezing them greedily.

"Yes. Yes," she said in a dreamy voice, lost to the sensations and craving more.

He grabbed again at her, fully yanking her dress from her body. She helped, grabbing at her undergarments and pulling them off. Then she was nude and helping him shed his clothes.

He pulled her on top of him with her back against his chest. They both looked up at the night sky and saw above them a universe of lights, scattered stars, long ago locked into their positions, petulant and flickering. She felt so exposed. To him. To the night air. To the universe above.

His hands ran down her torso, right to the center of her. When he touched that spot, that one little spot, she cried out, spread her legs and raised her hips into the air, opening herself more fully to touch. He seized the opportunity, and, with one hand, he cupped her buttocks while the other moved deeper, pushing two fingers inside her. She arced her shoulders against his chest. His touch was exquisite, and she couldn't help writhing about and bucking against him.

It didn't take long. Swiftly, Carrick lifted her and placed her beneath him on the blanket. He loomed above her, and she stared at him in wonder. Never breaking eye contact, he parted her legs and pushed himself inside of her. She felt a slow piercing that filled her and made her moan.

A long, drawn-out groan came from his throat. He lifted her hands above her head and pinned them to the ground. Then, he thrust fully into her, hard. Letting her know who was in charge. She was aware of an exquisite, full sensation. Again and again, he entered her with slow, powerful, deep thrusts until she experienced that delicious feeling between her legs and she met him thrust for thrust. Until she begged him, "Faster, please." He obliged until once more her cries silenced the crickets.

Afterward, their bodies lay knotted together on the blanket. Hours passed until fragile dawn gathered in the east. Half the sky was the inky color of night, and the other half was the peachy hue of the morning.

Light and dark were evenly balanced. The world held its breath. For a moment, it looked as if the light might change its mind and flee. But then, a crescent sliver of the sun appeared over the trees and night shrank away, defeated. She smiled.

Her clothes lay in the dewy grass, and she stood up and gathered them, shaking the moisture from them before dressing. Waking up Carrick, she said, "Let's go to bed." She blushed to hear her words. Because after just two nights, they already felt natural to say.

Once in his bedroom, Penrose opened the windows. She lay beside him and listened to the sounds of the morning settling in. In her heart, she knew everything was changing. The world would soon see his brilliant creation and learn his name. She fell asleep with a smile on her face, certain that the future was bright.

Chapter 10

When Carrick woke up in the morning, he announced that they would formally unveil the mechanical man that evening and attempt to power him up. His enthusiasm was contagious, and spirits ran high. Even C.J. was excited. Carrick surprised everyone by announcing he wanted to set Harris Two up in the great room. "A place of prominence." He smiled at Penrose. "Don't worry, Penny, I know it will work. Even if it doesn't, I'm not discouraged. Not one bit."

Carrick and C.J. fiddled with Harris for most of the early evening. They wouldn't let Penrose downstairs into the workshop, telling her, "It's going to be a surprise." When the clock struck nine, they brought the new Harris up from the workshop but made Penrose go into the other room until they had him set up and covered with the sheet. He sat in a place of prominence in the great room, right in the center, looking almost like a ghost with the sheet covering him.

Penrose had prepared a small spread of food—grapes, cheeses, cookies and bread with jam. On an impulse, she grabbed a bottle of wine she'd found in the kitchen. Since it was a celebration, she even made sure C.J. looked his best, telling him to go and change his shirt and wash his face.

While C.J. was gone, Carrick poured two glasses of wine.

The red wine was potent and stung her tongue. "Here's to second chances," she said, lifting her glass.

"Hear, hear," he replied with a smile as they clinked their glasses. "Penny," he said in a low, conspiratorial voice, running his hand around her waist. "After C.J. goes to bed, come outside with me. Let's lie under the stars again and turn one night of heaven into two."

"Yes," she said, smiling, her heart pounding in her chest.

Just then, C.J. came back downstairs, looking handsome in his dark trouser shorts and white shirt. They gathered around the mechanical man, staring at him in a quiet wonder. Then with a flourish, Carrick removed the covering, and Harris Two gleamed triumphantly in the candlelight, his wooden arms at his side, and his legs stiff as boards with rollers underneath him.

It was an amazing sight, and the three of them fell silent. "Should we start him?" asked Penrose.

Carrick nodded at C.J. "How about you start him up?" he asked.

C.J. stepped forward somberly as if it were a great honor. He went behind Harris, to the battery pack, touched the wires together, and everyone waited, eyes trained on Harris.

She heard the faintest buzzing noise. Harris shivered to life, jerked, hesitated and then began to move. He inched forward, rolling along, his stick legs straight and his barrel chest proud. His bright silver eyes gleamed with hope and promise as he slowly, gracefully, lifted one spindly arm. He waved.

Laughing with delight, she clapped her hands and said, "It looks like he's saluting the future." Raising her hand, she waved back at him.

Standing beside her, Carrick took Penrose's hand into his. "He is," he said.

C.J.'s head turned. He looked at them holding hands, and he smiled shyly at Penrose.

Harris continued to wave. It was such a simple movement, and anyone looking in might think it foolish. But Penrose knew better. Harris *was* the future. He was their hope and, better yet, he was their renewal. Two failed projects had come together to create a new vision. *Please let it last.*

They ate and drank, laughed a lot, and Carrick talked about his plans. It delighted Penrose to see him animated and happy.

Afterward, she cleared the food and dishes and carried them to the kitchen. Setting down the plates on the counter, she heard Carrick yelling in an angry tone and ran back to see what was happening.

C.J. stood in the doorway of the great room, a knife in hand, gouging a mark into the wood. Sawdust lay sprinkled around his feet. Carrick towered over him, a harsh look on his face. He yelled at the boy, "There are hundreds of marks here! How long have you been doing this?"

"Carrick," Penrose said, walking up to them.

C.J. looked from Penrose to Carrick and back again. "I... I can't explain it," he began to say, when suddenly he threw the knife down and ran from the room.

Penrose chased him into the foyer. "C.J.!" she shouted. But he ignored her, opening the front door, running outside and down the steps without looking back or closing the door. She was standing there wondering what to do, when Carrick called to her.

"Come back, Penny. It's okay, he'll be back."

Sighing, she went back to the great room and found Carrick standing and looking at the door frame. "Look at these marks," he said. "I can't believe I haven't noticed it before now. Some marks look old. Others are new." He shook his head. "He must have been doing this a long time."

"There has to be a reason for it," said Penrose, looking closely. She saw the marks that she'd noticed on the first day. The vertical hash marks in groups of five. She shrugged. "I don't know. I saw them on my first day here. But, because he's your son, there's a genius in his reasoning."

Carrick laughed. "You're probably right. I didn't mean to be so hard on him." He sighed. "I still have a lot to learn."

"Do you want to go outside and get him, or should I?" she asked.

Carrick slipped his hands around Penrose's waist and pulled her tight. "Let the boy go," he said. "I didn't mean to scare him. And, look, he ran outside, not into the tunnel. It's a step in the right direction. He has a lot to learn, too."

Pressing his cheek against hers, he whispered into her ear, "Plus, it gives us a moment alone. A stolen moment with your lips."

He leaned down and kissed her. He was warm, and his hands were strong at her back. She loved the scent of him, the feel of his stubble against her cheek, but nothing compared to his lips against hers. The second he kissed her, the world fell away, leaving the two of them, which was just fine by her. The kiss deepened. He pulled her closer, his hands all business.

She pushed back gently and whispered in a soft voice, "Later, Carrick."

"Promise?" he said.

Nodding, she laughed. "Of course."

He gave an exaggerated sigh. "Well, that leaves me with the chore of putting Harris away."

"I'll finish the dishes." She kissed him on the cheek. "We'll meet later," she promised. Returning to the kitchen, she began stacking the dishes, listening to the sounds of crickets as she worked.

Suddenly, the crickets stopped chirping. The silence was booming, overwhelmingly louder than their songs. She stopped, an eerie fear creeping up her skin. From the distance, there came a low roar. How strange.

She set down the dish and listened. A throaty, rolling growl came from somewhere far away, out in the night. It sounded like a train approaching from a great distance. She peered out of the window, half expecting to see the light from a train splitting the darkness. But there was none, just the twinkle of stars. A pungent odor rose in the air, almost like sulfur.

The sound grew louder, angrier and closer.

The plates on the counter rattled. The chairs vibrated around the table. Unsteady, Penrose held out her hands as her eyes darted all around her, trying to figure out what was happening. A rumble surged beneath her feet. The house shuddered. The dish she'd set on the counter fell to the floor and shattered.

Carrick yelled to her from the workshop, "Earthquake! Get out, Penny! Get out!"

Earthquake! In Charleston? Impossible.

But the ground heaved again and she knew the truth of his words. Then the sound of crunching stone and shattering glass as the kitchen window burst drowned out Carrick's screams. Another surge exploded beneath her feet, bucking Penrose into the air, and she fell to the floor.

The gas lamp shattered, plunging her into darkness. Her thoughts fractured into a thousand worries, but she focused on Carrick's words. She needed to get out—and fast. She stood and tumbled forward.

The house made horrid, loud protests to the shaking as she lurched into the hallway. She was dimly aware of her surroundings. Pictures falling, walls cracking and windows shattering. Her world had frighteningly turned very wrong. The ground could not be trusted. A particularly big tremor came, and she fell hard to her knees. It took a moment before she recovered, and when she stood, she saw C.J. at the front doors.

He stood there holding on to the frame for dear life. She watched in horror as the grandfather clock rocked from side to side, tilted, and then came crashing down.

C.J. was shouting at her, screaming, but the chaos

and wild noises drowned him out. He looked so afraid, in a panic.

She knew where he was going. The tunnel. The most dangerous place in an earthquake. Stumbling forward, she raised her hand to him. "Stop!" she shouted. "Don't go inside! It's dangerous!"

His face, contorted in shock and fear, seemed not to register her words. He let go of the door frame, and the shaking earth pitched him forward. He landed right in front of the door of the tunnel, which swung open and shut with the shaking earth. An eerie blue-and-white light flicked from within the tunnel, and above him the chandelier swung wildly.

A primitive scream tore from deep within her. She kept her gaze on C.J., willing him to turn back. Time slowed as she raced toward him, trying to stop him from going to the one place he considered safe. Horrified, she watched as he dropped to his knees and disappeared into the opening. She had to get him out. In a wild leap, she dove headfirst and slid across the floor, following him into the open door. The darkness swallowed her whole.

Part Two

Out of the night that covers me,
Black as the pit from pole to pole,
I thank whatever gods may be
For my unconquerable soul.

—William Ernest Henley

Chapter 11

The earthquake seemed unbelievable. But this, Penrose realized, looking around the kitchen and rereading the note, this was unreal. She held out a last, thin thread of hope that Carrick might be in the workshop, and she ran down the stairs that led to his space. The smells that greeted her in the stairwell were familiar and even comforting, and she breathed in the scent of metal, wood and grease. Finally, one thing that gave her hope.

When she reached the floor, the workshop was dark, and it was hard to see. After taking a few steps, she looked up and stopped cold. Shadows stretched across the walls, revealing a handful of dark shapes that loomed in front of her. Shapes that looked like people.

The forms stood stoic and motionless, like ghost soldiers standing at attention.

She stood still, her hands half raised, her legs paused midstride. Her gaze darted around the room.

She watched and waited for one of the mannequins to move, half hoping they would move, half hoping they wouldn't. But not a single one flinched.

After what felt like a million years, she crept forward, ready to bolt. When nothing moved in response, she burst into a run and fled up the stairs. Running without thinking, she sped down the foyer and up the grand staircase, heading straight to the one place she felt safe—her bedroom.

Barging into the attic bedroom, she saw that it too had changed. Her bed was gone. Tables crowded the space and were piled high with the chaotic look of junk. Even the safest place she knew petrified her. Leaning against the wall, she slid to the floor sobbing, not willing to get up, unable to take even one more step in that terrible house of shadows.

After an eternity of staring blankly at the still and strange room, she slept.

A dull gray light filtered through Penrose's eyelids. She opened her eyes. Dust motes flitted about her, glowing in the sunlight. Confused, she squinted and blinked, trying to understand what she was looking at. Her dress was filthy, coated with grime, and her hair hung in strands around shoulders. She looked at the strange sight that used to be her bedroom.

And then she remembered. Everything rushed back. She stood up, bones aching from sleeping on the floor, muscles sore, and looked, really looked, at the room.

The morning sun was harsh as it illuminated the room. Colorful metallic arms and legs lay strewn on tables and all over the floor. The limbs were very clearly fashioned after the human body but made of a shiny and hard-looking substance. Her nightmare was real.

Morbid curiosity drove her to walk over and touch a leg. A cool, hard surface greeted her finger, and she yanked her hand back. Why wouldn't this strange torture end? What had she done wrong to deserve it? She'd done one thing wrong. She'd stolen the destiny of another person. Perhaps this was penance.

Walking the room, she went to the closet and opened it. It was no longer a closet, but a washroom with a sink and a toilet. The toilet looked so very different, yet its purpose was immediately clear. She pressed a lever on the side of the toilet, and jumped back in shock when the water began to swirl and then disappear right before her eyes.

The sight and sounds of the water reminded her of the very real urge she had. A practical part of her urged her to go to the bathroom, and when her bladder agreed, she did so, making sure to press the lever afterward.

The very basic act soothed her. It reminded her that a person resided in the home. Not ghosts.

The sink impressed her as well, its steamy hot water shooting out from the faucet when she turned the handle. She washed her hands and face, brushed the dust from her hair and then smoothed it down. She tried to wind it back up into a bun, a task she abandoned when the house began to shake and she heard a thunderous roar.

Her first thought wasn't fear, but joy. The earthquake made loud unusual noises, perhaps another one was coming, she thought foolishly as she rushed from the washroom. Maybe it would bring her back to the home she knew. On shaky legs, hopping over limbs, lifting her skirts to do so, she made her way to the window. The sound intensified, became sharper, and the roar changed to an incessant thwacking noise.

She went to the large circular window, which was now covered by a drape. She craned forward but still couldn't reach the drape. The sound continued, loud and getting louder. Winds buffeted the window and rattled the panes. She had to find out what made that noise. Climbing onto the windowsill, she leaned forward, pulled back the curtain the tiniest bit and peered outside.

Charleston was gone.

The world had been scrubbed of life. Windblown grasses tumbled over a snow-covered prairie that held nothing at all to catch the eye except for shadowy mountains that lurked on the horizon. A huge swath of sky stretched in all directions, the bleak blue of a winter day. The green lawn, the duck pond, the ancient oak with its limbs dragging along the ground—they were all gone. In their place was a bonfire pit, and a road that snaked through the landscape—a black surface glistening in the sun, with clumps of snow clustered at the edges.

Clumps of snow. A sky of winter blue. Arundell Manor stood at the edge of the world.

The windows rattled again, and the roar grew so loud that the sound seemed to be inside the room with her. She looked up and saw a huge, metallic dragonfly speeding past her window. As she watched, it slowed, sounds chopping the air as it hovered over the ground before setting down gently.

Keat Carrick Arundell guided the helicopter low over the manor, visually inspecting his home. Everything was just fine, but then again, everything always was.

That was how he liked it, how he demanded it. The home had been well cared for during his year-long absence. The swimming pool covered for winter, firewood freshly stacked beside the garage, the snow plowed from the driveway and landing pad. On the patio, the hot tub steamed invitingly. Inside, he knew that the house would be spotless and completely stocked for his arrival. Everything was in order—as it always was.

After all, his staff knew his habits, knew to have the house ready and to make themselves scarce for the month. Every December, he lived at Arundell. Like a programmed robot, his life operated on schedule, as it had since the day he was born. As heir to the Arundell fortune and CEO of Arundell Industries, he lived according to standard operating procedure. And the user manual dictated he spend every December at Arundell because it was what he'd always done, ever since he was a kid. He liked things that way, orderly and under his command. Control was vital.

He guided the chopper to the landing pad, passing the garages where he stored his toys, and the Range Rover waiting in the driveway for his use. His gaze swept over the house again. It was a major production to move the house, but it had been worth it. As Arundell Industries grew into the largest robotics company in the world, the family fame and fortune grew with it. Security became a real problem.

Thirty years ago, his father, Carrick Arundell IV, who loved the family home as much as he did the family history, came up with a solution that kept their ancestral home intact while providing them space and privacy. As an added bonus, it gave them a shorter commute to

Silicon Valley, which became a necessity when the robotics industry exploded.

Now, coming to Arundell was his annual retreat. In order to run the company, he had to live in the valley—and he loved all of the excitement it brought him. But he also loved to unwind and get away. To be Zen with his ideas. This month-long retreat to his beloved home would give him countless hours free of distractions to do what he did best. What every Arundell did best.

Create robots.

He now set the chopper down gently, listening to the engine as it spooled to silent. He removed his helmet, revealing a thick head of jet-black hair, clipped short. He looked out at the skies. Clouds towered behind the mountains. He'd beaten the storm, but not by much. Once the clouds made it over the ridge, they'd bring plenty of snow. Wouldn't bother him one bit. Hibernation sounded just fine.

Grabbing his bags, he jumped out of the chopper and walked around it, checking the landing gear, and once satisfied that everything was in order, he began to walk to the house.

A shrill cry split the cold winter air. A woman's cry. Looking up, he promptly stopped in his tracks, his gaze locked on the attic window. The bright sun fell on the window, illuminating the unmistakable outline of a woman. A pale hand held back the curtain, and a porcelain face peered out at him. A china doll with jet-black hair.

It couldn't be. It must be a trick of the light. Increasing his stride, he ripped the sunglasses from his face and watched a ghostly silhouette recede into the shadows.

"What in the hell?" he said, and stormed toward the house.

* * *

Penrose watched the jaw-dropping sight of a dark-haired twin to Carrick jumping down from the flying contraption and walking toward the manor. In this strange, mixed-up world, white had turned to black, summer warmth had turned to winter cold, and her hope now turned to despair. Still, she wanted to believe. They were almost the same height, with the same lanky, muscular body and, most disturbing of all, the same sharp features.

Perhaps it was Carrick, she thought, half convincing herself. She was too nervous and too scared to feel anything but relief at his familiar form. She couldn't stop herself from reaching out, touching the window in longing and yelling, "Carrick!"

Instantly, the man's head snapped in her direction, and he stared up at the window, wearing strange glasses that blackened his face.

He began walking in angry steps toward the house, looking right at her window as he did so. Incredibly, this man's hair was dark, raven-black just like her own. The hairs on her neck rose and dread filled her soul as she realized he was not Carrick. Where Carrick brooded in anger, this man striding toward her prowled, eating up the space between them.

The curtains fell from her fingers. She was in danger. He was coming to her, she felt it. She edged away from the window inch by inch, hoping her slow movements would conceal her. She'd never been so afraid and yet so drawn to a man before.

The front door opened, once a familiar, comforting sound. But now it now petrified her. A moment later, it slammed shut, hard enough that she felt vibrations under her feet. Footsteps pounded up the stairs.

She had to hide. Scrambling, she leaped from the windowsill and tumbled onto the floor, knowing she had only one place to turn: the dark tunnels that she swore she'd never enter again. Jumping up, her feet a blur of motion, she careened forward, arms outstretched, and dove for the tunnel door, scattered the strange limbs in all directions. Her hands slammed into the door, and she desperately grabbed at the seam, trying to open it, but a thick coat of paint sealed it shut.

Like a drum, his footsteps continued to beat up the stairs. She could tell by the sounds of his footfalls that she had only seconds to disappear. The door she pressed on was as stubborn as always. It refused to open.

"Please," she begged, slamming her fist into it again and again. It wouldn't budge. Desperate, she flew forward, shoulder first, ramming her body against the door, and heard the quiet click that she once feared. The tunnel door had opened.

The door to the attic rattled just as the darkness revealed itself to her, and without looking, without thinking, without pausing, she dove into the blackness, knowing it was her one hope. She yanked the door closed behind her and flung herself to the floor, panting, shaking and shivering. Waiting.

The bedroom door creaked as it opened, and she heard footsteps. "Hello?" The voice was velvety. Deep. The rich timbre of it startled her. "Who's in here?"

Keat paced the attic. The room crackled with an energy that told him someone had just been there. No doubt about it. It angered him. He felt violated.

Raising his voice, he asked the question again. "Is anyone in here?" There had to be. He'd even heard noises as he came up the stairs. "I'm warning you to come out now."

There was no answer, but there was a presence. Christ, there was a presence.

He walked into the bathroom, looked at the sink and saw faint droplets of water around edge. He ran his fingers over the cold drops. Someone was here. Enraged, he stormed back into the attic, stood in the middle of the room and shouted, "Whoever you are, come out right now!"

But no one answered. Nothing moved.

He went to the window, lifted the curtain and looked outside, thinking through the possibility a person had actually been in the room. The way he saw it, the odds were somewhere between impossible and not a chance in hell. No one could slip past the perimeter. It was patrolled. It was digitally monitored and had a laser beam to detect anyone crossing over the boundary.

With such a fail-safe system guarding the perimeter, Keat never felt the need for a security system inside the house. The only technologies at Arundell Manor were Keat's robots and his cell phone. He liked it that way. It had never been an issue. Until just that moment.

He looked around the room again. Maybe he was wrong. It was possible that his assistant, Valerie, could have used the sink up here when she prepared the house for his arrival. It was entirely possible, now that he considered it. He dug in his pocket, whipped out his cell phone and called Valerie.

"Hello, Keat," she said, answering on the first ring

in her no-nonsense voice. "Did you get my note in the kitchen? Is there a problem—"

He cut her off. "Did you use the attic bedroom upstairs?" He sounded harsher than he intended.

"No, of course not. No one was up there."

"You're certain?"

"Yes, of course. Why, what's the matter?"

"I'm trying to figure that out. I'll be in touch," he said, ending the call. He spoke out loud, not knowing exactly who or what lay hidden in the room and was listening to him speak. "Someone or something was here and I promise I'll get to the bottom of it."

He stormed from the room, trying to keep his emotions in check. Really, he should be reasonable. The chances were so very slim. He had a lot to accomplish and couldn't waste time chasing ghosts. Besides, what were the odds?

Chapter 12

Penrose heard him leave the room. Then the only sound was the beating of her heart. It was so very black in the tunnel. But the darkness was a blanket that comforted her, kept her hidden, and for the first time, she understood why C.J. hid in the walls. Better to hide in a secret place than to be in a world that was so very frightening.

She lay there, overwhelmed, wondering how two men could be nearly identical in features, and yet the difference was night and day. Try as she might, she couldn't forget the sight of that man or the deep timbre of his voice. But he sounded like a Northerner when he spoke.

Hidden, she waited uncountable minutes, thoughts tumbling as she crouched in the space. Every creak and groan in the house traveled to her in eerie waves. Scratching noises came from somewhere behind her, and she tried not to imagine what was causing them.

Minutes turned to hours. Dust and darkness were her only companions. She hardened her mind just as she'd done when her mother had died, shoving out feelings, coldly tallying needs and necessities. She shuddered at what she had to do. It was almost unthinkable, but it was her only hope. She had to get to C.J.'s little room in the tunnel where she could safely sit and think. She must go even deeper into the tunnel.

Taking a shaky breath, she began. She crawled blind, afraid to stand, moving along inch by agonizing inch, unsure if her eyes were open or closed. Sticky cobwebs grabbed on to her fingers as she swept her hands back and forth in front of her. More than anything she wanted to yank her hands away, but she couldn't. The ladder lay somewhere ahead of her, and she needed to find the notches in the floor so she wouldn't fall into the hole. It seemed that she crawled for hours, but finally she felt the rough grooves under her fingers. Turning around, she gathered her skirts about her waist and began to descend into the belly of the house.

Down, down, down she went until she was convinced that the ladder stretched straight into hell. Then her foot touched solid ground. She took a few steps, sliding her hands along the wall. The cold, damp stone scared her, but she needed to have something to guide her.

She pressed ahead until her breath didn't echo back as quickly and she didn't feel as contained. The space had opened up. Fairly certain that she was in C.J.'s room, she ran her hands along the wall again until she bumped into something.

Something wooden. Her fingers danced over the object figuring out what it was. C.J.'s desk.

She rummaged over it. She gave a tiny shout of joy

when her hand bumped into the familiar tin box that held the candles and matches. Nervous, she fumbled with the matches until she managed to strike one. It sputtered and went out. She tried again, and the flame arced to life.

For the first time since the earthquake, she smiled. Light. It was the sweetest thing she'd ever seen. Touching the flame to the candle, she looked around her. The space was exactly as she remembered it. Even the wooden mannequins were slumped against the wall in one corner, the mechanical bird placed almost lovingly between them.

C.J.'s makeshift bed lay in the other corner with the covers all bunched up. She rushed over to it, hoping he might be asleep under the covers. When she pulled them away, the fabric came apart in her hands. She was left holding nothing but shreds and looking at an empty bed.

"No!" she cried, the word echoing in the stony room. She thought of Carrick and C.J. In her heart, she knew with absolute certainty that they weren't here. Where were they? She didn't want to acknowledge the awful thought that swirled in the back of her mind. She had to believe that they were alive, that they had survived the earthquake and were right now comforting each other. It didn't seem very likely.

She sank to her knees while the candle beside her burned brightly. The last thing she wanted to do was cry, but she couldn't stop the hot tears that splashed onto the ground. She would rather rage than cry, but she didn't want that man to hear her. He wouldn't exactly come running to her aid. Wiping the tears from her cheeks, she resigned herself to the truth of her predicament. Something terrible had happened, and though she didn't understand it, she needed to accept it. Possibilities streamed through her mind, each one too frightening to consider.

Not long after that, she heard the man, Keat—he must be the man from the letter—thundering down the stairs. Since C.J.'s room was beneath the stairway his steps sent booming echoes into the space. The front door opened and then, a moment later, it banged shut. She listened keenly, waiting for another noise. Everything was silent, and she knew he'd left the house.

She huddled in the orange glow of the candle, her hands linked together over the flame, seeking a comfort the fire couldn't provide. She had to face some facts. She couldn't be dreaming, or even dead. Her body was still alive. Needful. Hunger gnawed at her, and her dry mouth tasted like chalk. Thank goodness, she'd used the strange washroom, but right now, she needed to find some way to eat.

The only real choice was to wait until the middle of the night and sneak out to find necessities, and hopefully gather some information about what exactly had happened to her. Maybe find a way home, a little voice inside of her whispered. That little voice felt very fragile and what it said seemed almost impossible to achieve.

The front door opened again. She heard his footsteps and the muffled noises of a house coming to life. Very normal sounds, ones that shouldn't scare a person. Yet they scared her senseless. She listened for every noise, trying to guess his whereabouts and what he was doing. Even though she was scared, she knew that she needed a plan and, at the very least, more information.

Convincing herself that she should know the layout of the tunnel, she grabbed an extra candle and some matches and made her way out of the room. Moving quietly, she explored, discovering that vents lined the walls. She didn't notice them at first because they were all closed, shut tight and hard to see. But little streaks of light coming through the slats drew her eye. She figured out that if she wriggled her fingers between the slats, she could force one open wide enough for her to peek out. The tiny opening provided slips of light that illuminated the crawlspace.

Using her candle, she spent the afternoon moving from vent to vent, peering into each room. The vents gave her a birds-eye view. Each room she saw was like looking at a perverse painting of the home she knew only yesterday. Except for the workshop. She found the vent to the workshop and approached it hesitantly, still nervous about the shadowy human forms she'd seen. She pressed her face against the vent, peered out and saw the men from the night before.

Lined up in straight rows, a half dozen men stood lifeless and still. They wore matching dark jumpsuits, were the same height, and their facial features were identical. The expressions on their faces were smooth, too smooth. The longer she stared, the more oddities she noticed. Their skin was too waxy, their hair looked painted on.

Instantly, Penrose knew what she was looking at. Mechanical men.

Her grip around the slats tightened. These mechanical men were fantastical, almost unbelievable. The thoughts in her brain whipped around like a tornado. Possibility after possibility leaped into her mind, and her hands shook with delight. She couldn't wait to tell Carrick.

Carrick. She couldn't tell Carrick anything. Just to think the name caused an ache in her soul.

Just then, the man—Keat—strode into the room wearing denim jeans and a black shirt. Her heart stopped at the sight of him.

He resembled Carrick with one profound difference beyond the jet-black hair. Carrick was driven, the need to create etched into tight expression that was always on his face. This man? He was driven, but he had the satisfied look of a man who had achieved his goals. He didn't have the burning look of need. He had achieved. There was no other way to describe the cool confidence he displayed. He looked fierce, yes, intense, yes, but this man had the easy, almost sated expression of a man at the height of his achievements. She couldn't tear her eyes away.

A five-o'clock shadow shaded his jaw and outlined his perfect lips. A longing swept over her, hot and needy, surprising her with its fierce intensity.

But there were too many similarities between Carrick and Keat to ignore. Face pressed against the vent, she studied him closer, looking for discrepancies. But the differences were minor. Keat's lips were a fraction thinner, his height an inch taller.

She shuddered as chills ran through her, which deepened to goose bumps as she considered what it all meant. So similar, yet different. Just like the strange and scary Arundell she now hid in compared to what she had left behind.

There was only one explanation for this similarity. It was hard for her to accept the impossible, but the resemblance between the men was so strong that she couldn't deny it. This man was related to Carrick. No doubt about it.

The incredibly complex mechanical men, the flying contraption. Keat. She must have come forward in time. Because she certainly hadn't gone back in time. Somehow, the earthquake must have propelled her forward—as unbelievable as that sounded. Yet the proof was all around her—she just didn't know how far ahead she'd come. But, staring at all the strange things in the room, she knew it was a significant amount of time.

It was hard to accept. It would be far easier to think herself gone mad—or dead—but the facts came together in support of one hard truth. She was witnessing the proof of it.

She watched as Keat sat down at a workbench, sipped a cup of coffee and stared at a small white device he held in his hand. He kept touching it, swiping his finger across it. Occasionally he'd frown at it and Penrose found herself wondering what captivated him so. Finally, he set it aside, stood up and went to a large chest against the wall by the fireplace. He opened the doors and pulled something out.

She saw a quick flash of blue before he turned his back and blocked her view. Whatever it was, he hovered over it for a few minutes and then he spoke out loud.

"Power up, Harris," said Keat.

Harris. He'd spoken the name *Harris*. She leaned forward intently, straining to hear every word. But all she heard was odd whirring noises. Keat stepped away, revealing another mechanical man. This one was different than the others. It was smaller, half the size of a person, with metallic blue skin and a helmet for a head. A black screen covered the front of the helmet. He was like a shiny, miniature human. Childlike.

An image illuminated on the blank screen that covered the mechanical man's face. Its facial expressions sprang to life and looked like a painting in motion. Its eyes blinked, and its mouth moved, and the mechanical man—Harris—spoke. "Hello, Keat," it said in a droll, monotone voice that was unsettling to hear. "Good morning to you."

"Good Morning, Harris," said Keat. "Are you ready to begin work?"

"I'm always ready to work, Keat."

Harris. This was a newer version of Harris. She remembered the first Harris, her Harris, with his stout iron body and his lantern eyes. That Harris seemed childish compared to this version of Harris. But that didn't matter at all. What really mattered was the truth of what she was witnessing.

Carrick had done it.

He'd changed the world. He'd left a legacy. If only she could tell him. She hoped that he survived the earthquake to witness it. It pained her to have such a morbid thought, but that was the truth of it. The horrible reality.

She watched for hours as Keat worked with Harris and the other mechanical men. She learned a new word for them: robot. Again and again she heard Keat use the word. It was a thing of beauty to watch Keat in the workshop, and the afternoon sped by. It was a strange thing to assess a man so similar in looks and demeanor to her Carrick. It was stranger still to be attracted to both men.

She noticed other differences. Where Carrick was an artist at heart when he invented, this man was a conductor. The robots around him were like musicians in an orchestra, and he was constantly moving, jumping from table to table, pushing buttons and pulling levers. He had dozens of robots turned on at once, all of them performing different tasks, moving with elegance and grace. Like a colorful band, they performed their tasks.

Penrose was riveted. This man was impassioned, sexy and at ease with himself. She recognized another similarity between the two men. They were happiest when they were deep in thought, creating robots. He seemed to be focusing on Harris, the blue robot. Whenever Harris talked, the screen lit up on his helmet.

Every time she saw the familiar smile tug at Keat's lips, or the tight, intense expression on his face as he worked, she remembered the same expressions from Carrick. She couldn't help comparing the men. Keat was different. He didn't seem angry at the world.

After Keat had left the workshop, she made her way back to C.J.'s room. Once there, she ran her fingers over the wooden mannequins. The wood was dry and aged. They seemed so lifeless; dead.

She couldn't help remembering the conversation that she'd had with Carrick on her first night at Arundell. When she asked him how he gave the mechanical man life, he told her that he simply made them move.

Thinking of the bright-eyed, newest version of Harris, she realized that Keat had some essential element that Carrick didn't. For Keat didn't just make the mechanical men move, he gave them life.

Chapter 13

Keat loved the workshop. Maybe it was because it offered direct connection to his memories of his childhood and with his love of inventing. He'd spent countless hours next to his father in this very spot. The space soothed him. He could've built a bigger, modern workshop, but it wouldn't be the same. It wouldn't have the same scuff marks on the floor, the same smells and the same rusty tools.

Even though there was a massive, subzero storage facility beneath him, housing all the computing power he'd ever need and countless spare parts and previous prototypes, he preferred to work in this space.

He communicated via email and text to corporate every morning. After that, he turned his phone off to work on Harris. Harris #142, to be exact, the latest prototype in development.

Robots would soon be in every household, and Keat

intended to be the front-runner. He worked on it every moment he could and fell asleep thinking of it.

The project was a daunting one. The prototype had problems from day one. The newest trouble was with voltage regulation. It demanded his full attention because everything came to a halt if the battery pack wasn't working right.

Removing the plastic casing from the back of the robot, he grabbed a pair of needle-nose pliers and threw himself into solving the problem. For the first time since he'd arrived, he was able to wipe thoughts of the dark-haired woman from his mind. She'd haunted his thoughts.

Starving and thirsty beyond reason, every minute felt like an hour to Penrose as she waited for the house to quiet down. Finally, the velvety chimes of the grand-father clock struck two in the morning. She slipped her shoes and stockings off and opened the little door that led to the foyer. Slowly, cautiously, she crept out into the hallway. Keat could be around any corner or hiding in any shadow, waiting to pounce on her and…and what? She didn't even want to think about the answer to that question because every outcome seemed awful.

The marble felt cool and hard beneath her feet as she padded silently toward the kitchen. Once there, she grabbed a banana and three apples, careful to take what wouldn't be noticed. She used her skirt to hold the fruit. A closet door was open, and by the faint blue light that shone from one of the strange devices in the room, she saw a box with the word "cookies" on it. She impulsively grabbed that, too. Even though she was hungry enough to take much more, she knew she shouldn't, and began to walk back to the tunnel.

She stopped in front of the great room. The flickering light that shone from the room still called to her. Needing to know what caused it, she entered the room and looked around, ignoring the pit of dread in her stomach that told her to run. But she couldn't run. She had to know.

The light came from an enormous picture frame that hung on the wall. There were images inside of it that looked as real as the world she stood in. And the photographs moved. The images were in motion. Penrose went closer and, when she saw what the images contained, her knees almost buckled.

A man carrying a gun chased a group of people on the street. They screamed in horror, soundless. The image faded, switched, and she saw a person sitting at a desk, the words "evening news" spread out underneath.

A rustling noise startled her. She whipped around. Keat lay sleeping on the couch. As she watched, he rolled over and his hand slid to the floor with a thud. His eyes fluttered open.

Penrose stood frozen, afraid to move, waiting for him to close his eyes again. His unfocused gaze slid over her body, and she felt undressed and exposed. For one brief second, he looked into her eyes, and she saw something register in them. His eyebrows lifted, and he looked at her the way a man looked at a woman he coveted, and her pulse raced in response.

Please, she willed him, *fall back asleep.* Finally, his gaze moved away, and his lids shuttered closed.

Keat was having a dream. A very good dream. Normally he dreamed about designing robots, but this dream was a welcome change. It featured a beautiful woman. The dark-haired one that he had seen in the window. He dreamed that he could see all of her features clearly, down to her perfect pink lips and neon-blue eyes. The dream was so good he didn't want to wake up even though a warning came from deep inside him.

For the first time, in the dream, he was able to see all of her. She wore an old-fashioned dress, severe and tight in the bodice, and he wondered how a waist could be so small. And that hair, wild and free. He wanted to tangle his fingers in her hair, to grab it and pull her down on top of him. But something stopped him. An expression of fear—no, of horror—marred her features. In his dream, he realized that the woman was afraid of him. That he was the monster she so dreaded.

Something wasn't right. The feeling boomed in him, finally rousing him from sleep though he kept his eyes closed. He was aware of everything around him. He waited, his instincts sizzling with readiness.

There was a quick swishing noise, and a small gust of air rushed over him.

His eyes snapped open.

For a split second, he was certain he saw a woman, but when he looked again she was gone. And it was the woman from his dream. With the same sharp, classic features. The same dark hair and eyes so blue he could make out the color in the dimly lit room. There was nothing there. Damn, the dream felt so real.

Too real. He shot up from the couch and looked around the room. Everything was in perfect order. The news still played on the television. Nothing was out of place. From the coffee table, his iPhone blinked at him, reminding him of the hundreds of messages he had to respond to. He ignored it.

He must be going crazy. There was no way in hell he'd seen the woman just now. He must have dreamed it. An exceptionally lifelike dream. It was too bad because she was exquisite. She looked so very real and had a mysterious, chiseled beauty. Keat settled back into the leather couch and closed his eyes, trying to conjure up the dream again. Snippets of it came back, teasing him.

But now his lust burned hot for her. Part of him wished it wasn't a dream, because if it wasn't…oh, the things he would do to her. Unmentionable things.

Only a moment later he heard the distinct sound of footsteps running down the foyer. He jumped up instantly, grabbed his phone and bolted across the room. He flew down the hall to the foyer and looked up the staircase. Nothing. Christ, was he going crazy?

With a surge of fury, he shouted, "Wherever you are, I will find you! And you will regret it!" He yelled so loudly the crystals in the chandelier rattled. Wherever the woman was, she most definitely heard him. Even if she was still in his dream, she heard him.

A new possibility occurred to him, one that was so ridiculous he almost laughed it off. What if she was a ghost? The house was 250 years old, after all. The perfect age for a house to be haunted. Besides, he'd seen a ghost already in this house, long ago, when he was a child.

"Dammit," he mumbled to himself at the creepy absurdity of the whole situation.

Climbing the stairs, he whipped out his phone and texted his director of corporate security. He wrote, Can you do a sweep of the video from the cameras around the perimeter of my land? Worried about a breach.

There was only one road to the manor. One way in

and one way out, and it was protected by a guard gate. If anyone came over the fence, it would be on those recordings. He'd know for certain how that woman got inside. Or if he had a ghost, instead.

He stood in the foyer, chest heaving, enraged. "You'll regret the day I find you," he roared into the dark and empty house. At least, he hoped it was empty.

Penrose crawled to the door and pressed her cheek against it, listening. The wall seemed paper-thin. His anger easily penetrated through it, and the heat of it rolled over her in waves.

It wasn't just his anger. She was coming undone. The sight of him lying on the couch had taken away her breath. Her entire being responded to the sight of him, and that scared her almost as much as the man did. How could she be desperately frightened of a man and still attracted to him?

She curled into a ball, right there by the door, holding back sobs that racked her, afraid that Keat would hear her.

Carrick. C.J. Keat. They all blended in her thoughts. The one thing that shone brightly as a beacon in her mind was Arundell Manor. Even though she couldn't make sense of what was happening, she knew to the depth of her soul that she could always count on Arundell. It might be the only thing she could ever rely on.

Her bones hurt when she finally made her way back to C.J.'s room. Without bothering to light the candle, she felt along until her hands bumped into the wooden mannequin. She lifted him gently and brought him over to the bed, sitting him upright next to her. Even though he was a wooden man, she felt safer with him beside her. It was a piece of the home, the man, and the little boy she missed so much.

She ate her fruit in silence. The food tasted like dust, but she forced it down anyway. Then she curled herself into the tattered blanket, and tossed and turned until sleep claimed her.

Chapter 14

A few days later, Keat carried a cup of coffee into the workshop and began his day by removing the motherboard from Harris #142 and checking it for defects. He felt a kinship with the robot. He understood its nature.

It felt good to get away from Silicon Valley and reconnect with the robots he loved. Plus, he avoided Christmas.

It sounded silly, but there it was. He hated the sight of the wreaths and trees, the holly, and even the Christmas songs. They were constant reminders of the life he didn't have. He could hole up and hide out without seeing one single Christmas decoration. Not one reminder.

For the rest of the day, he drank his coffee, fiddled with the motherboards and circuits, and played his music at full volume. On the surface, everything seemed normal. But he was unsettled. He couldn't shake the feeling that someone was watching him. It affected his concentration, and he found himself making foolish mistakes. What should have been an easy fix on Harris was now testing him to his limits.

All he could think of was that tiny waist of hers. His little ghost. He longed to wrap his fingers around that waist and pull her close to him. Ridiculous, he reminded himself, pushing the thought from his head. He needed to focus on Harris's electrical problem.

Over the next hour, Keat tried numerous things to fix Harris, but nothing worked.

Nothing was going right, and the least of his worries was that wreck of a robot.

Blood pounded in Penrose's temples, part in fear and part in anger at Keat. If this was a dream, then he was the monster of her nightmares. But, no, it was real. He was agitated yet again—hands darting in the air, shouting sharp words that vibrated straight through the walls. He was a sight to see, a dark-haired version of Carrick and in the bright light of day, no less. And his passion—the same intensity, the same brooding quality. And, yet, something truly sinister emanated from him.

He stood in front of the robot. Waves of anger emanated from him. "I'm done!" he yelled, "Why can't you operate the way I programmed you to? What the hell is wrong with you?"

The mechanical man's head turned and he opened his cartoon mouth and spoke. "I'm sorry, I do not understand your request."

"I'm tossing you right into the snow!" he said in a roar, yanking the robot up, pitching it over his shoulder and storming from the room. As soon as he left the room, she flew like a bird through the tunnel and emerged into the attic bedroom. Racing to the window she pulled back the curtain, not caring if he saw her.

Keat strode across the snow. Harris lay draped over his shoulder, his metallic legs sticking straight out, his small head bobbing with Keat's quick steps.

The distance and the falling snow blurred Keat's image. He stood like a shadow figure on the bleary landscape. With a rage-filled roar that she heard all the way in the attic, he hoisted the mannequin over his head and threw it in a huge arc. Harris landed with a thud on the ground.

"No!" she shouted, clutching the window helplessly. "Please, Keat! No!"

Without looking back at the house, Keat stormed toward that terrible vehicle of his, jumped inside, and with a roar of the engine he drove away.

Penrose looked at the helpless robot. He didn't move, just lay there like a doomed man resigned to his fate.

The thought of stepping outside struck pure fear into her, but she felt she had to. She must save Harris.

She fumbled at the latch before finally opening the door. "My God," she said, for it was so different than balmy Charleston. The cold was deep. The world was white and crisp, and even the blue sky looked brittle. This land of the future was cold. Very cold. She stepped out into a crusted pathway that led to the bonfire pit. But before she got very far she turned around and look back at the house. It was and it wasn't Arundell.

The manor sat on this blank land, oceans of it that stretched in all directions. She looked at where the pond should be, and yet there was nothing but flat white ground. She hurried her steps, dancing along an icy path until she knelt beside him, and with a gentle push turned him over. He stared lifelessly up at her, the strange lights in his eyes gone dark. His screen was slicked with icy mud, and she wiped it away gently.

She scooped him up. He was light in her arms. With quick but careful steps she walked back to the house and brought him into the tunnel with her. When she finally reached C.J.'s little room, she set him down, fumbled around in the darkness and lit a candle.

She felt wild, giddy from her crime. Her cheeks were hot, her hair and dress damp from the snow, her fingertips numb from the bitter cold. She studied the robot.

Her prize sat motionless. His presence in the room made for a strange party, with the wooden mannequins in the corner, the mechanical bird and now him, too. A giggle escaped her. She couldn't help it—it just felt too good to claim something from Keat.

And the robot looked magnificent. In the cloistered space with the flickering warmth of candlelight playing on his metallic blue skin, he seemed alive. There was a vibrancy to him. It warmed her to look at him, and all of a sudden she didn't feel nearly as hopeless.

She set about clearing him off, wiping the mud from his body and patting him dry as best she could with her skirts. Finally satisfied, she tried to wake him up. "Power up," she said.

Nothing happened. Turning him around, she ran her fingers over his back. There was a small door on it. Lifting it, she felt the cables and metal frame that lurked underneath. But she could feel no lever or buttons.

Perhaps if she lifted him, she might find something. Slipping her hands underneath his arms, she hoisted him. Then a sharp noise came, startling her.

It was the front door opening and shutting, followed

by a shout of hot anger from Keat. She dropped the man a second time, watching as the side of the wooden table thumped him hard, right on the side of his torso.

He landed loudly, faceup on the floor. Lights flashed numbers and letters across the black screen where his face should be. "Rebooting," he said.

"Hello?" she asked, confused.

A series of beeps and whirring noises continued. It was funny, watching the lights that played across the screen. And then a cartoonish version of his face appeared. He blinked.

Gently, she lifted him upright and leaned over him, studying him closely. "Hello?" she said.

"Hello," said Harris, blinking at her.

Tears pricked her eyes, and for the first time, she allowed herself a vulnerable moment. There'd been precious few in her life. Penrose wiped the tears from her eyes, leaving spiky black lashes in their wake. Her heart pounded in her chest. "Please," she said. "Talk to me."

"Harris responding," it replied in his strange voice. "Request?"

Keat drove wildly across the countryside, trying to cool down. His life was out of control. Of all the things he hated, this was top of the list. To make matters worse, a storm was coming. He saw the clouds building dark and high over the mountains. He had to get back to the house and take the robot inside.

He turned his Range Rover around. As he pulled into the driveway, his phone buzzed with a text message from his head of security. It read: After reviewing the recordings, there have been no breaches in the past six months. He sighed. There wasn't an easy answer.

He went and looked for the robot. It wasn't there. He'd thrown it down, right there, not thirty minutes before. Walking back and forth in disbelief, his boots crunched the snow. His lead robot was missing, and he wasn't even sure what to make of it. He couldn't shake the feeling, ridiculous as it was, that he knew who had taken the robot. With suspicion pounding in his veins, he went to the house. He could find out for certain in a few minutes.

Once inside the workshop, he sat down on a stool, pulled his phone out and launched Harris 142's interface app. Hoping, praying, that the robot's battery would still be functional, Keat connected to its internal receiver. He activated Harris and crossed his fingers that the battery still worked.

It did.

The black screen on his phone brightened as the image came into view. He saw movement, blurred images that appeared as white streaks on the screen. Then, a bright, glowing ball came into focus. He stared at the odd sight until he realized what he was looking at. A candle. How odd.

Not a moment later, a face appeared. The face he'd been dreaming about. His ghost. Except she wasn't a ghost. She was real. Real.

Rage pounded in his veins, but her beauty was undeniable. High cheekbones. Wide, scared eyes that glowed brightly in the light of the camera. "Tell me about Keat Arundell," she said. Her voice came to him scratchy and muffled, as if she was speaking from the moon, only she wasn't. She was speaking from somewhere inside of his house.

"Dammit," he whispered. He felt sick to his stomach as he stared at the woman on his screen. She wasn't a ghost. She was a living, breathing person inside the manor. Clenching the phone in hand, he vowed to catch her right away, and when he did, he'd make her pay. But first, he wanted to introduce himself. After all, she was a guest in his home.

She was so happy when the robot began to speak to her. A garbled squeal escaped her mouth. Harris. Her Harris. Her hands shook so violently that she had to hold them together. She said in a shaky voice, "Hello." Then she asked foolishly, "Who are you?"

"My name is Harris 142. I am an assistive device for humans. I was conceived and designed in 2015 by Arundell Industries as a personal project for Keat Arundell, CEO."

"Harris," she whispered.

"Yes," he replied. "Harris. Prototype number 142. May I ask who I am talking to?" His voice never rose or fell, rather he spoke in a monotone.

"My name is Penrose." She smiled at those strange eyes, unsure of herself, and she resisted the foolish urge to hold out her hand and offer it in greeting.

"Pen Rose," said the robot in a halting voice. "A pleasure to meet you, Pen Rose."

She smiled. Hearing her name, even incorrectly, made her feel more human. Safer somehow. The man's strange, picture eyes moved and then settled on her face.

"Tell me about Keat Arundell," she said impulsively, not even expecting him to answer.

His voice surprised her. "The following is a Wikipedia entry. Keat Carrick Arundell," said the assistive device. "Born October 18, 1984. Fifth generation Arundell, CEO of Arundell Industries. Known for his genius and his reclusiveness. He reportedly lives in Montana at a location so secret even his own company doesn't know the location."

Penrose grew quiet, trying to absorb what she was hearing. The creature stopped talking. Quietness settled in the room, except for her heavy breathing. The robot's words had flitted through her mind again and again when, suddenly, a different voice came from the robot. A familiar voice. Keat's.

"Hello, little ghost, did you know I can see you?"

Darkness blinded her. It had nothing to do with the tunnel, and everything to do with the fear that threatened to make her faint. Choking for breath, she leaned closer to the robot, trying to understand how it could speak with Keat's voice. Sudden realization hit her. Carrick was never a wicked man of magic. Keat was. She scurried away, deep into the tunnels, knowing that trouble lay ahead.

She was somewhere in the house, but where? Keat raced through the rooms, searching for her but coming up empty. He was missing something. Was there a passageway? God, he should have paid more attention to the relocation of the manor. He never bothered with details about such things, he only cared about his robots. But he remembered that he stored all of the architectural plans in the safe. Right in the workshop.

He raced to the workshop, passing a window and noticing that the snow was really coming down now. It would be a whiteout soon. Good. She'd be trapped for real. Only this time she'd have him to answer to. He opened the mammoth safe and dug through the family papers, journals, pictures, pulling them out and carelessly throwing them to the side. The fire blazed hot enough that beads of sweat ran down his face. Finally, he found the large, rolled-up architecture plans. Unraveling them as he walked to the kitchen, he spread them out on the table and studied the drawings. When he saw the tunnel and its two doors, a slow smile spread across his face.

"Showtime," he said softly, already anticipating the shocked look on her face as he caught her. He would win. He always won.

His plan was simple. He'd crawl into the tunnel, find her and bring her out. After that, he was undecided. Call the authorities, certainly. But he wanted to hear from her own mouth why she would do such a thing.

Keat gathered random tools, uncertain how the doors would open. He took a flashlight, an ax in case he had to break through the wood, and a rope. His plans for the rope involved her. His heart felt like ice, his soul blackened by the ire that someone would think to violate him like this. Screw his fantasies about her. Those were over. All of that paled next to the cold, hard and sickening truth about her.

Now that he knew there was a tunnel, it was surprisingly easy to find both entrances. He decided to enter the tunnel from the attic. Whoever had built the tunnel had been a talented craftsman and hidden the seam perfectly in the wainscoting. After giving the little door a hard shove, it opened.

The blackness was absolute, like a void in the universe. He feared nothing. Or thought so, but staring into the tunnel, knowing that woman hid somewhere inside of it, he felt uneasy. Every man had his limits.

He flipped on the flashlight. The white beam split the darkness and illuminated the rough stone walls. Dropping to his hands and knees, he paused just outside the door. It took a force of will for him to enter the tunnel, but he did, flashlight in one hand, the beam bobbing ahead of him.

Six foot three doesn't fit easily in such a tight space. His shoulders brushed against the wall, and his back scraped against the ceiling. His breathing was loud and too fast. The tunnel widened, surprising him, and he could stand.

At full height now, and feeling more confident, he swung the flashlight around the tunnel. The meager light was worthless. A thin beam against the hungry dark.

He moved deeper into the bowels of the house, and every step was a struggle. How had he lived and grown up in this house when it had a secret like this tunnel? He came to a hole in the floor and shone the light down into it. The beam illuminated halfway down the shaft. Beyond that, the bottom remained a mystery.

A sound echoed from deep within the innards of the house. A feminine gasp. Surprised, his grip slipped from the flashlight, and it fell, a ball of light sailing down until it hit the floor with a loud crack and then shut off. Blackness reigned again. Now the light came from behind him, weak sunlight streaming in from the attic window.

"Forget this," he said. There was no way he would crawl around in the dark. Cupping his hands together, he called out, "I'm coming for you, little ghost. I know you're in here. You're going to regret the day you started living in my walls. That's my promise to you." His voice traveled down the hole and echoed deep into the shaft.

Backing away from the hole, he turned around and crawled back out.

As he walked down the stairs, he devised a plan for getting her out. The cat-and-mouse game, only just begun, was over. He had to trap her inside so she couldn't escape from one door or the other. Or force her to pick one door while he lay in wait.

Coldly, calmly, he went outside to the garage and began gathering supplies. He grabbed an ax, electrical tape, another flashlight and a metal washtub. With a chilling look of determination on his face, he stormed back to the house. Dumping all of the items onto the floor of the foyer, he went to the workshop and grabbed thin, green pieces of wood, which he stacked in the washtub.

He knew the best way to get rid of rodents. By smoking them out.

Penrose listened to him retreating from the tunnel and couldn't help the tiny smile of satisfaction it brought her. When he'd shouted at her from inside the walls, it had turned her blood cold. Knowing the tunnel was intimidating enough to send him away gave her a sense of pride. He'd be back, of course, so she knew it was foolish. Still it was a victory, and that mattered to her.

But it didn't change the fact that he knew where she was hidden. The tunnel was now a trap. Her options had dwindled to nothing. Something bad was going to happen. *Run*, her instincts told her. But to where? Out the front door into the cold, featureless land that stretched on forever? She pushed her hands through her dark hair, wondering what to do, but every single option seemed hopeless. There would be no running. She had to fight.

A moment later, she heard the downstairs entrance to the tunnel open, and a dull gray light shone into the crawlspace. He was coming, just as he'd promised. She inched ahead, uneasy, and peered down the hall. Sunlight streamed into the space, illuminating the walls. All of a sudden, his arms appeared in the doorway pushing a metal tub piled with wood into the tunnel. Then once more as he dumped crumpled paper onto the pile of wood. She saw the small flame from a match as he tossed it onto the wood.

"No," she whispered to herself, "not that. Not fire."

As if he could hear her, he said, "Hello, my pretty little ghost. The game is over. It's time to come out. I'm smoking you out like a rodent. Your only escape route is up and into the attic, where I'll be waiting for you." The door slammed shut.

He was forcing her into his trap. Penrose stifled a scream that if started would never stop. She watched, horrified as the flame licked to life, bright and happy, unaware that it would bring about her doom. Tendrils of white smoke curled higher, hit the low roof, flattened, and spread along the ceiling.

It took a moment before the pungent trail reached her room. The acrid smell burned her lungs when she breathed. As she watched, the fire was growing and smoke billowing out thickly.

Panicked, she grabbed Harris and dragged him down the hall, deeper into the tunnel. No matter what, she wasn't leaving Harris behind. Ever. She came first to the kitchen vent. He had closed the vent. When she pressed against the slats, they didn't budge. He'd secured it shut.

Without a candle, and with the vents sealed tight, she couldn't see the smoke. But it hung thick as a cloud. A deep fit of coughing overtook her. Eyes burning, she pressed on. Every vent was tightly closed, and no matter how she clawed at them, they wouldn't open. He was right. Her time was up.

Panic came easily. It would be so much easier to give up and lie down, let the smoke suffocate her. But she wanted to live. The need beat within her. She knew that trying to escape might be futile—he could catch her, and if he did, he'd kill her. No, she had to try to escape.

Three thoughts repeated in her head. *Get to the attic, lock the door, and don't let him in, no matter what.* She had to lock him out and then she could escape through the window or perhaps compromise with him. Mind made up, she scurried, holding her breath, using both hands to pull her along to the attic.

She'd never moved so fast before. She determinedly refused to let go of Harris. He scraped the floor as she ran. She dropped him once and almost left him, but she couldn't stand the thought of abandoning him.

When she reached the ladder, she heard Keat on the stairs, pounding up them. It was a race. She had to reach the door before him. Awkwardly tucking Harris under one arm, she climbed as fast as she could. When she reached the attic door, she listened for a moment and heard nothing. Punching the door open, she fell sprawling onto the floor. Smoke poured from behind her.

Hacking, stumbling, taking deep gulps of air, she reached the front door to the attic bedroom. He was so close. She heard his breathing. Quickly, she threw the lock and leaned against the door, partially stopping the smoke from pouring in. A small win.

He was on the stairs, climbing closer. There was still so much smoke. She had to be quick. She darted to the window, grabbing a limb of the robot from the table, and she smashed the glass.

Cold air poured in and sucked the smoke outside, sending a plume of white into the gray cloud-covered afternoon sky. Brutal, unrelenting snow slashed sideways. Snowflakes and ashes swirled around the room and landed on her. The snow nipped at her and disappeared, but the ash clung to her, mottling her skin and dress.

She was numb, disconnected from the world. Every difficulty, every challenge in her life paled before this moment, and, yet, it didn't seem real. She heard his shouts coming closer. His voice sounded hollow. Distant.

She stood, turned and faced the door, tucked a stray hair behind her ear and smoothed her skirts. She felt wild and crazed as she waited for him. The moment she feared most was at hand.

The door handle rattled, followed by four vicious strikes of his fist against the door. Then, his soft voice called to her through the door frame. "Hello there, ghost. I know you're in there. Why don't you come and say hello to me? Are you shy?"

Words would not form on her lips. Her hands began to shake, and she stood foolishly, mute and dumb.

"Come now," he cajoled. "Won't you open the door for me? I just want to say hello. To meet my guest face-to-face."

Knowing the end was near, she spoke the first words she'd ever said directly to him, "I would rather be dead than meet you face-to-face."

Chapter 15

Keat's anger made him crazed. "So harsh!" he said. "Here you are, a guest in my home, and you throw insults at me?" His fingers rattled the door handle once more before he slapped the wood with his open palm. "An uninvited guest, I might add, and I'm getting impatient." His velvety voice barely concealed his rage.

She didn't answer him.

"Answer me this. How could you get inside my house? Forty miles to the nearest building and guards protecting the perimeter twenty-four hours a day? How did you manage that, ghost?"

His ghost was quiet. He hoped she was afraid. He leaned forward, his shoulder first, and barreled forward, smashing into the door. With a loud thump, it bounced against the frame, trying to break open. But the lock held fast.

She screamed. He heard her scurrying and, with

a thump, she pressed against the door. He heard her breathing. Trying to hold it shut.

Foolish.

He collided with the wood, and the force of his blow made her bounce off. He heard her fall to the floor. A moment later she was back at the door, pushing, panting. She took quick, feminine breaths. But he wouldn't be stopped.

He pressed his lips against the door and spoke. "Maybe you are really a ghost. Why don't you prove to me that you're not?"

Her soft voice surprised him. "I'm no ghost. I'm human."

"Then prove it. Let me see you. Give me proof that you are flesh and bone. Or if you prefer, I can use this ax I brought along, split this door in two and find out for myself whether you live and breathe. One way or another, you better prove it."

He lowered himself to the ground and slid his hand underneath the door. "Shake my hand, ghost. Introduce yourself."

Penrose leaned forward and watched as four fingertips appeared underneath the door and slid back and forth.

"Don't be rude," he said in a mocking voice. "Shake my hand."

She examined his fingers. The whorls in his fingertips were oval. He had the skin of a working man. Calloused. Nicked. Her face screwed tight, she reached out and light as a butterfly's wing, she ran her fingers over his. His touch was warm.

With a pounding heart she snatched her hand away.

As soon as he felt the warmth of her skin against his, he jumped back and stared at his hand as if he'd been burned. The tingling that lingered on his fingers was all the proof he needed. She was real. Flesh and blood. And it deepened his rage. "Open this door!" he demanded, banging against it loudly. "Open it right now!"

Penrose listened as he spoke in a low voice. "Please. Listen to reason. I will not hurt you. I promise. I need you to open the door."

Lies. She was close to breaking. She shook her head wildly, covered her ears and tried with all her might to wish her way back to the real Arundell. Through her covered ears, she could hear him, his anger rising in intensity.

"I suffered with you here. With you hiding in my home." His voice grew louder. "With you spying on me. With you stealing my food. Worst of all, you convinced me that I was crazy." He gave a low, maniacal laugh that sounded crazy to her. "Don't you have anything to say to me?" Then a moment later, he continued. "No? A cat has your tongue?"

She whimpered.

"What's that?" he said in a soft, lulling voice. "Do I hear a little bird in her cage? Or do I hear a criminal, someone doing things they shouldn't? I'm going to give you five minutes, little ghost, and then I'll break this door down. Your time is up. Though I do enjoy hearing your feminine whimpers that ring of fear."

"I am afraid," she said.

"I'm holding an ax," he said through the door. "I'll give you to the count of five. Then I'm splitting it wide open. If I were you, I'd back away."

She scooted back, all the way across the attic until

she reached the little door to the tunnel. Even though the tunnel was closed, smoke streamed through the doorjamb. Harris lay in a heap. She grabbed him and propped him in front of her like a little soldier trying to protect her.

Keat began counting. "Five."

"Four."

"Three."

"Please."

It was quiet for a moment. "Open the door," he said.

"I can't."

"Two."

"One."

He heard a scream as his shattering blow hit the door, sending splinters flying through the air. The ghost made a last-ditch, foolish effort to save herself. Throwing open the door to the tunnel, ignoring the plume of smoke that poured from it, she dove into the crawl space, covering her mouth as she scrambled.

Again and again Keat swung the ax and struck the door—too hard and too wildly—but he didn't care. Each blow brought him one step closer to a resolution. When the ax finally split the wood, he reached inside the room and unlocked the door. He turned the handle, but the door wouldn't budge. It was jammed on the splintered wood. Stepping back, he lifted his leg and kicked it open. And he saw his ghost as she disappeared into the tunnel.

Penrose screamed and clawed the floor as strong hands grabbed her ankles. She was trying to dig in, to prevent him from pulling her out. He had the grip of an iron vise and wrenched her from the tunnel. "You won't get away from me," he said.

She emerged kicking and screaming before he dumped her onto the floor, his hand a shackle around her leg. She stole a peek into his rage-filled eyes. He seemed beyond anger, as if he had gone to some deep and awful place in his mind.

His gaze slid over her face. "I cannot believe there is a woman hiding in my walls!" he screamed. "A person! I knew I wasn't crazy!" His hand squeezed her hard as he spoke. "And look at you. Wild hair, wild clothes. Disgusting. What are you doing in my walls? My house?"

"I don't know," she whispered, her eyes wide, and shaking her head. "I really don't know." If only she knew what to do, how to respond to a monster like him. She could barely look up at the man.

"Don't mess with me," he replied, grabbing her by the wrist and yanking her to her feet. He spun her around, dug the rope from his pocket, and wrapped the cord around and around.

He pointed at her dress. "What are you doing, dressed like a creepy ghost? Are you a nutjob, or what? Crawling around in my walls? Are you spying on me? And the prototype? Why would you steal my prototype?"

She was afraid to look up at him, as if the mere challenge of eye contact would send him over the edge. That rage was so explosive. "I had no choice," she managed to whisper before her voice failed her.

He sounded deceptively smooth and gentle as he said, "Who are you and where are you from?"

"My name is Penrose Heatherton. I'm from Arundell Manor," she said in a wavering voice, her face contorted in fear. It almost hurt to tell the truth but, somehow, she couldn't stop herself. "I work for Carrick Arundell, helping him design a mechanical man."

"In what year?" he asked.

"Eighty-six," she whispered.

"You expect me to believe that you came forward some thirty years?" He laughed.

"You mean, it's 1916?" She shook her head slowly as the impossible sunk in. "Oh, my God," she whispered.

"No. It's 2016."

She saw it then. Something inside him snapped as the disbelief on his face etched in deep, and his features twisted down and hardened into uncontrolled fury.

Keat felt as if he had been kicked in the gut. There she was—living, breathing proof that a person hid inside of his home. There were no words to describe the level of anger he felt.

Temples pounding, chest heaving, he stood and took in the sight of her, for she was a sight. A sorry one. Her face and hair were smeared and grayed with ashes. Why did he ever think she was beautiful? He'd never seen an uglier creature in his life. She looked like an old woman. "You're coming with me," he said, his voice thick with disdain as he grabbed her by the arm.

Dragging her down the stairs, he took her to the workshop. It was the room he felt most in control, and right then, he needed to be in control. More than ever, he needed that control.

Careful not to let her fall but not showing any kindness, either, he led her down the stairs. Her dress felt foreign to his touch, the cloth too thick and the fabric rustled, heavy as a drape, as she walked. Together, they barreled into the workshop. He pushed her forward until she stood in front of a table.

"Down," he said, his iron grip forcing her to the floor.

The robots watched with disinterest as he tied her to the leg of the table with the cord. He made sure she was close enough to the fire to warm her and to dry her clothes. She sat in a crumpled heap, grayish hair hanging limp over her face, her eyes trained downward and her skirt a black bell around her.

"Look at me," he said. He wanted her to look him in the eye.

She shook her head.

"Look at me," he repeated.

She lifted her head and looked up at him through wild tufts of hair. She held his gaze with a tight expression of malice on her face. The blazing fire behind her gave her an evil, witchy look, and he was taken aback by the sight.

He dragged a chair across the floor, spun it around and sat in front of her. Staring at her with crossed arms, and close enough to reach out and touch her, he said, "Tell me who you are. And be honest."

She tossed her head, moving her hair aside, and he saw her bright blue eyes more clearly. "I told you my name. My name is Penrose Heatherton." She spoke harshly. "I already know yours."

"Aren't you cute?" he said. "Giving me attitude when you're tied up." He tilted the chair forward until he hovered right above her. "So, Penrose Heatherton. You said you worked here before?"

"I did." Her gaze swept over the room, and she said, "I created robots with Carrick in this very room."

He laughed outright. "You're entertaining, I'll give you that. A wild ride." When his laugh died away, he simply said, "Or you're crazy."

"You are mistaken on all accusations," she said, her eyes a blue flame. "I have no delusions about what happened. The last thing I am is crazy. Trust me, it would be a blessing if I were crazy, a far better fate than this."

"Penrose Heatherton, your fate is about to get a lot worse."

"Call me Penny," she said.

"Oh, you're no Penny. I'll stick to Penrose."

In the light of the fire, it looked to Penrose as if steam rose from Keat's skin. He looked so angry, staring at her with the darkest eyes she'd ever seen.

For the past week, she'd known him from afar. In that manner, it was easy to cast him as a monster. But standing there, shaking with rage and something more— something like fear—he looked like a man, a very powerful, very angry man. One pushed to the edge. By her. It was a thousand times scarier than a mere monster.

It wasn't her fault, however. At least that's what she wanted to believe.

"Why don't you just admit that for some sick reason, you chose this house to break into? Because who would head out into the middle of nowhere to live in the walls of a house?"

"I don't even know where this house is!" she screamed. "Or why we aren't in Charleston? Why are we in this strange winter land?"

An eyebrow lifted. "We moved it," he said. "But I think you already knew that. This home is not one a person would accidentally find, or even seek out. There's something wrong with you breaking in here to live. Don't you think you're laying on the Southern accent a bit thick? You sound like a *Gone with the Wind* rerun."

"I don't know what you're talking about!" she said in a shrill voice that couldn't be her own. Everything collided within her, all of her fear, panic and anger at the situation. She leaned forward, arms taut from the cord, until their noses almost touched. When she spoke, it was low and threatening. "How dare you," she spit the words out. "I am at my worst. Reduced to crawling about like a rodent in your walls, and you think I chose you? That I snuck in here of my own free will?" She took a ragged breath and continued, "I would shave my head to be free of you. Chop off my limbs. You frighten me more than any man."

"Don't tempt me," he said. "And I frighten you? You haunt my house and want to blame me for freaking out over it?"

Her eyes ticked back to his, saw the cold disdain in them. That was the worst of all, the disdain. For as she'd spied on him, she alternated between fearing him and desiring him, but never ever disdaining him. And she was surprised to discover that hurt her. "I don't haunt this house. I'm alive."

He snorted. "Yes, you're alive. It's not the nineteenth century, darling. Which means you're no ghost. You're merely crazy."

Impossible. Yet there she was. The woman, Penrose, lay in a heap on his floor, her black skirt billowed out like some bad dream. Insisting she was from the past. Insisting he listen. Worse, that he believe her. The sad thing was, she looked so earnest that he was actually tempted once or twice.

He needed to think. While she was tied up, he went and doused the fire and boarded up the tunnels, and while he worked, he thought about everything she'd told him. Her story was impossible. Utterly impossible. But he knew that she hadn't crossed the perimeter of the land. Yet, there she sat, on the floor of his workshop, in an old-fashioned dress. The whole damn situation was creepy and odd.

When he came back to the workshop, he asked her, "Why didn't you just come out of the walls and tell me?"

"Because I watched you. When you first chased me into the wall, I was scared to death. You're a horrid man. You don't know how frightening it is for me to be here. Until you suddenly appear in a different time, you won't know the fear I face."

"I don't believe you," he said. She was beautiful. No denying that. Once he looked beneath the grime, he saw the china-white skin, dark lashes, full pink lips. He knew there was some kind of body underneath that crazy gown. But she was a nut. Or a stalker. He'd already been there, done that with a stalker. No repeats, thank you. He'd find out for sure. It was a mission.

"Listen to me," she said. "Just listen. I don't know how I got here, only where I came from." She leaned back with a strangely pretty expression on her filthy face. "Hear me out. I am speaking the truth. I came from Arundell Manor. In Charleston."

She knew far too much about Arundell. "That's impossible."

"I know. It is impossible. Yet here I am." She looked

away with a pained expression. "There was an earthquake. A terrible earthquake that came out of nowhere. Everything shook. Everything. I was trying to save C.J. Carrick was there, too."

"An earthquake? Everyone knows that South Carolina doesn't have earthquakes. You've got your states mixed up. California is what you meant." But for the first time, the hairs rose on the back of his neck when she mentioned the name C.J.—Carrick, Junior, the founder of Arundell Industries. Carrick Arundell was the original inventor, but his son C.J. was the real genius, the one who founded Arundell Industries.

With all of his instincts on edge, he urged her on. "Continue."

"C.J.," she said. "He lived in the walls. He felt the safest there. When the quake came, he ran right into the tunnel. It was dangerous, and I had to get him out. That clock, that grandfather clock kept on ringing as the house shook, and I darted into the tunnel with him." Her tears were so thick he couldn't see her eyes through the glisten.

He asked warily, "Then where is C.J.?"

"I don't know! He could be dead! I just don't know!"

"He didn't die young."

Her head snapped up with such a look of joy that the creepy sensation returned full force.

"Okay, so let's assume that's true," he said, partly to appease her, but more to keep her talking until the truth finally came out. "When was this earthquake?" he asked.

"August. August 31, 1886."

He stared at her. "In 1886? You really expect me to

believe you came here from one hundred and thirty years ago?"

"If there were some way to prove it to you, I would."

"How convenient that there's no way to check."

"As I said, I'm not lying."

"Okay, I've had enough," he said. "I'm calling the police. They'll haul you away."

"No!" she shrieked with an urgency that made him jump. "I can't leave the manor! Please, it's the one thing I can trust. I need to stay here. I feel it in my bones."

There was something about her tone that struck a chord in him. He stared at her, hard. Finally, he nodded. "Okay, for now you can stay. It's a whiteout anyway. Lucky us, we can enjoy each other's company for a while longer."

Chapter 16

Penrose watched as Keat left the room. He returned a short time later and sat down on the chair right in front of her, holding a bowl in his hands. The smell of soup filled the air. Her mouth began to water. It'd been days since she had real food.

He lifted a steaming spoonful of the hot liquid and held it in front of her mouth. "Eat." It was an order. "You looked hungry."

His kindness surprised her. Wary but starving, she tilted forward and clumsily came down, mouth open, on the spoon. The hot liquid scorched her lips. She hissed and fell back on her heels, soup in her mouth, gasping for air to cool it down.

"Blow first."

"It's hard to get the motions right, tied up as I am," she answered once she was able to swallow the soup.

It felt so good sliding down her throat. Hot and filling. "More, please," she said greedily, her stomach practically forcing her to beg.

He held up another spoonful and she blew hard, making little waves on the surface before she took another bite.

"Right now, we're going to have a heart-to-heart. If you need help with something or if you're having personal problems, there are other options." He spoke slowly, always spooning more liquid into her mouth.

"The only problem I have is that you don't believe me."

"Penrose, people don't travel through time." He almost looked like an adult trying to reason with a child.

"I did."

He set down the half-empty bowl of soup and sighed. "Aren't you growing tired of this?"

"Yes, I am. I'd like nothing more than to be in my home. My real home. To wash up—"

"God, you need to wash up." She shot him an angry look and he lifted his hands in the air. "I'm just saying. Maybe it's not such a bad idea. Do you want to take a shower?"

"A shower." She said. "I'd love to," she blurted out.

"Okay." He nodded, his dark hair gleaming as the firelight played off it. "But no funny stuff, all right?"

She didn't know why he was suddenly a nice guy, but she wasn't about to turn down a shower. She felt like the world's dirtiest creature just then, and a clean body sounded heavenly.

"Do you have a change of clothes?"

"No. All I have I'm wearing on my body. And I'm not sure I know how to use your shower stall."

"I have to hand it to you. You're good." He came and untied the cord from her arms, then helped her to stand up. "So, I suppose I'll teach you how to use a shower, and get you something to wear." He stood beside her as she stretched her arms. "Let's call a truce. A temporary cease-fire."

He led her upstairs, one hand holding an elbow, the other rested on her waist. "Will I have to escort you everywhere? Or can I trust that you won't run away? You won't be going back into the tunnel, that's for sure."

She stopped abruptly. "I'll never run away from Arundell," she said fiercely.

He looked at her long and hard. "Why do I believe you?" he asked before urging her forward again.

They stopped in his bedroom along the way, and he gathered some clothes for her. Handing them over, he said, "I'm sorry, I only have men's clothes." Gesturing at her body, he continued, "I'm short on old-fashioned dresses at the moment. They're mine, so they'll be too large for you."

"Thank you," she whispered, taking the clothes from him. He was so imposing that she felt flustered next to him. Unsure of herself. "Whatever you can provide is welcome." She held up the pants. "What are these?"

He laughed harshly. "You're good. They are sweatpants, as if you didn't know. And feel free to drop the Southern drawl anytime now."

"I couldn't even if I wanted to, and I don't want to. It's who I am," she said stubbornly.

They entered the bathroom. He took a few towels from the closet and handed them to her. They stood side by side in the large, tiled space. The wide tub in front of her looked more appealing than the shower, but he seemed intent on her taking a shower, and she didn't want to cross him. He had just started to show a sliver of compassion.

The shower stall was huge with glass blocks all around and two nozzles. He stepped inside and guided her by the elbow until they stood side by side. He looked at her with those dark, thickly lashed eyes. Almost pretty, except for the gaze. Finally, he said, "Are you certain you need directions on how to use a shower? Don't you think the show has gone on long enough?"

"Please," she said, answering both of his questions with one single word.

"I take it you've been in here, too, right?" he asked.

"I have." It sounded like a confession, being in such an intimate room in his house without his knowledge. She hated the feeling.

"Did you watch me in here?" He stepped closer, merely an inch, but it was a step intended to intimidate her. She knew that. It infuriated her that it worked.

"No," she assured him. "I didn't. I tried not to invade your privacy."

"So you've never seen anything you shouldn't?"

"No."

"Too bad," he said, sending a hot thrill through her body.

He studied her. "Maybe you want to see something now?"

She stepped back from him, nervous.

"Never mind, I have my answer." Instantly, he was all business again.

No you don't, she wanted to say, but the words didn't leave her lips. It was too risky with a man like him. Too dangerous.

In a cool voice, he showed her how to turn the hot water on. He began to explain the shampoo and conditioner to her, but once she lifted the bottle to her nose and sniffed, the feminine part of her understood instinctively what these were for. She was a quick study in girlie indulgences.

"I'll leave you alone," he said, "I'll be just outside the door, waiting for you when you finish."

After he had left, she undressed, gladly letting the tattered black gown and underclothes drop to the floor. She stepped into the shower, turned the handles and felt the icy shards of cold water rain down on her. She screamed at the top of her lungs.

From the other room, she heard him bellow, "It takes time to heat up!"

She stood shivering as she followed his directions. When steam began to billow in the air, she stepped inside and fell instantly in love. Hot water on demand. What a glorious thing.

Needles of hot water pulsed over her skin. She turned slowly, letting the water burst over her skin from above, flooding her with heat and invigorating her all the way down to her soul. She had never imagined such decadence, a hot shower with soaps and lotions to slather over her body.

Time ceased to mean anything. Her skin turned bright red. She used the shampoo, the conditioner, the soap, and scrubbed her skin raw with the washcloth. She stayed until the water turned cold.

After the shower, wrapping herself in a thick, luxurious towel was a second treat for her. She brushed her hair, feeling cleaner than in God knows how long.

She went to the pile of clothes Keat had laid out for

her. They smelled so sweet, as if they'd been washed in perfume. The first was a man's soft cotton shirt, and she slipped it on, acutely aware that it belonged to Keat. Her stomach flipped at the knowledge his body had touched the same thing. And it was so soft. Her wet hair hung in strands down her back, but even that felt like a luxury.

How long had it been since she'd had wet hair? And she'd never had wet hair that smelled as good as this. She picked up the other article of clothing. Sweatpants. They reminded her more of soft pantaloons as she slid them on, but they too were heaven. She felt clean and pretty, with clothes as light as air on her body as she left the bathroom.

Keat waited for her in the sitting area of his bedroom, two overstuffed chairs on a thick rug in front of the fireplace. His iPhone in hand, he was using it to run searches. When he discovered that there really was an earthquake in Charleston, he'd gone cold. He planned on searching her name, but when he typed in Penrose, the autofill feature suggested something called a Penrose staircase. Intrigued, he clicked on it, and promptly wished he hadn't.

According to Wikipedia, a Penrose staircase was an impossible object, a staircase that looped around and around upon itself. A person could climb it forever and never even rise one flight. He sighed. He just wanted some answers. And all he got in return were riddles. Sickened, he set the phone down, tired of searching.

He went downstairs and grabbed two sodas for them. At least he could test her at every turn, to find some way to trip her up. Even the sodas were an attempt at that. It was almost midnight, but he wasn't ready to let go of his intention of forcing her to admit the truth. He wanted more information before calling it a night.

After the longest shower known to man, she finally emerged from the bathroom. "Come and dry yourself by the fire, little ghost," Keat said to her as she walked toward him.

His intentions were noble. Mostly. At least they weren't indecent. Until she stepped into view. As soon as he saw her walking toward him cautiously, looking shy, any nobility he had instantly disappeared. Her jet-black hair gleamed a long trail over her shoulder. Beneath it, the T-shirt was wet, and either she didn't know it was transparent or she was very clever at her game. He drank in the sight of her, and when he saw the dark outline of her nipples beneath the shirt, his cock responded immediately. Her breasts were small. The perfect shape. Her skin was red and shiny from being scrubbed, and she was the sexiest thing he'd ever seen.

The sweatpants were baggy on her and as she walked they fell down. She was fast about yanking them back up again, but that didn't stop him from seeing the curve of her hip.

The intensity of his reaction surprised him. How had he been so enraged at her before and now wanted her so fiercely? There was no easy answer, and, right then, he didn't care to analyze it. All he knew was that he wanted her. From the moment he first saw her as she haunted him, he couldn't get her out of his mind. Before he could stop himself, he made a vow. He would have her.

Handing her the can of soda, he said, "I brought you a drink. Have a seat."

"Thank you," she said, taking the can. She sat down, crossed her legs formally and analyzed the can in her hand.

"Don't tell me you don't know how to open a soda can."

"I'm sure if I look at it a moment, I'll be able to. I just need to study it."

"Hand it over," he said, holding his arm out.

She gave it to him. He cracked it open and handed it back.

She took a sip and promptly spit the soda out everywhere. Wiping her mouth, she looked at him and said, "It burns."

"It's a good burn, though," he replied. Another test passed. Point in her column, he supposed.

Trying again, she took a small, dainty sip and stared straight ahead at the fire.

After a few minutes of silence, Keat asked, "What are you thinking of?"

"I was thinking of Carrick and C.J.—Carrick, Junior."

"Tell me about them." He wanted to hear what she had to say, and see if it lined up with the Wikipedia entry. Or the corporate website.

She began to talk. Her Southern accent was pronounced. It gave her voice a lilt that made it sound musical and very sexy. The soft orange light fell on her features. Her hair had dried wild and curly, and her lips were rosy pink and tempting.

"Carrick is an artist," she said. "He's an inventor, like you, and very intelligent. It's a family trait."

Christ, it bothered him that she spoke of a long-dead man in the present tense. What the hell could he do to shake her conviction?

"He has such a passion for inventing robots—I mean mechanical men," she said with a smile, and then laughed. "I get confused now. You say robot. We say mechanical men. I think Carrick coined the term," she said wistfully.

Suddenly he realized something. "You were with him." It was a statement, not a question.

She blinked, and the blue of her eyes disappeared underneath a fringe of dark lashes. She looked so pale that even the warm glow of the fire gave no color to her skin. "Yes," she said. One quiet little word. One big giveaway.

"You loved him."

The fire crackled and snapped as he waited for an answer.

Finally, she opened her eyes. "No," she said. "But oh, I don't know… I've known him for such a short time. It's more like I'm in awe of him and overwhelmed. He's almost a force. He's moody, and can have a sharp tongue. He's obsessed with his work, and anything that interferes sets him off. But when he talks about his ideas…oh, you should see him. He uses his hands, painting pictures in the air trying to get me to understand. I have this one memory of him standing over a table in the workshop, his white hair tousled, his clothes disheveled. Nothing else mattered but that mechanical man. If I had dropped a glass, he wouldn't even have looked up."

Keat was confused. "Wait. He's old? He had white hair?"

"No." She shook her head. Her brows came together, and she looked at him, confused. "Don't you know?"

"Know what?"

"Carrick has albinism, and so does his young son, C.J. They were incredibly pale skinned."

An uneasy feeling gripped him. A nagging sensation that something was right there at the edges of his memories. "I had no idea," he finally said, after struggling and failing to figure it out.

She gasped. "There's a reason you don't know," she said, looking at him with wide eyes. "I can show you," she said excitedly.

"How?"

"Follow me," she said, and jumped up from the chair. He was hit with the sight of the sweatpants falling down again, and this time he caught a glance of the downy hair between her legs before she yanked them back up. It was too damn late, though. He was instantly hard. Thankfully, she walked in front of him, and he followed her, trying to push that hot image from his mind.

Holding the sweatpants up with one hand, she led him down the hall to the row of portraits. He'd never noticed the pictures before. They'd always been there, and he'd stopped seeing them many years earlier. She walked up to a large painting with an ornate gold frame. It was a long-ago portrait of Arundell Manor, and judging by the bell skirt that the woman in the picture wore, it was painted around the time of the Civil War.

Two older boys chased their younger brother on the lawn. Not one of them had albinism.

"I don't see him," said Keat.

"Exactly," she said softly. "But he's there. In fact," she traced her finger along a mended tear in the middle of the youngest boy, "this is him. His parents wanted to portray him as having normal coloring." A sigh came from her. "I was with Carrick when he tore this. Jabbed his finger right through the fabric. It burned him—being rejected, hidden away, and colored over. Painted a different color for the world to see, and all by his own family. Imagine this wonderful child with bright white hair and pale white skin."

He stepped back in shock. The memory that had tugged at him but not risen to the surface only a few minutes earlier came on hard. It all happened so long ago, he'd long forgotten it. Though for years it haunted him. He was a boy himself when it happened. The house was still in Charleston, not yet moved, and he woke up one night to see a white-haired boy standing over his bed and staring at him. The boy looked so much like himself, a ghost version of himself, that he lay frozen in his bed, unable to move. Finally, the ghost ran—not floated—but ran from the room. Though Keat was petrified, he followed, running out into the hallway. But the child-ghost was gone.

He felt sick and angry. There was no way he'd ever mention that memory to her. Hell, with this woman standing in front of him saying those things, he never wanted to think about that again. He lashed out at her. "But all of this has nothing to do with you, does it? And it certainly means nothing to me."

She whipped around, her face pinched down with anger. "Nothing to you? I'll tell you what it means," she hissed at him. "What it should mean to you. Carrick's biggest fear was being remembered the wrong way." Her chest heaved. "But maybe his biggest fear should've been that he'd be forgotten completely and that nobody could trouble themselves to care."

Keat said, "He's dead anyway, Penrose. It doesn't matter anymore."

"It doesn't matter?" Her features fell. "Were you even listening to me?"

"Penrose," he began, "they're all dead. Gone!"

Tears shone in her eyes, but her cheeks blazed an angry red. "No, they're not! They live! I saw them not one week ago!"

He opened his mouth to speak, but she cut him off. "And maybe they are dead. Maybe you're right." Her voice hitched. "But they should live on. In your heart, at least. They certainly burn brightly in mine! And I'll tell you why it matters. His pain at the way the world treated him—that pain pushed him, drove him to create the first mechanical man. That one thing about him, his affliction, the thing everyone tried to hide…" She swept her hand in a wide arc, indicating all of Arundell Manor. "Well, it brought about every single thing you have today. He envisioned mechanical men, beings who would be judged by their abilities rather than their color. It was a blessing. Never a curse. I wish he knew that. I wish he could see with his own eyes what he accomplished."

Feet apart, shoulders thrown back, she leaned forward, and her ice-blue eyes stared hard at him. "Everything you are, you owe to him, and it makes me sick to hear you say those words. To deny the gifts your ancestor plopped right into your lap. The gifts that you so casually disregard." She spun around and walked away, somehow managing even in sweatpants to look proud as she strode back toward the bedroom.

He didn't know what to make of her. From the walls

of his house, he'd pulled out a strange woman with fierce blue eyes and strong convictions, and the strangest story ever. And against his better judgment, against every smart thought he'd had, she made his heart pound and his cock hard. Keat stood perfectly still and stared at the painting. The whole thing was pure insanity, and yet he couldn't take his eyes off the boy with the scar running across his body. Keat raked a hand through his hair and sighed. "What the hell is happening to me?" he asked the boy. But the child ran down the hill with that damned expression of glee on his face.

He walked along the hall with slow steps until he came to his bedroom. Closing the door behind him, Keat saw Penrose sitting in front of the fire. She looked gloomy and stared at the flames with a blank expression. He sat beside her, but she didn't look at him.

He cleared his throat and said, "I'm sorry. I didn't mean to be harsh. But you have to understand that this whole thing is nuts, and you...just plopped into my lap. I came here to get away, to go on my annual retreat. I do this every December."

Her gaze shifted warily from the fire to him.

"I came here expecting great things this year. And look what happens." He laughed, a hollow sound, and shook his head. "I can't help but think of my father. He died, you know."

"I'm sorry." Her voice sounded very small.

He shrugged. "I can't decide if my father would be delighted by you or scared to death of you. Both, I suppose. He did love family history. I never listened to him talk about it, though. It just wasn't important to me." He kept it to himself that he still wasn't sure if he believed her. But he couldn't ignore the feeling in his gut, or how she knew so much and how passionate she was about it all.

"I forgive you," she said. "Trust me, I'm just as shocked as you are. If I could wish it away and then return to my time, I would."

No. It was more than a word that popped into his head—it was a force. No, he didn't want her gone, which made everything even stranger. "Tell me about them," he urged.

She seemed hesitant.

"Please," he urged. "Help me understand."

She cleared her throat, a tiny sound, and then began to speak. At first her words were soft and shy and tinged with her Southern accent. As she spoke, the light of the fire danced with the shadows on the walls, and soon her words took on an almost dreamy quality. He stared into the flames as she spoke, and he saw her memories come to life.

She explained everything to him. Carrick and C.J. became real to him, not merely names listed on paper or a corporate feel-good story recited to shareholders. They were his family, trying and failing and trying again to succeed. Now, 130 years later, he was still part of the legacy. A rush of pride, sentiment and humble awe filled him. He couldn't remember ever having such feelings.

He knew she could be deluded or lying, or both. But the intensity of his response to her stories made him not care. She spoke words that his soul needed to hear. Fabrications they might be, but it felt too good listening to them to stop her. He often thought of his father, of the times they'd spent together here at Arundell creating robots. Much like Carrick and C.J.

The realization left him unsettled. His thoughts raced ahead of her words, recalling the stories his father had shared with him. He wished he'd paid better attention. When his father died, all was lost, and he'd never thought of those stories again. His entire focus became creating the next invention or reading the next profit report. The hollow reality of loss settled inside of him. Would his father be forgotten, too, one day? Would he?

It would've been easier if he'd never seen her and faced these emotions. His thoughts returned to the present, and he realized that she'd grown silent.

She slept. Sitting upright, leaning against the side of the chair, with her chin tucked into her chest, she looked soft and beautiful. He checked the clock. One in the morning. Quietly, trying not to wake her, he scooped her into his arms. She weighed nothing, and as soon as he felt her soft body against his, he realized his mistake.

Sighing, stirring slightly, she leaned against his chest and whispered, "Carrick."

He felt that familiar, hot rush of jealousy as he carried her to the bed. It drove him crazy, because the last thing he should be feeling was lust for her. He laid her down. Seeing her body sprawled out on his bed made him wicked hard, and it took a force of will to cover her with the blanket, but he did it. Then, with his lips set in a grim, disciplined line, he pulled down a few pillows and a blanket and lay on the floor in front of the fire, staring up at the ceiling.

He listened to her breathing. She took the most feminine little breaths, and it captivated him. Settling under the covers, she let out the softest sigh of pleasure.

Groaning, he rolled over and stared at the fire, and only when the flames turned to embers did he fall asleep.

Chapter 17

Last night hadn't been a dream, after all, Keat realized as he woke up with aching bones from sleeping on the floor. His ghost lay sleeping in the bed. She was buried so deeply under the covers, all that was visible was the dark waterfall of her hair. Her breathing was heavy and even, and he knew she would sleep a bit longer.

He didn't know exactly what to do with her. But he knew what he didn't want to do, and that was to call the authorities. Not yet. He wasn't about to hand her over to anyone else until he found out the truth. He had no fear that she'd try to escape. Unless she was going to walk countless miles on ice and snow from last night's storm, she was stuck.

Which, he realized as he stared at her, didn't bother him one bit.

But did she travel through time? Last night, listening to her talk it seemed not just possible, but definite. She knew so much about that era, subtle nuances that only someone who had lived during that time would know. He felt the strong emotions behind her words and stories. She had lived those experiences, or at least thought she did.

But, there, in the bright light of morning, without the seduction of the fire and her words, his doubts crept back again. The whole thing was insane, and yet he still wanted to believe her. And the strangest thing of all was that he felt connected, rooted in history and part of a legacy.

He padded downstairs, lit the fire in the workshop and made a pot of coffee in the kitchen. Using his phone, he checked his email and on impulse messaged his assistant, Valerie, to find out everything she could about a woman named Penrose Heatherton who lived in Charleston in the 1800s. He didn't want to look anymore. If there was anything to be found, Valerie would find it—she worked miracles every single day.

His stomach grumbled. He pulled a packet of bacon and a dozen eggs from the fridge and began to cook.

Penrose woke to the morning smells of coffee and bacon. In her whole life, she hadn't ever been as comfortable as she was at that moment lying in the big, fluffy bed. Opening her eyes to the sunlight, she blinked at the strange sight of it before quickly closing her eyes and snuggling under the covers to savor a few more minutes of heaven. The dark tunnel was behind her. That was one good thing at least.

For a moment, she felt she was at Arundell with Carrick, and he was downstairs making breakfast for her.

She indulged in the fantasy, enjoying the rush of happiness it brought her. It was such a sweet reprieve from the anguish she'd known since the earthquake. She let the minutes tick by, listening to the distant sounds of him banging around in the kitchen.

But the persistent sunlight shining in her face forced her back to reality. It was a reminder that this would never be the Arundell she knew. If this were her real home, she'd be sleeping right beside Carrick instead of waking up, bright eyed and ready to face the day.

Everything was the opposite of what it should be. There was nothing she could do about it, and she wasn't sure she minded, she realized as she lay there.

The smell of the coffee tempted her. Well, there was one thing she could do, she could get up and have some coffee. After so long without it, it sounded glorious.

She went to the bathroom and washed up. She brushed her hair until it glistened and the curls were no longer wild, but smooth. She wound her long hair in a bun and tucked a strand in deep to lock it in place. Checking herself in the mirror, she was glad to see her reflection in the light of day, not always in the shadows. She looked alive and felt better than she had since the night she'd arrived.

Her dress hung on the back of the door. She intended to put it on, but when she got close to it, the rank odor almost choked her. It reeked of smoke and filth. There was no choice for her but to leave Keat's clothes on until she washed the gown. Gathering the dress and her underthings, she went downstairs.

Keat stood in the kitchen wearing denim blue jeans and a white button-down shirt. He huddled over the stove tending to the bacon that sizzled in the pan. She took her time and watched him. He was surprisingly graceful and looked even more handsome this morning. Seeing him up close suddenly made her shy and nervous.

The look he gave her as she approached made her even more nervous. He stood still, and his eyes traveled the length of her body. "Good morning," he said, holding up the coffeepot. "Want a cup?"

"Please," she said, sounding almost desperate.

While she stood holding the cup, he poured the steaming coffee to just under the rim. "You look much better this morning."

She smiled. "I feel much better."

"Cream and sugar are over there," he said, nodding at the table.

"I like it black," she said. "I have a favor to ask of you. My dress is filthy, and I need to wash it so that I can have something to wear. Can I use your washtub?"

His lips tilted up in a smirk. "We use machines nowadays. Follow me. I'll show you. I have to be fast though because the bacon's almost done."

She followed him down the stairs to a little space in the back of the workshop where two square machines stood side by side.

"Here they are," he said, opening the door of one of the machines. "You simply put your clothes in here," he said, and then pulled open a little drawer near the top. Nodding at the bottles and boxes on the table, he said, "And you put the soap in there. Shut the door, hit the blue button, and easy as that you'll have a clean dress."

She nodded, looking at the machine in wonder. "I think I understand it," she said.

"Okay, let me run back upstairs. Bacon needs me."

After he had left, she pushed her dress and underthings into the opening, shut the door tight. Then she chose a bottle of soap and poured it in the cup right to the top. Pushing the blue button, she watched through the window as her dress began to tumble around, and water filled the tank.

Immediately, the water turned inky black. Her dress must have been filthy.

"Breakfast is ready!" called Keat from upstairs.

"Coming," replied Penrose. She patted the washing machine to thank it and then headed upstairs.

Keat sat drinking his coffee and watching her eat. She took a seat, politely asked for a napkin and calmly unfolded the paper over her lap. As she ate, she took small bites and chewed daintily. Watching those rosebud lips barely move as she chewed her food drove him crazy. He couldn't explain it, but damn, it was sexy.

She even cut her bacon with a knife and fork. *Who cuts their bacon?* he thought. She did. No doubt about it, she was a strange bird. Oddly, knowing these curious habits of hers pleased him. He could almost imagine the genteel Southern upbringing that would bring about such polite eating. But just because she had old-fashioned table manners didn't make her an old-fashioned woman.

He wasn't buying it. Oh, he wanted to believe her. More appropriately, a certain part of him already believed her. That part of him had bought into her story lock, stock and barrel from the moment she opened her rosebud mouth.

Watching her eat, it was easy to imagine her, sitting at a table 130 years ago, eating in the same manner. But if that were the case, she wouldn't be sitting there driving him wild with that mouth.

He was almost sad when she politely, delicately, placed her napkin on her plate and pushed the plate away.

"Your dress is probably clean by now," he said.

Her eyebrows lifted perfectly as if in total shock. "Really?" she replied. "That fast? That's amazing!" she said in what looked like real surprise. She could win an Oscar. "Is it dry, too?"

"No. It might be too delicate to put in the dryer." He decided to play along with her game of not knowing anything. "Let's go get it."

They went down into the cellar together, but when they reached the washing machine, she slowed and said, "Oh, no!"

"What?" he asked sharply, responding to the shock in her voice. "What is it?" Then he saw it.

She'd bleached her dress. "Why did you put bleach in?"

"I put in the soap that you pointed to." A sharp aroma came from the washer. "What did I do wrong? I didn't know it would take the color out."

"You put bleach in the washing machine. It whitens everything. All colors."

She pulled the dress from the machine and held it up. It was almost uniformly white. A couple of gray splotches. The aroma of bleach was unbearable.

"It's ruined," she said.

"Not necessarily," he said. "Let's wash it again and get the smell out. We can lay it over a chair in the kitchen to dry. It's warmer in there than the workshop. Give it a few days. Then you can decide whether to toss it or not."

"But I have nothing to wear."

He smiled. "I bet women have been saying that for centuries. Never fear. We'll take a trip into town."

After making Penrose don a black winter coat that swam on her small frame, Keat led her outside and opened the door to the Range Rover. She looked a little odd wearing filthy boots and sweatpants that were too big on her, but she was still sexy. Her cheeks glowed rosy red in the bitter cold, and with her black hair long and free, she was unforgettable.

"Are you sure it's proper?" she'd asked him in a serious voice when he suggested she leave her hair down.

"It's more than proper," he said. "It's expected." Even if it weren't entirely proper, she looked too damn good with it down. It was so shiny and bouncy, like a dark, swirling halo around her beautiful face. Even without makeup, she aced out any woman he'd ever met.

Helping her into the front seat, he shut the door. She looked at him with a face of utter fear, and he smiled encouragingly at her as he walked around to the driver's side. He'd play her game and win.

He was determined to trip her up, to catch her making that one small mistake, one slip of familiarity that would prove he was right and she was lying. He knew it would happen. He just had to be patient.

The way he saw it, she deserved far worse. If he turned her in to the authorities, she'd be carted away, and besides, he might get in trouble himself for failing to report her right away.

Even though he still felt rage pounding in his blood, he didn't quite want that for her. He was so used to winning, so used to being triumphant that her calm, sweet smile as she steadfastly refused to budge from her story drove him insane. He would win this battle. It might take time, but he would win it.

Sitting in the seat, he turned to her and said, "Are you ready to have fun?"

She looked flushed. Excited. "I think I am. You're sure this is safe?"

"Most of the time," he said with a wink. He fired up the engine, did a three-point turn and drove away on the snow-covered road.

Not five minutes later, he had to fend off her requests to go faster and faster.

"It's snowy, Penrose, we have to keep it pretty tame."

She looked around, eyes wide with amazement. "We have to go faster," she said passionately. "I love it! I cannot believe things can travel this fast!"

"Watch this," he said, as he pushed the button that lowered the windows. Cold air whipped into the car, making her hair fly all in all directions. She squealed in delight and for the first time in a long while, he laughed—a great big belly laugh.

How long had it been since he laughed? Too long by far.

Chapter 18

Penrose felt wild and out of control traveling so fast. Once, when she was eleven, she'd taken a train ride to Savannah with her mother. She had sat on the train, forehead pressed against the window, the world sliding like a backdrop screen behind a play. The images captivated her. Riding in a car, the images assaulted her. Demanded her attention. She gladly, willingly, gave it. "There's no feeling in the world like this!" she exclaimed. "It's amazing!"

"Oh, my dear Penrose," he said with a smug look, "you have no idea what fun this century can be." He gave her a wicked grin. "We're just getting started."

When she looked at him, her stomach flipped. Her black hair whipped around and stung her face, and she smiled at him.

When they came to town, she was surprised by some

things but unsurprised at how similar one town seemed to another. Keat assured her that was because she was in a small town. "You should see New York City," he said.

"Oh, I'd love to. My mother told me tales of the city. She's from New York, you know."

"I didn't know," he said. "What was your mother's name?"

Was. What a terrible word to hear. It reminded her that not just her mother was dead, but everyone she ever knew. "Her name was Diana Heatherton. She died six months ago." She looked at him apologetically. "I mean…you know…one hundred and thirty years ago." It pained her to say those words and to think about her poor mother, so very long in the grave by now. Forgotten by all.

Keat seemed to understand. He reached out and patted her arm. "You don't need to talk about it. I know it's hard to lose someone."

She blinked away the sharp tear that poked at her eye. "Your father?"

"Yes." He grew still and silent, and she felt his mood turn dark. He didn't elaborate, and from the intensity of his gaze she thought it best not to pry.

"I'm sorry," she said.

"Thank you," he said. "We're almost there. I'm taking you to the finest shopping establishment backwoods Wyoming offers. The Supercenter."

"The Supercenter," she repeated after him. It sounded as exciting as New York City.

Once in the store, Penrose had to recall a simple trick from her childhood to cope with things that frightened her. Just keep putting one foot in front of the other. *Stare at your feet,* she commanded herself. She concentrated on doing that as Keat led her through the enormous store. When she first walked in, everything shouted at her. Lights brighter than a sun shone down from the ceiling. Goods and supplies were jammed on every shelf and stood in piles in the rows. People jostled against each other, pushing their carts.

"Get whatever you want," he told her when they got to the makeup and grooming section. "Get two if you like. It doesn't matter to me."

"I have no way to pay you back," she said.

"You were lucky enough to haunt the house of a very rich man. So trust me when I say get whatever you want."

"Thank you," she said.

"I'm going to get a salesclerk to help us buy some clothes for you. Stay in this section, and I'll be right back."

"I will."

With Keat gone, she indulged all of her urges, marveling at every single product. She put lipstick, hairbrushes, hairpins, ribbons, lotions, creams and body spray into the cart. Next came mascara and blush. In the hair-color aisle, she stood in front of the rainbow of available colors, hardly believing what she saw. She picked colors that appealed to her and tossed them into the cart. She read every package with awe, learning of all their unbelievable powers to make her beautiful and change her whole appearance.

Keat returned with a salesperson, and they went to buy clothes. Once they figured out her size, she was off and running. Jeans were a problem. She couldn't quite get the hang of walking in them, and strode up and down the dressing room in an odd, hitched gait.

But the rest she loved. From blouses to bras, skirts and panties, sandals and heels. Even a pair of sneakers. She adored them all, and when she left the dressing room, she thanked the clerk who had helped her.

"No biggie," said the woman in a bored tone, and shrugged. But to Penrose it was very much a biggie.

When they were paying for their items, Keat picked up the boxes of the hair coloring. "You can't buy these," he said.

"But I love the idea of changing how I look," she protested sadly. She really wanted to experiment.

"You can change how you look. I don't know too much about beauty routines, but I can tell you that your hair is too beautiful to risk on a box of color. I'll make an appointment to have it colored at a salon."

It sounded exciting to her. "Thanks," she said.

After shopping at the Supercenter, Keat said to Penrose, "How about a bite to eat?"

"Sure."

He took her to Trixie's Diner, a mom-and-pop establishment with silver siding and a neon sign. "Now you're in for a real treat," he said. "One of the many benefits of living in this century."

A waitress sat them at a booth near the door. The seats were red plastic, and the table white and full of dull gray scratches. They each slid into the seats, and Keat noticed that she smiled and bounced a little bit, testing the seat.

She was like a child in some ways. Not in the ways that counted, that was for sure. But this innocence, the willingness to explore the world and the sheer delight in doing so, amazed him.

He took a menu from the stand and handed it to her. She spent as much time running her fingers over the clear plastic as she did looking at the items on the menu.

"I'm not usually one to make decisions for another," he said, "but Trixie's diner is famous for their cheeseburgers." He smiled at her. "And will you split a chocolate shake with me?"

"A cheeseburger?" Her eyebrows drew together.

"You haven't heard of a cheeseburger?" he said, making a mental note to research it later. But he appeased her by saying, "I suppose they hadn't invented those yet. What about a milk shake?"

"I haven't heard of that, either."

"Well, then, you are in for a real treat."

An older lady in a yellow uniform came over to take their order. "What'll it be?" the waitress asked, holding a pad of paper and a pen.

"Two cheeseburgers with everything and a double chocolate milk shake. Extra thick. And two straws, please," he said.

A short time later, they sat sipping chocolate milk shakes and eating their meals. Penrose took extra delight in the French fries, swirling them in ketchup until they were dripping before popping the whole thing in her mouth. "These are the most delicious things," she said. "And, yes, I'm familiar with them."

She was adorable. She sniffed the cheeseburger and then tried to take it apart to eat it.

"No, no. Try it like this." He took a big bite, motioning at her to try it.

Raising it to her mouth, she opened wide and took a bite. She nodded to show him how much she liked it.

He took a sip of the shake. "Try this." Pushing the glass over to her, he held out her straw. "It's heaven."

She put her lips around the red straw, and his cock stirred at the sight. He could tell the moment the milk shake hit her mouth because her expression completely changed. Her eyes widened, and her mouth began to work overtime to suck up the sweet concoction. After a few moments, she said, "I think I've died and gone to heaven. This is the most delicious thing I've ever tasted." Pulling the straw from the glass, she ran it through her lips.

He hissed under his breath to see her red lips wrapped around the straw. "I'm glad you like it," he managed to say.

Later that evening, Keat sat at a table in the workshop, reading an email from his assistant, Valerie. There wasn't much new information on Penrose Heatherton, but what little facts Valerie found supported what he already knew, or rather, what Penrose already told him. She was born on May 10, 1865, in Charleston, South Carolina. Her mother was listed as unmarried on her birth certificate. Her father was listed as James Penrose. She appeared in both the 1870 and 1880 census, but there were no records of her after that, save for the listing of her name in the Charleston newspaper as one of the missing in the days after the earthquake.

Seeing her name as one of the missing was new, but beyond that there was frustratingly little to go on. His jaw twitched. That itch was rising up in him. Once he set his mind to something, he wouldn't let up until he got what he wanted. And what he wanted from her was the truth.

Was that all he wanted? An image of that perfect hip, of which he'd caught a glimpse when her sweatpants slipped off, came to mind. He thought of those blue eyes and the way they glittered fiercely at him and the way her face lit up when she laughed, which happened far too rarely.

Maybe it was something else entirely. When she spoke about his family, it made him feel whole again. He knew it was just an illusion, him believing her stories, but whatever the reason, he wasn't about to let her go. If it was an illusion, he wanted it to linger on just a little bit longer.

A sound drew his attention away from his cell phone, and he looked up to see Penrose standing in front of him.

God Almighty.

Her modern look completely surprised him. Her hair was a glossy black cloud. Wearing just a touch of lipstick, she looked hotter than most women looked with a full face of makeup. She wore a blue sweater and a long, formfitting skirt, and the way it clung to her body left no doubt as to the perfection he saw on the first night. She held her now-white dress in one arm and, remembering her in it, he had a definite preference. Modern. All the way. Standing there with those rose-colored lips, she was a temptation like none he'd known before.

"I just went to grab my dress. I'm going to dry it upstairs."

If she was really from another era, then she moved effortlessly between the two centuries. The only indication something wasn't quite right was the uncertain, almost apologetic expression on her face. As if she wasn't comfortable in her own skin.

"You look wonderful," he said, speaking the truth.

She visibly relaxed. "Thank you," she said in that Southern lilt of hers. Taking a few, maddeningly sexy steps forward, she came in front of his table and said, "What are you working on?"

He held up his phone and watched her expression.

"What does it do?" she asked with a curious expression on her face.

"Come now," he coaxed. "Isn't there anyone you'd like to call?"

"To call? No."

"Oh, you'd rather text."

"Please stop," she said. "I don't know what you're talking about."

He looked at her long and hard. "I'll stop for now," he said. "But what I was doing before you walked in was making an appointment at the salon for you to have your hair done."

"Really?" She looked suspicious. "But why are you so nice to me?"

"You're my guest, remember?" he said simply. The truth was, he wasn't entire sure why he wanted to indulge her. He had to run a few errands anyway, he told himself. It didn't hurt anything and, besides, he rather liked the modern Penrose that was blossoming before him.

"Thank you," she replied, tucking a strand of her black hair behind an ear. Her eyes darted around the room. "I was hoping that maybe I could help you with something. I'd like to feel useful." She bit her bottom lip.

That was enough to make a man crazy. She stood there, looking so eager, so hopeful, that he couldn't say no. "I could use your help with a few things."

She blessed him with a million-dollar smile in return and damn if it didn't turn him into a lovesick teenager, his heart fluttering like mad. It was a smile to move mountains for.

He set her up at a workstation and had her organize the hardware—he was always messy when it came to those things—and she sat patiently, sorting through the nuts, bolts and screws. Her presence in the workshop pleased him, which was a surprise. He usually liked to work alone. After that, he had her clean up the lines on some of his drawings so that he could scan them in and upload them to the 3-D rendering program. When he handed her the bottle of white-out, she seemed fascinated by it.

"You mean, you can just paint white and erase these stray marks?" she asked.

"Yeah, no big deal, Penrose."

"Hmm," she said, reading the bottle with such a studious look he burst out laughing.

He found himself telling her about his ideas and plans. It surprised him. She sat there quietly, her small fingers sorting through the bits and pieces, and soon enough he began talking. She listened eagerly, asking smart and pointed questions that caused him to rethink more than a few things. Which, of course, brought about new ideas.

She inspired him. And maddened him. If only she would admit who she was. It didn't matter where she came from, he just wanted her to tell the truth. He could live with that.

They worked side by side until well past dinnertime and then ate sandwiches in the kitchen. During dinner,

Keat received an alert on his phone that a severe winter storm was headed their way and expected within hours.

It was late when they finished dinner. Penrose looked as if she could work all night, but Keat was tired. "Let's go to bed," he said.

Penrose wasn't sure exactly what she was expecting when he mentioned going to bed, but getting her own bedroom wasn't it. His face was stony as he led her up the stairs. "I've moved your belongings to a spare bedroom," he said. "I think you'll be more comfortable there, and you'll have privacy."

"That's fine," she said, trudging behind him, running her hand along the railing, trying to hide her disappointment. The knowledge that he didn't want her in his bedroom hurt. It was foolish, of course, but it still stung to hear it. Not that she wanted anything to happen. No, of course she did. After being alone in the tunnel and watching him from afar, his nearness only intensified her longing.

He brought her to a room a few doors down from his and opened the door for her. Doing her best to keep her face neutral, she thanked him. The room was fine, comfortable, with a twin bed and a dresser, and she'd be safe with him nearby. But she wanted to hear his breathing, his footsteps, and the muttered curses when he was frustrated. She craved his presence.

After he had left, she went to her pile of new belongings and pulled out a nightgown to wear. It was the lightest blue color and slipped over her body like silk. It was so thin she'd have to snuggle under the covers to stay warm.

After crawling into bed, she was restless and sleep

wouldn't come. Images of Carrick and Keat kept popping into her mind and blending together, confusing her. And arousing her. Each of them held a different appeal. Finally, she gave up. She sat up, sweating and wiping her brow, wishing that they were the same man. A foolish wish, she knew, but her heart still desired it. She wanted both men and yet she could have neither. Keat distrusted her, seemed bent on proving her a fraud, and she would probably never see Carrick again.

Finally, she fell into a restless sleep.

The next afternoon, Keat drove her to town. They walked side by side along the main street until they came to The Spiral Curl Salon. Penrose stood in front of the window, staring at the pictures of the models that hung in the window.

"What are you staring at?" he asked her.

She couldn't believe how beautiful the women were. "I could never look like that," she said. "I can't believe how all the women are so perfect in the future."

"Penrose, you outshine them all."

Her blue eyes darted to meet his own. He changed the subject. "Come on, let's go inside and see what they can do for you."

The beauty parlor had a bell on the door that jingled loudly when they entered. It was at the end of the day, and the shop was quiet. It smelled of spice and perfumes and a stick of incense burned by the checkout counter. From the back of the shop came the clack-clack-clack of a pair of heels as a woman approached the counter.

"Can I help you?" she asked.

Looking at the woman, Penrose thought of a rainbow. In her late forties, she had rich brown hair and wore a collage of colors, from her red vest to her black fancy shoes. Gold rings gleamed from her fingers. There was something so coiffed, so perfect about her. The woman took one look at Penrose and said, "My word. I have two things to say to you. Trim and eyebrow wax." She smiled warmly. "And I say that with love, darling."

Penrose looked at Keat for help. She was hopelessly lost.

"We have an appointment," Keat said, barely containing a smile.

"I've cleared the decks. A complete makeover. And my pleasure." She turned to Penrose. "And look at you. You're like a blank canvas." She walked around the counter and circled Penrose, analyzing her hair. "How long has it been since you had a haircut?" She spoke sharply before adding in a kinder tone, "My name is Ophelia, and I'm the owner. And, honey, what rock have you been hiding under that you've gotten this far in life without at least highlighting your hair?"

Penrose wasn't sure how to answer, and again Keat had to speak up. "She's been out of touch with modern times. That's the easiest explanation," he said.

Ophelia looked at Penrose. "You poor thing. You mean like a cult?"

"Something like that," said Keat.

"Come on back," she said to Penrose. "Let's sit you in the chair and find out what you're interested in." She pointed at Keat. "You can either make yourself comfortable or make yourself scarce. Your choice, mister."

"Scarce," he said, chuckling.

"Come on now, darling," Ophelia said to Penrose. "Have a seat."

* * *

Keat finished his errands and returned to the shop. He walked inside and then stopped. He stood there staring stupidly at her, trying to absorb the shock of seeing her as a hot, modern woman. Not just any hot modern woman, but the hottest one he'd ever seen. He had loved her black hair, but it didn't hold a candle to her as a blonde. God wasn't supposed to make mistakes, but he sure made one with her—she was meant to be a blonde.

"I told you," Ophelia said proudly. "He'll be eating from the palm of your hand." She beamed from behind the counter.

Penrose stood up. She looked anxious, standing with her hands in front of her, wringing them together. He knew he should say something, give her a compliment at least, but damn if he couldn't speak.

"Yep. That's the best compliment of all. The speechless kind."

Keat looked at Ophelia and then at Penrose. "She's right. You look amazing. Beyond any compliment I could give you."

A tiny smile pulled at her mouth. Her cheeks turned the faintest pink, and she stared at her hands. Keat looked at her hands. Eating from her palms sounded mighty fine to him.

Chapter 19

Penrose lay in bed later that night, marveling at her new hair color. The blow-dryer had impressed her, the magical hair color impressed her—everything did. Except for the dragging hollowness that she felt with Keat.

There were bright spots, like the rush she got when he looked at her a certain way. But he maintained the foolish insistence that she was putting on a ruse. Or worse. It made her angry, the way he played with her. Nice one minute but cruel the next. She wasn't crazy, as he accused her of being, but she would be soon if he kept it up.

The two centuries were so different; yet, there were things she loved about both of them. She thought of home—the scent of pine in the air, the green trees that crowded every piece of land they could. It was so lush, so beautiful that she longed for it. She looked out of the window. Another storm.

Snow never seemed to end here.

She wanted to go home. The longing came on strong. If only there were some way she could. But maybe…

After all, there were so many amazing technologies in the present. Maybe she was missing something, some kind of science that could send her back in time. Back to the Arundell she belonged in. The idea took hold. Of course, she wouldn't ask Keat. She knew the answer he'd give her. No, the only one she could ask was Harris.

She decided to try it. Slipping from her bed, she walked across the cold marble floor, quietly opened the door and made her way down the hall. The clock struck two in the morning, and she noticed the snow falling even heavier outside. No wind, just big, fat flakes dropping heavy and fast.

It was cold downstairs, and she regretted not putting on a robe, but she wasn't about to turn around and fetch it. She went through the kitchen and down the cellar stairs to the workshop.

In the workshop, it was colder still, and her skin puckered. The robots were lined up like soldiers. She saw Harris over by the fireplace. No fire burned. He seemed almost lonely, waiting there. She went and knelt in front of him, and the stone floor hurt her knees. She said, "Power up."

The black screen on his helmet flashed bright white before the image of two blinking eyes appeared. "Hello, Pen Rose," he said in a loud voice.

"Shh," she urged him, pressing her fingers to her lips. "Can you talk lower?"

"Yes, of course I can," he replied in a softer voice.

Penrose looked left and right as if she was about to commit a crime, and then whispered, "Harris, can you tell me how to travel back in time? I want to go home. I can't stay here anymore."

Keat opened his eyes with an uneasy feeling. He'd had lots of uneasy feelings lately, but this one had teeth and put him instantly on edge. Something wasn't right. Rolling from his bed, he threw on a pair of jeans and went to check on Penrose.

She wasn't there. His first thought, when he saw the empty bed, was that she'd gone back to the tunnel. He flew down the stairs two at a time, racing to the entry door of the tunnel. When he opened it, the lingering, offensive odor of smoke rose out of it, sharp enough to turn him away. The reek was too heavy in the air to tolerate. He was sure of it. Then, as he was shutting the entry door, he heard the faint monotone voice of Harris coming from the workshop, and he went straight there.

When he came to the stairs, he saw Penrose. The sight of her on her knees in a nightgown that was thin as paper stopped him in the doorway. He saw her in profile, saw the teardrop shape of her breasts, the swell of her backside and her hair trailing down her back. The look on her face, earnest and pleading as she whispered to Harris, should have brought about pity, but instead it angered him. Damn her. He stood there, breathing hard, emotions pushing and pulling at him, and he heard her ask, "Harris, can you tell me how to travel back in time? I want to go home. I can't stay here anymore."

The foolishness must stop, and it would stop right here, right now. He felt a tidal wave of sickening emotion. And worry for her. He had thought she stuck to her guns because she was lying, but that look on her face was too eager, too hopeful, to be lying. She truly believed that she lived in that era, and that angered him even further.

She was his little ghost. But she was disturbed, and he had to face that fact. He pawed his face in despair. He should have known better. He was a bit of a celebrity. Whenever he went out with a woman, her face appeared in the magazines, with some crazy title that the reclusive billionaire might have found his bride. His team had always cautioned him to have a security force around him. God, it made perfect sense. She had just hit him sideways with all of her passion and facts about his family.

She was a stalker. The knowledge hit him like a ton of bricks, and it didn't sit well. He stepped into the room and said in a cold voice, "Harris."

Penrose gasped and turned sharply. He should have empathy for her, with those big eyes and that scared expression, but he ignored the feeling. Once and for all, he would prove to her, and to him, that she was deluded.

"Hello, Keat," said Harris. "What can I do for you this morning?"

"Harris," said Keat, walking into the room. "Can you tell me everything you know about Penrose Heatherton, born in 1865?" he asked the robot, knowing the files had been uploaded to the server by his assistant.

"Of course, Keat," began the robot in a chillingly dispassionate voice. "Penrose Heatherton was born in Charleston, South Carolina, on May 10, 1865..."

With cold disinterest and a monotone voice, Penrose listened as the robot recited the facts of her life. The stone floor beneath her knees was softer than the truth. She watched the bright, happy eyes of Harris fade away and pictures of Charleston in the aftermath of the earth-quake began to flash across his screen. She felt numb and almost sick to her stomach to see the images that flashed across the screen. Her beautiful hometown destroyed. Lives lost. But whose lives? She choked back a sob and looked at Keat, unable to hide her despair. He was cruel.

Without a trace of passion or life in his voice, the robot continued. "Penrose Heatherton is found in the 1870 and 1880 census as living with Diana Heatherton. According to the *Charleston Observer*, she was listed as a missing person in the aftermath of the Great Charleston Earthquake, and there are no further records of her."

"Enough," said Keat. He strode over to the pile of firewood, picked up a few logs, tossed them into the fireplace and lit a fire. His back was to her, and she had the urge to push him into the flames.

"You're cruel." She leaned back and rested on her heels. She felt crushed. Furious. Her voice shook as she spoke. "If you think those facts will convince me that I'm not her, you couldn't be more wrong." Tears stung her eyes, and she pressed at her eyes hard, trying to stop them. "It breaks my soul in two. Because my life has been broken in two." *And now my heart*, said a little voice deep inside of her. She'd only just begun to realize the depths of her emotions for him.

"I can't decide if you're a schemer or if you're crazy," he replied, turning around slowly to face her. He looked cold, dispassionate. Like a robot himself. "I'm still not sure. But I'm sure of one thing, Penrose—if you are who you say you are, and if you were born in 1865, then you are a ghost. According to the newspaper, you were never seen again. And the man you ask for is dead, as well. Look at the calendar. Carrick is long dead. You are, too. Which makes you a ghost in my home." He sighed, deep and heavy, and strode forward until he stood above her. "But you know the real truth."

His words took a moment to sink in. Of course, looking at the calendar gave a simple truth, but one she never really dwelled on. The truth hurt, more than hurt. It destroyed her. Everyone she'd ever known and every person she'd ever seen was dead. C.J. was dead. Carrick was dead.

Carrick was dead. Of course he was, but still she found it hard to breathe. It was so strange, the way the fact kept pounding, swirling in her thoughts. She stood up slowly, her knees screaming in protest. "I know what you say is the truth. But, Keat, inside of me, I know what I say is also the truth. Nothing you can do to change it. Nothing. The truth stands alone, and it stands in my heart."

"There are only two possibilities. The first and factual one is that you are someone else, and that you suffer from a severe mental problem. The second is that you are dead and a ghost—"

Angry, she cut him off. "I'm not dead! And I'm not lying, either!" She was defensive, taking steps backward and shaking her head. "I'm right here, Keat. Alive. Not dead, and I'm telling you the truth." Something inside of her broke open. "You think that you have it all down, don't you?" Her hands shook as she ran them through her hair. "You have all the facts. You have robots. And fancy things. Machines. And now you're going to stand there and tell me what I am. So, tell me, do I look like a ghost to you?"

He didn't answer but stood there with a clamped-down expression on his face.

She was tired of trying to understand everything, to make the best of the mess she was in. "I'm not crazy. I'm not a ghost." But her voice wavered as a sick little thought came into her head. Suddenly, she needed to prove she was alive. She needed to feel. Taking a few more steps, she spun around and ran to the doors of the workshop, flung them open and ran out into the snow-storm wearing nothing but her nightgown.

The whiteness swallowed her up, and the cold was a million thorns on her skin. Flakes swirled around her, eddied and blew past her. She ran as far as she could, kicking up rooster tails of powder until she couldn't see the manor anymore and the world was merely a blur of white and gray. Breathing heavily, she stood letting the cold eat at her, bite her skin, trying to savor every sensation. Even the pain. "I'm alive," she said, and it felt right to say those words. It felt affirming. So she raised her voice, and over and over she repeated, "I am alive. I am alive. I feel this. I feel this," until her voice rose to a shout.

The wind whipped higher as if it agreed with him and she screamed in reply, "Aren't I alive? Doesn't my heart beat?"

There was no answer but the wind.

A shadowy figure appeared through the curtain of falling snowflakes.

"Penrose!" Keat called out, moving in her direction. "There you are," he said, coming to stand in front of her. He rubbed his arms over his bare chest. "Come back to the house."

The snow swirled around them. "No," she said,

angry. Everything hurt. Moving hurt. Shivering, she took one step forward, close enough that she reached out and jabbed him with her finger. "I've had enough," she whispered. "Enough of your taunting. Your jabs. Your eyes on me every second, waiting for me to slip up. I've spoken the truth since my first word to you."

Her chest heaved as she spoke. "You call me ghost. The newspaper calls me missing. The calendar calls me dead." She shook her head back and forth wildly. "But I live. I'm alive. Aren't I?" she asked in a hopeless voice. "How can I be dead and feeling all of this? I'm not dead, Keat. I'm alive, and I'm not lying."

Flakes of snow clung to his hair and his eyebrows. Looking up at his eerily familiar face and snow-white hair, for one brief moment she saw Carrick. An anguish filled her soul.

"Please, Keat, I want to go back. I want to go home. You can keep your lightbulbs and your helicopters and your washing machines. I want the Arundell I know and love." She stepped closer, close enough that their chests touched. "I want the duck pond and the oak tree," she whispered. "I want people around me who believe in me."

Carrick was a damaged soul, but he needed her. Keat was whole and strong, yet he rejected her. Life wasn't worth living unless you lived it in the company of those who valued you.

She shook so violently from the cold that she could barely speak, and her words came out in a pathetic whisper, "I want a man who looks at me and believes in me. You distrust me and look at me with disgust. So yes, I want to go home. Can you blame me?" She was numb and cold. Burned with cold. Burned with anger. But she reveled in the feeling because it was proof she lived.

She raised her finger and pointed at him accusingly. "You. Do you think that I came here to be with you? You're wrong. My body may want you, but my mind knows what you are. A monster. The sad truth is that I'm stuck with you, and I'm stuck in this damned new century."

She called him a monster. Keat didn't care. It was what she said before that that mattered. She wanted him. The second he heard those words it was as if an iron band that had constricted his chest for the past few days had been cut and he could breathe again. Hope again.

He hands slid behind her head, and he lifted her face to his. Her hair felt icy, but her skin hot. Hot and most definitely alive. Suddenly, nothing mattered but that one fact. "You are alive, Penrose," he said. "I promise you that and I can prove it."

"How?" she cried in a desperate voice. The snowflakes on her hair created a white, lacy shawl around her face. Her cheeks were flushed pink, her lips even pinker. She looked up at him with anguished eyes, a desperation he'd never seen on a person before.

It was a fear so deep and a pain so real that any lingering doubts he had about her story disappeared. Facts and science no longer mattered. Only she did, and the sudden, booming certainty inside of him. He believed her. He felt it in his bones. He'd never been so angry, so scared, or so taken by a person before. From the moment he saw her, his emotions had been wild. Fear to lust, hate to longing, and now something deeper.

She looked up at him. She seemed so small, shivering

as she was in his hands. He felt a fierce need to protect her and an even fiercer need to kiss her, to claim her in some way, as if that might lock her into this century. "I want you. I believe in you. Come inside and let me prove it." He kissed her, his lips coming down hard, his hands gripping her.

Chapter 20

Keat's lips took hers, descended on them and claimed them. A flame came to life within Penrose. If she weren't alive, his lips would've coaxed her back from the dead. She had ice on her fingers, her feet had turned to stone, and her body was frozen. But her soul burned with life. The sensation of his lips on hers was stronger than any snowstorm, any sting the world could give her.

The kiss traveled to the bottom of her soul and back again. She most certainly lived. The smallest whimper escaped her lips, and Keat seemed to understand what she said. Yes. She'd said yes. He scooped her into his arms, crushing her body to his for warmth, and carried her through the snow back to Arundell Manor.

"You need a bath," he said. "You need to warm up." Melting snow dripped onto the floor as he carried her up the stairs to his bathroom. It was all she could do to cling to him. Her thin nightgown was plastered to her body, and she felt the heat from his skin.

He didn't turn the bathroom light on as he entered. The dim light from the hallway spilled through the open door and made the bathroom shadowy. With his foot, he kicked the tub faucet and water streamed into the tub. They stood while the water filled the tub, and he held her in those strong arms of his.

It seemed that in an instant everything had changed. The way he looked at her was different. The way he held her was protective. It was hard to know how to react, and she felt a bit shy. Uncertain. Fluttery.

When the bath was almost full, he placed her, standing upright, into the tub. The warm water swirled around her shins. "Don't go," she said.

"Penrose, I'm not going anywhere." His voice was low. Standing right beside the tub, he put a hand on her shoulder and slipped a finger beneath her strap of her nightgown. She tilted her chin, the slightest nod, and his fingers worked their way down her shoulders, taking the wet fabric with them. Looking down, she saw her chest rising and falling rapidly. His hands were so warm and seemed to sear her cold, damp skin.

Her breasts were bared. He looked down and sucked in his breath, and a rush of pleasure flooded her at his reaction.

His fingers moved again, and, with aching slowness, he peeled the fabric away from her stomach. The nightgown dropped into the water at her feet.

He took a huge breath and exhaled in a soft whistle. "The sight of you," he whispered.

The mirror beside the tub reflected their image. The faint light illuminated every curve of her body. Her nipples were dark points jutting out, and a dark shadow was visible between her legs. Keat looked tall, imposing. Dark. His jeans were soaking wet. They revealed every muscle of his strong legs and the stiff tent that bulged at his crotch, and suddenly she shivered from head to toe.

"Water," he ordered her, putting his hand on her shoulder.

"It's not from the cold—"

He interrupted her. "I don't care. Down." Putting his hand gently on her, he pushed her down. She slid down, right in front of his jeans and saw his erection more clearly. Immediately, her eyes darted up to meet his dark gaze.

"You do that to me," he said in a low voice. "Even when I thought I'd imagined you."

A tiny thrill of sensation rushed between her legs as she slipped into the steaming water. Penrose wasn't embarrassed or shy lying down in front of him. Maybe in some way she invited his gaze. After all, she'd been hidden for so long, and spent her days secretly taking in the sight of him. It thrilled her to have him taking in the sight of her. She lay in front of him as if to say *here I am*.

He took a deep breath. "Sometimes I think you enjoy making me insane. You know I'm coming in that water with you."

"Yes," she said.

Suddenly there was a fierce gust of the wind that shook the house, and the lights went out. The room was plunged into darkness. The house, which hadn't seemed very loud before, was suddenly as quiet as a tomb.

"Keat?" she whispered. Her heart punched in her

chest, and all she could think of was the tunnel. "Keat?" she asked again, her voice rising to a whine.

"It's okay, Penrose." He moved. His voice came to her from a different place. "Stay there," he said in a calming voice. "It's just a blackout. A power outage where the lights go out. It's temporary. I'm going to get some candles. I'll be right back. Be calm."

He was gone. The room was too quiet. When she moved, the rippling water sounds seemed unbearably loud. Breathe, she reminded herself. Dim moonlight came through the window and lit the tendrils of steam that rose up like ghosts from the water. Her eyes adjusted.

Something nagged at her, a sense of doom that some fact had been overlooked.

"It's nothing to worry about," Keat said. "I'm back," he called from the hallway. Then she saw his familiar form carrying a tray filled with a dozen candles flickering with little flames. He continued, "The power will be back on soon, I'm sure of it. I thought we'd have some fun with it."

Penrose watched as he approached the tub, sat beside her and set the tray down. "You look beautiful in the candlelight," he said. "Like a fiery angel."

Candles.

She said nothing, merely watched silently, in shock, as he lifted a candle, placed it in the water and gently nudged it in her direction. Oh, she thought, fate was cruel. Things were repeating. Dear God, things were repeating.

It twirled out straight toward Penrose. Keat took a few more candles and scattered them over the water.

"Stop," she said in a quivering voice. She was instantly split in two centuries. "Please, stop." She froze, barely even able to draw breath. Panic rose inside of her, and she couldn't understand why. She couldn't let those candles go out—with all her heart she knew they couldn't go dark. If those candles went dark, something very bad would happen. "Please, take the candles from the water. Please."

"Penrose," he said with a look of concern on his face. "What is it?"

How could she explain it to him? That she and Carrick had placed candles on the dark water, and that the indifferent darkness had snuffed them out? She looked at him with every ounce of emotion she had, willing him to understand. "Please," she whispered in a voice that didn't sound like her own.

"Sure," he said, "no problem." He scooped his hand into the water to lift a candle. The motion created a wave that rippled out, reaching first the nearest candles, which wobbled and then flipped.

"No. No. No," she said softly, and covered her mouth with her hand. Other candles began tipping into the water and flipping over. She closed her eyes. "Make it stop. Please. They can't go out!"

"They're just batteries. Open your eyes. There's nothing to be scared of. They won't go out."

She opened her eyes the tiniest bit and peered out through the fringe of her eyelashes. A fuzzy yellow glow greeted her, and then her eyes flew wide open. And she saw the miraculous sight of the candles hanging upside down, yet still burning. The little flames flickered, illuminating the dark water and casting wavy rays of yellow light on her skin.

"Look," he said. "I'll show you. I'll turn it over." He reached for a candle, his hand sliding under the water and brushing against her thigh. It left a trail of heat on her skin. "It's okay, look," he said. He turned the candle right side up, and the strange light still burned perfectly.

"You don't understand," she whispered, and shook her head, unwilling to believe what was happening. She spoke without thinking. "What if this is our brief chance at heaven?" she said, remembering the words that were once spoken to her by a different Arundell man. Carrick's words. The words seemed to hang over the water of the bath.

It was not Carrick who replied, though. It was Keat. "If this is our nirvana, then I've died happy, Penrose."

The world had turned inside out. She was staring at candles that burned under the water. They were a different kind of fire.

She looked up at Keat. He was a different kind of man. Not a dark twin to Carrick. And what if this really was her brief nirvana? What if this was the only happiness she could grasp? Wouldn't Carrick want it for her? Of course he would. Carrick himself had said, "Fire has no choice but to grab its moment, whatever moment it's given, and burn."

A different century. A different kind of fire. A different man, one she couldn't help but to burn for. Was this the moment she'd been given? It was. She turned to Keat and said, "Take me to bed now."

"My pleasure," he replied, and reached down for her.

They went to his bedroom, and he laid her dripping wet on the bed. By the light of the fire, he saw her. She was magnificent, Keat thought. The sight of her body was a shock to his system. He sucked in his breath like a dying man. He was so used to plucked and perfected women.

Christ, he wanted her, wanted her like no other woman before. His cock was stiff and ready to bury itself inside of her.

She reached up to him and touched his stomach. He peeled his cold, wet jeans off and climbed into the bed.

Her skin was hot. His was cold. A groan came from some dark, primitive place within him. Their bodies slid against each other, exchanging high temperature and cold, settling on a burn that pleased both of them.

He kissed her. She had the sweetest little mouth he'd ever felt. Good God, her mouth could drive a man to insanity.

She whimpered and moaned, and her hands were everywhere on his body. There was a wildness in her that reminded him of a winter storm, fierce and determined. He moved with deliberate slowness, taking her mouth slowly with his own, thrusting his cock against her bare thigh. He kissed her for so long that her mouth became swollen from his kisses. Now she was no longer fierce but softened, ripe and willing. Every time his hands touched her body, she arched her back and opened her legs.

He was torturing himself. It took all his will not to slip his hand over her downy hair and between her legs. Once he felt her hot and wet and waiting, he would be unable to resist. And he wanted this to last, because he felt alive. Wholly alive. Her body bloomed under his hands. His touch coaxed moans and whimpers from her.

With other women, he was mechanical, like a robot. With her, he was alive.

* * *

Penrose wanted him. She closed her eyes. She wanted to savor his touch and block out everything else except the trail of heat he left along her skin. Her awareness followed his fingertips.

He came to her breasts first, caressed them and brought her nipples to fine points. Then his hands traveled over her stomach, lingering and gripping her pelvic bone. She thrust upward, inviting him lower. But he denied her, skimming lightly over her curls and down her thighs.

Need consumed her. She wanted to be taken by him. Claimed. The rest could wait.

"Now, Keat," she begged him when she couldn't take it any longer.

As he settled over her, she realized that there would be two moments in her life. Before and after, and she was in the very last moments of before. "Hurry," she whispered, not wanting to chance fate, grabbing his hips and urging him on. She was ready for the after. For the ever after.

He spread her legs, positioned himself at her entrance and then thrust inside.

Heat consumed her, a deep passion made fierce what they had endured together.

"Yes," she whispered, trailing the word in a long sigh. It felt as if she'd waited a century for this moment.

How strange that she felt so comfortable with Keat, Penrose marveled. It was a different century, after all. Of course, it wasn't simply the change on the calendar. But the feeling she had when she was next to him was a timeless contentment. It didn't matter what the calendar said when she was next to him. She felt whole. For an entire week, they indulged themselves in the bedroom, spending long, lingering mornings twisting in the sheets before they made their way downstairs to eat breakfast.

Penrose often accompanied him to the workshop. At first, she watched him and did small jobs, her mouth open in awe at every bit of technology the robots had inside of them. After a few days, she began to ask questions and then graduated to offering her opinions. Which were usually wrong. But it was still exciting to discuss ideas with Keat. He reminded her of Carrick in that he loved a good discussion about inventing.

Every moment felt sweet but stolen. All of her emotions for Keat came with the small but still-present baggage of guilt attached. Everyone she knew was gone. Carrick was long dead, and though her emotions were poignant, they'd certainly dimmed. Her short time with him felt almost like a dream. He was gone, but she vowed to never let his memory die away.

Some of her favorite moments were in the bathroom, sitting at the vanity and trying out new looks. Keat bought her magazines, and she flipped through the pages, looking at the glossy photos with awe. She experimented.

Sometimes, when she emerged from the shower and looked at herself in the mirror, she barely recognized herself.

Later that week, Keat set up a movie on the large-screen television, grabbed some blankets and settled on the couch with Penrose to watch a movie. It was his new hobby—watching Penrose as she watched movies. Her reactions delighted him. For that night, he'd chosen *The Hobbit*.

When the movie started, he sat back and watched Penrose. She had no filter. She looked at him with absolute awe as she watched the strange creatures, peppering him with questions about how real they looked. Every emotion tore through her. She cried and laughed and screamed in fear. And every reaction entranced him.

He savored rather than distrusted her genuine delight at the world around them. He wanted to run from thing to thing and show them to her. He found new love in old, everyday items, and in visiting old ideas, he discovered new possibilities for his robots. She was like magic to him. He wasn't ever going to let her go. It didn't matter that he'd only known her a few weeks. His heart had longed a lifetime for her.

They drove into town later that week to do some shopping. On the way back home, she begged Keat to take her for a long drive. He indulged her, speeding up and down the roads, taking her deeper and deeper into the mountains. They drove for hours. He played music for her. All different kinds. She surprised him by liking pop music blared at high volume. They passed through a huge meadow covered in snow. Keat pulled the Range Rover to the side of the road and asked her, "Do you want to go play in the snow?"

She gazed out at the wide-open, perfectly untouched sea of white. She grinned wickedly. "Of course, I do," she said, and then, without hesitation, she opened the car door, stepped outside and ran straight into all that white powder.

Her breath came in great, steaming bursts. Cold air

sounded different than the warm summer air of Charleston. Keat yelled to her, but his voice was muted, and she kept on running. She'd been so trapped, so cooped up in the dark tunnel that the blindingly white open space felt like heaven. No. Better than heaven. It felt like life. With Keat at her side, she was fearless. She'd never been happier in her life than at that moment.

Something hit her back, and white powder exploded into a cloud all around her. She did a swift about-face, her hair whipping around. He ran toward her. Quickly, she scooped up a ball of snow and aimed it at Keat, who ran at full speed toward her. Her snowball didn't make it very far. It landed with a soft plop a few feet away from her. He ran faster, a solitary man in a winter wilderness. He took her breath away.

She scooped up another handful of snow and made her last stand. Widening her stance, she patted the ball tight as she'd seen him do and cocked her arm back. He barreled toward her, snow flying, his long legs eating up the ground between them. Her blood whooshed like mad in anticipation, and she focused on timing her snowball just right.

Counting out loud, she tried to pace his run to her throw. "One." Her hands packed the ball again. "Two." She trained her eyes on him. He was right there. "Three!" she shouted, throwing the ball.

Her timing was terrible. He was already in front of her by the time she let go. An explosion of white powder burst in front of her eyes. Before she even understood what happened, a tall, hard body enveloped her and then she was falling, falling.

The ground came up fast, but the snow was soft. His body was hard on top of hers. Warm, too. The snow stole all of the sounds and swallowed the whole world. Their breath was ragged, and he rolled her over so that she lay on top of him.

She leaned down to kiss him, draping her hair around his face. His lips were cold when hers touched his. A grunt of satisfaction rumbled from deep inside him. His hands wound through her hair, pulling her tight against him—and his tongue. That hot tongue slipped into her mouth.

Her whimper went nowhere. His mouth stifled it. Strong hands roamed her body, pressing against her and forcing her as close as possible to him. Grabbing her rump, he thrust her up and down on his very rigid cock.

"Oh," she said when she felt it through her jeans.

"*Oh* is right," he said. "See what you do to me? Winter has nothing on you, Penrose. You heat up any man's blood."

"Do I?" she asked, loving to hear those words from him and craving more.

"Take these pants off," he said. "I need you right now."

"Here?" she asked. "It's so cold." Her nipples were already hard points. Even her nose had numbed.

"I'll keep you warm."

She looked around, but all she could see in every direction was a white canvas. Only his black car stood out.

Only them. His hands began pushing her pants down her body.

"Off," he growled.

She complied, and happily, too. Her feet easily slipped out of the boots, and she stood towering above him, enjoying the view of his body stretched out right in front of her. Proof of his desire was the bulging in his denim pants and the intense look on his face.

He was so handsome. Everything had changed so much in the past week. As she stood before him, a little throb of anticipation pulsed between her legs. She shed her jacket, then her shirt, and quick as lightning she shimmied out of her jeans. She was getting better with wearing jeans.

"Oof," he said. "I've never been so damned cold and so damned hot at the same time. Get over here, Penrose."

She went and lay on top of him. His hands cupped her buttocks again. He urged her higher. "I want to taste you," he whispered. Rising up, she scooted higher, her knees burning in the snow. Her goose bumps tightened. Her stomach fluttered. She hovered with the most intimate part of her body right above his mouth.

A wicked smile teased on his lips. "This I like. No, this I love." He slipped two fingers between her legs and opened her lips. The bitter air swirled around her heat as the fingers of one hand slipped inside her and the other buried itself in the flesh of her backside. He held her firm. He wouldn't let her go. Or even move. His hands forced her down onto his mouth, and he locked her in place.

She cried out. His tongue. His mouth. Right there. She was forced to endure. To give in. To fly.

Her whimpers and moans, dampened by the heavy air, fell to the ground as soon as they left her lips. Dimly, she was aware of the world. A herringbone sky above. Pockets of melting snow dimpling the blanket around them. All bright images against his dark looks.

His lips were soft, pulling, sucking on her clitoris,

gentle and welcoming. But, beneath his lips, his tongue darted insistently, almost cruelly, flicking against her again and again. She bucked. Or tried to, but he held her still. As best she could, she rode him and thrust against him in minute motions.

A deeper need ruled her. She leaned down and twisted her hands around his head, dug her fingers into his hair. His eyes were closed, his mouth on fire. A delicious numbness gathered. Desperately, she tried to stay ahead of it, moving faster and faster until it overtook her, and in a fit of whimpers she went completely still. Then she fell forward, burying her hands in the icy snow, panting for breath as waves of pleasure flooded her.

He held perfectly still with his hands clutching her thighs. His mouth was gentle once more. Every touch of his tongue made her quiver, and he waited until the little waves passed. Only then did he release her.

Hovering over him on all fours, she said simply, "I never knew."

It took a moment for him to speak. He gripped her thighs and moved her lower onto his torso. She saw the glisten of her moisture on his lips as he spoke. "I never knew, either." He pulled his hands away, and she heard the sound of his zipper.

She lifted up so that he could lower his jeans.

"God," he said. "That's cold."

Moving her hips down his body until she was right over his hardness, she settled over him, legs wide, eyes on him, and pressed down.

Oh, that. It was a piercing. A hot and quick surrender and then he was buried. She couldn't move. She needed to stretch to accommodate him. He moaned and threw his arms to the side, clutching fistfuls of snow.

He arched, contorted and hissed, "Dammit, Penrose. You're torturing me."

That was all she needed. She buried him deep in her belly and began circling her hips. She was sated, still numb and throbbing but no longer needy. So she taunted him—pulled back her hair, exposing her body to his gaze.

She rolled her hips around, watching his reaction. He looked driven, almost angry. It made her wild. She bit her lips and rolled again, stretching her breasts higher. Reveling in it.

A blur of motion. Icy hands at her hips. Grinding, demanding, forcing. On and on, bucking her around. He roared, primitive and claiming.

It was his turn to pant, to close his eyes. But not for long. He exploded in a roar. Only a moment later, he said, "I hate to do this—" he lifted her from his still-throbbing hardness "—but my ass is frozen solid."

They crammed into their wet and frigid clothes and laughed all the way back to the Range Rover. Now that their passion was sated, the cold announced itself with a vengeance. She shivered and walked as fast as she could, trying to force the jacket on. He ran, half-naked, and got to the car before her.

Once she reached the car, she was greeted by the sight of him pantless, sitting in the driver's seat, not even bothering to try to dress.

"They're heated seats," he explained with a wry grin on his face.

Chapter 21

After they returned home, they ate dinner and worked on the prototype. Penrose felt his eyes on her more than once. Finally, Keat went upstairs and called down to her from the landing, "Come on up, Penrose!"

"In a minute!" she replied. She had something she wanted to do. She had to look for it, but she finally found the white-out on Keat's table. Taking it upstairs with her, she padded down the hall until she came to the painting of Carrick as a child. With tender, gentle strokes, she painted his hair white and then stood back to look at him. It still wasn't quite right, but it made her feel better. The past mattered. These moments would matter, too.

She went to bed, and they made love by the light of the fireplace. The last thing she remembered before she'd fallen in the snow was the rising wind and heavy snowfall. She watched the flakes spin by the window until her eyes closed.

When she woke later, the fire in the bedroom had gone out, and the room was dark and chilly. Keat still slept beside her, happily hogging the covers.

A restlessness that she couldn't shake kept her awake. It was no use. She couldn't sleep. Carefully, she lifted Keat's arm and slipped away from his embrace. Putting on a robe and slippers, she went to the kitchen. After making herself a cup of tea, she sat at the table, letting the steaming mug warm her hands, and listened to wind circling around the house. The wind blew hard and seemed full of purpose, like a living thing, and it filled her with trepidation.

But it wasn't just the winter wind that scared her—it was the future. She wanted to be with Keat, and that hope warmed her more than the tea did. But everything was so different. *One step at a time*, she reminded herself.

Her dress still lay draped over the chair next to her, where she'd left it earlier in the week. Setting the mug down, she ran her finger along the dress. Everything had changed in the new century. Even her dress had been made new again. She sighed and suddenly wanted Keat next to her, and the reassuring warmth of his body.

She put the mug in the sink, turned off the light in the kitchen and, at the last minute, retrieved her dress from the back of the chair to take upstairs and hang in the closet. With her dress in one arm, she began to climb the stairs. As soon as her foot hit the first riser, a particularly fierce gale buffeted the house. It was a strange wind, a low growl. She stood on the stairs, hesitating, a tight nervousness taking hold.

There came a soft click. The tiniest noise, but one as familiar to her as her own heartbeat. The hair on the back of her neck rose and she slowly, reluctantly, turned around. Lightning flashed, and in the brief, flickering light, she saw a small, white head of hair emerging from the tunnel door.

"C.J.?" she said, hardly believing what she saw. It was him. It was C.J.

His face remained hidden in shadow, and a strange light came from the tunnel behind him. He turned toward her, hesitated for a moment, and then she saw his skinny body scurry back past the little door.

"No!" she shouted. Without hesitation, without so much as a thought, she rushed forward. Wearing a bathrobe, arms laden with her dress, she did what she promised Keat she'd never do. She entered the tunnel, and the darkness swallowed her whole.

Keat rolled over in bed. His hand reached out to find Penrose and grabbed nothing but empty sheets. He bolted upright in bed and looked around. The storm raged outside, and the howls sounded angry and vengeful. He rose from bed, slipped on a pair of jeans and walked down the hall.

"Penrose?" he called.

An eerie white light glowed up from the foyer, and he approached the landing with a deep sense of dread. When he reached the stairs, he saw the tunnel door open, strange light spilling from it and Penrose disappearing through the doorway. In that instant, he knew he loved her and couldn't live without her.

"No!" he roared, and flew down the stairs. "Come back!" he shouted at Penrose. It was too late. She was already gone. Without thinking, Keat landed hard on the floor and leaped forward, sliding into the tunnel to follow Penrose.

Penrose counted as the grandfather clock rang out ten chimes. Soft, reassuring sounds. But to her, hidden as she was in the tunnel, the sounds were anything but reassuring. Time had lost all meaning to her. She held her breath until the last chime died away, leaving only the ticking of the pendulum. The ticking was like a heartbeat, but the rhythm was unfamiliar. She didn't fear the darkness that surrounded her. No, she feared the light that snuck underneath the door, for she knew in her bones there would be a different world out there.

Waiting and hiding weren't options. Better to know than to wonder. She pushed open the door, stuck her head out and whispered urgently, "C.J.?"

There was no reply. She crawled from the tunnel, still holding the gown in her hand. The air hung thick and sweet and warm in the foyer. The sharp, tangy scent of yellow pine lingered and she heard the night calls of crickets.

She was home. *Home* meaning Arundell in Charleston. The scents and the sounds rolled over her, calling her back, though her memories felt distant. They were hard to recall, almost as if they belonged to someone else. Every breath she took felt stolen.

"C.J?" she said. "Carrick?" Saying his name made her nervous.

Yes, she knew she was back at Arundell, but in what time? The answer wasn't obvious. She took a few steps. Everything felt unreal, sights and sounds amplified. Out of habit, she began to walk toward the kitchen and the stairs that led to the workshop. Carrick. It was night. He would be down in the workshop right at that moment, working away. Why did she feel so scared, so unsettled? "Better to know. Better to know," she whispered.

Through the kitchen and down the stairs she slunk along, dress in her arms, and clinging to the shadows. At the foot of the stairs, the workshop came into view. The fireplace blazed with light and heat. But the room felt cold to her. The tables were piled high with odds and ends. Everything was familiar, but she couldn't shake the fear that clung to her insides.

In the middle of the room, standing with a childlike glory, Harris number one gleamed in the firelight. His gas-lamp eyes were dark. His power lay hidden and dormant, but she still warmed at the sight of him, knowing all of the potential inside of him. Not in his clunky body or his fiery eyes, but in the dreams he carried within him. The dreams and the vision of one man, the one man who had started everything. Then she realized she was back to the time before he fell and was destroyed. Knowing this made her feel a little better, but it still left many unanswered questions.

Carrick. There he was, sitting with his back to her, bent over a table, his white hair a wild halo. She brought her hand to her mouth and covered it to prevent her from crying out. Time meant nothing to her heart. Whether it was one beat or a million in the time since she'd last seen him, it didn't matter. She still had a fondness for him.

But it wasn't the same. Not anymore. Not after Keat. Layers of love and life collided in her mind, and she stared numbly as the man she never thought she'd see again as he toiled lovingly, obsessively, over some small component. It was bittersweet, the sight of him. Her feet began to move across the floor in his direction.

Then she stopped herself. Wait. She needed to think. She remembered the calendar that hung on the wall. It read August 18. She hadn't even started employment at the manor yet. In fact, she'd be arriving in the morning. In merely a few hours. And yet, there she stood. What did it mean? She didn't know.

He turned around suddenly. He wore his thick glasses and they made his eyes appear huge as he stared in her direction. The sight of those kaleidoscope eyes and their swirling colors made her want to cry. She was scared, too, unsure of what was happening. And Keat, oh, what about Keat? He'd be all alone, wondering if she'd ever return.

She froze, grateful for his limited eyesight. Some instinct told her she needed more information.

"Hello?" His familiar voice carried right to her heart. "C.J.? Is that you?" He stood up. His long, lean body rose to full height.

Her heart began to pound in her chest. He would think her a stranger. An intruder.

She had to leave, and right away. Turning, she ran up the stairs, careful to keep her footfalls light, her white gown still hanging in her arms. In a panic, she raced through the foyer, out the front door and into the night.

She tore down the gravel path that led away from Arundell Manor. Lightning and thunder crashed overhead and though it hadn't begun to rain, it would soon. There was only one place she wanted to go—to The Winding Stair, to get answers. More than anything, she needed answers. Could she just start afresh and simply circle back to the manor? The only way to know was to start at the very beginning.

The scents of the honeysuckle, gladiolas and jasmine that perfumed the air were as familiar to her as the back of her hand. Though she couldn't predict each gust of wind, the moment it came upon her she recalled it in full detail. Memories came back, far stronger than any déjà vu.

She stopped running and slipped out of her nightgown before hurriedly putting her dress on. It was humid out, and she was sweaty, so it was a struggle to don the gown. She fumbled with the buttons at her back and eventually had to settle for the top three remaining open. Her dress smelled of bleach, sharp in the perfumed summer air. She tossed the nightgown deep into the woods and wished that she'd worn her boots rather than the nighttime slippers. But they'd have to do.

As she walked through the woods, the moon bobbed between the trees, and a strange, persistent wind gusted against her. She leaned into the wind and pressed on, lost in her thoughts. She thought of Keat and Carrick both, and her memories of the men were twisted and tangled, overlapping in her mind.

Keat. It already felt as if he was slipping away from her. The future seemed far-off, a distant thing that she wouldn't see again. The impossible had happened twice. Perhaps it could happen a third time, and she would find Keat once again. She had to believe that.

And Carrick. How it tore her heart to see him, the emotions lost, never to be recovered. Even if she started again, how could she love him when Keat had her whole heart now? It was agonizing, and there was no easy answer.

It was late when she entered Charleston, the moon already halfway across the sky and peeking through the clouds. A haze covered the city, brought on by the rain, which had now lessened. That strange wind still blew, now at her back, curling the misty haze around her. She walked along the cobblestone streets, turning away from the few people who passed her by, unable to meet their gaze for, in a way, they were already dead.

Once you've been to the future, things change. Yes, everything was familiar, exactly as it should be. Yet she felt like a foreigner.

She walked until she reached the street that The Winding Stair Inn stood on. All of the buildings were dark except for one. Golden light from the streetlamps washed over the inn. Perhaps it was the way the light fell upon the glass, but the building seemed to shimmer for a brief moment, almost glimmering, and her eyes fell on a second-floor window. There, like a china doll, a woman with dark hair stood leaning against the window frame, looking up at the moon.

She watched as the woman—her—dropped the want ads. They fluttered to the ground. Oh, my God, she thought, realization dawning on her. She wore a white dress and her hair was now blond. Her gaze fell on the girl again—Penny—for she knew in her heart it was a different version of herself. Just like Harris the robot. Was she the newest model, or the oldest? Fate was cruel.

Chapter 22

Penrose opened the door to the pub. Charlie stood behind the bar, rag in hand. His head dipped in greeting. "Welcome back, dear," he said with a humble smile. "I said you can start again, and you can if you like."

Emerging into the modern-day Arundell had been enough to stretch her mind thin. This outright shattered every belief she ever knew. If she couldn't trust something as basic as her very existence, what could she trust?

She heard the scrape of a mug on wood and turned to see Mrs. Capshaw, her cheeks reddened after working in the kitchens. Penrose knew that because she'd worked beside the woman that very night, all those weeks ago. Weeks ago. No, minutes ago. The world was tilting, and she was sliding off it.

Without looking up from the warm cup of tea in her hand, Mrs. Capshaw said to her, "You're late. I was beginning to get worried." She turned to face Penrose, and there was little kindness in her expression. She had the fierce, calculating look she'd always had. "Time's wasting. Let's get on with it."

Penrose stormed to the table, shaking, and stood towering over the woman. "I'm late? Time's wasting?" Penrose said through clenched teeth, standing above her. She was so angry she could barely see straight. "You knew. The whole time, you knew."

"Of course I did," the woman said matter-of-factly, stirring her tea with a spoon and setting it aside. "I like the new hair color, by the way. I always forget how much blond hair complements your blue eyes until I see it again."

Penrose sank deeper into despair. *Until I see it again...* Her cheeks burned and her fingers tingled as she said, "And again? And again?"

Mrs. Capshaw smiled up at her. "On and on and on."

"What are you saying? What happened to me?" The horrible truth that was revealing itself seemed too big for her mind to swallow.

"What happened to you? That is a small question with a great big answer. Let me just say that my job is plugging leaks. And you, my dear Penny, are a leak."

Penrose took a step back. "I'm not Penny anymore," she said, lifting her chin. "Call me Penrose."

"How appropriate," said Mrs. Capshaw with a strange smile. "Because Penny is upstairs as we speak. But you're still a leak, whether you're Penny or Penrose. Think on it. A midnight baby. Born on such an auspicious day. A foot in two worlds. Cursed. And I of all people should know, for my story is similar. It's not your fault, dear. Fate hands out life sentences blindly. There's nothing you could have done."

Penrose sank into the chair beside her old landlady. If Mrs. Capshaw had dropped a boulder onto Penrose's head, she'd have been less surprised. It seemed too awful to consider. She put her head on her arms.

"Come now, Mrs. Capshaw. Must you be so cruel?" said Charlie from behind the bar. "What an awful way to break the news. Haven't we talked about this?"

"What does it matter, Charlie? It never changes. Never." She seemed so awfully practical about the whole thing.

"She and I—the same person—will be here, in the same room, at the same time?" Penrose asked in a weak voice. "When I...when I stole her position—"

Mrs. Capshaw put a hand on her shoulder, and Penrose lifted her head from the table, sitting up and violently shrugging the arm away. Mrs. Capshaw seemed unfazed. "You stole nothing. You gave a future to yourself. You gave a chance to yourself. You gave love. Hate me if you want, but I'm not the cause of it. I merely keep things in order. I'm a gatekeeper. There are plenty of us around. We tend to very few, but our job is of utmost importance."

Penrose felt the ground move underneath her, far stronger than any earthquake. "How...how can that be?"

"It just is. To question it is to court madness. I should know. I did that once."

"What if I choose not to go through with it?" The question came out limp and weak as it left her lips.

Mrs. Capshaw laughed. "That's the last thing I worry about. Every single person in your shoes does exactly what they should. You simply won't be able to stop yourself. It will be a compulsion inside of you. It's after this moment I worry most about. That's when it gets dangerous." Her dark eyes swept up and down the length of Penrose's body. "Don't you feel it right at this moment? Pulling on you? Can you deny the girl upstairs? Yourself? All that, painful as it was—can you deny her the same chance you had? The same love?"

"I can't," she said. She shook her head. "I can't deny her." The pull inside her was so strong. She detested it fiercely but was powerless to fight it. Love, real love, deep and parental, thrummed inside her for the girl upstairs. Lost and alone. Unloved by all, except her. Being unloved was a crime above all things. Worse than being forgotten.

"Well, then, shall we get started?"

Without even thinking or trying, Penrose sat more proudly in the chair, smoothed down her cheeks and rubbed her tears away. Penny must see her looking her best.

Mrs. Capshaw stood up, her beady eyes resting on Penrose a moment too long. "Look," she said. "You're already falling right in line. I have good news for you. All is not lost. You want to return to where you came from, I assume?"

Her gaze shot up and hope burned in her eyes. "I do. Keat. I need Keat. And more. I want to somehow save everyone from the earthquake and get back to him—"

Mrs. Capshaw held up her hand. "The man you love— you might, just might, be able to return to. The other— that is something you cannot do," she said. "You can only save yourself. It's your only hope. If you fail, you are doomed."

"How am I doomed?" asked Penrose, wondering if things could ever get any worse.

"Take a good long look at me," Mrs. Capshaw said, rising to full height. "Take heed of my loveless eyes. I was once in your shoes, and I failed in my quest to return. I wanted so badly to save others, but instead I ruined everything. When it was over, I had two choices available to me." A look of anguish flashed across her face. "I chose the less courageous path. I should have chosen the braver but final path. Now I am trapped here forever. A gatekeeper for the lost. If you'd arrived in a more timely fashion, I could've told you my own tale of endless woe. I'll just say this. Listen to me well, Penrose Heatherton, and do exactly as I say. Everything depends on it."

"I made the wrong choice when you first approached me. I should've refused." It was a sad, soft confession. "My greed condemned me. It has made me suffer."

"Everyone suffers, Penrose. Everyone makes choices— bad or good, they're just choices. A path taken. A coin spent. You were no different, you committed no crime. You didn't ask to be put in this position. It's just that your choices stretched across centuries. They always will."

"At least tell me I can get back," asked Penrose. "I need to get back."

"You can. Possibly. Though, after a few days, you might not want to. Hearts change."

"No, they don't," Penrose replied hotly.

"Didn't your heart change when you slipped away from us?"

There was nothing to say in answer to that, for it was true. All she could think of was Keat, the man she had left behind. Or in the future, depending on how she looked at it. Either way, he was no longer with her. "Keat needs me," she whispered. "And I need him."

"Right now, I need you. But she—" Mrs. Capshaw jabbed her fingers in the direction of the upstairs bedroom "—needs you most of all. Do not fail me. Make her want what you have. And she will, oh, she will. For the compulsion that's sweeping over you right now, the compulsion to help her, the same will rush over her. She'll not be able to resist. Once she's on her way, I'll explain how you can get home and get back to Keat. So, let's get started." Mrs. Capshaw stood up. "Time's wasting. Always wasting. We have to hurry and do something about that hair," she said. "Oh. You've no bonnet. I always forget that."

"I never do," said Charlie, and he tossed a blue bonnet toward her. It landed perfectly on the table, in exactly the same position she first remembered seeing it as she descended the stairs.

"Now," said Mrs. Capshaw. "Here's what you'll do." Her gaze held Penrose's and seemed to be admonishing her, warning her to follow orders exactly. "When Penny comes in, you must play your part perfectly. You have one chance to close this loop. One chance to seal the hole, and everything you do from here on out impacts that. When Penny comes in you must not turn around, and you must never look at her. Keep your chin up and look happy. I'll do the rest. When I walk upstairs to speak with her, you are to speak to Charlie. Don't worry. You'll remember your words. Under no conditions are you to get any clever ideas. I'll take care of everything."

"You'll take care of everything," repeated Penrose numbly. "You always were an enterprising woman, weren't you?"

"You'd have to be, in my position. Try to understand. That's all I ask." She went to the stairs and began climbing them, looking back at Penrose one last time.

"Don't worry, dear. She always has to scare the person. It works best that way. The good news is that it works."

"Always? It always works?"

"Well…" he said, his voice fading away to nothing.

"Charlie," she whispered. "I have to know. Why did you warn me against Carrick?"

"Ah, I had to try. I think of you as my own child and I keep trying to protect you from a broken heart. It never works, though."

She heard a noise upstairs. Hushed voices from the top of the landing.

At that moment, everything changed. As soon as she heard Penny's soft voice whispering, unsure and afraid, her entire being focused on the sound. Penny. No longer Penrose. Still, they were entwined. The same. Again, that strong rush of love and protective instincts surged through her.

She started to recall the words from that fateful night, and then she began to speak them. Repeating perfectly word for word. Charlie nodded, encouraging her and replying exactly as he should. She played her role. Back straight. Look proud and happy. It was like déjà vu but a thousand times stronger. She walked a razor's edge. She had to play it perfectly.

She felt Penny's presence on the stairs, the lingering, hotly jealous gaze on her back. *Don't worry,* she willed the woman to understand, *it will all work out. Maybe. Hopefully.*

She felt the cold hand of fate slide up her spine as

Penny swept past her, and she suddenly knew what it must be like to have someone walk upon your grave. She collapsed, head down on the table, as soon as Penny stepped outside. Charlie patted her on the shoulder as he walked by. "There, there, dear. You did just right. Breathe easy." The door shut behind him and she was alone. She put her head down and sobbed openly.

The grief and uneasiness was a feeling she couldn't shake, no matter how she tried. The colors of the world were off now that she knew the truth. Everything seemed dangerous. Even something as simple as opening the door was fraught with peril. One misstep, a slipped boot, and down she'd go, and the future would be in jeopardy.

She couldn't explain that feeling, the sense that she needed to be cautious. It was just there, part of her, like the need to be careful when crossing a busy street or handling a hot pan. The fear was folded into her soul, yet she still had to function.

The door creaked as Mrs. Capshaw returned to the pub. "Oh, child," she said in a weary, ancient-sounding voice. "Come with me up the stairs and sleep. I'll explain the plan along the way. Trust me. You'll feel better in the morning."

Penrose put up no fight. She followed her landlady up the stairs, listening to the plan. She was to return to the house on the night of the earthquake and no matter what, she was to prevent Penny from entering the tunnel. She alone must enter it. When she reached her old room, she collapsed on the cot. After Mrs. Capshaw had left, she stared out at the moon. One moon. Two

Penroses. She closed her eyes and waited for the nothingness to sweep her away.

But the nothingness never came. She slept fitfully, plagued by dreams of Carrick and Keat. When she rolled out of bed in the morning, the realization that right at that moment Penny was now arriving at Arundell hit her hard. All of the emotions were knotted inside her. Remembering Keat, she held on to the conviction that it was possible to return to him.

Afterward, she dressed and went down the winding staircase to the rear of the shop where the kitchen was and found Mrs. Capshaw. She felt like a traitor because there was something she had to do.

She had to go back to Arundell. Just one more time. To see Penny. To make sure she was okay. The need burned inside of her. Mrs. Capshaw seemed to sense it and had kept a ready eye on her all day, but Penrose was careful and concealed her intentions as best she could.

The opportunity came at a strange moment. Late that afternoon, a woman came striding into the pub, creating a ruckus as she tried to rent a room. Luckily, Charlie wasn't around. And when a grumbling Mrs. Capshaw escorted the woman upstairs, Penrose slipped from the pub.

Chapter 23

It was twilight as Penrose approached Arundell Manor. A raven cried out a coarse cackle from somewhere in the forest. She shuddered. It seemed a bad omen. When she first came to Arundell, the road had taken her closer to her future. Now, it took her closer to her past.

Emerging from the tree-lined path, she looked at the house. The sight of Arundell, its smooth marble glowing under the moon, a mansion of forty-one rooms and hidden passages crammed with secrets made her heart seize with gratitude. For when she fell into the gray area of destiny and everything had turned slippery and uncertain, it was the manor upon which she depended most.

A few windows glowed orange with light, and she thought of Carrick, C.J. and Penny inside the home. Suddenly, she couldn't move fast enough. Lifting her skirt, she ran. Carrick and Penny would be downstairs in the workroom. Penrose knew she was in danger-ous territory, but she couldn't help it. She had to see them. Taking a wide path, she hugged the trees until she reached the gardens behind the house.

Penrose crept closer to the workshop until she saw inside clearly. The room blazed with light. The mechani-cal man stood imposingly, the center of attention in the room. Even from afar he looked magical.

Suddenly, the tall, lean figure of a man crossed in front of the window. Carrick. He was so handsome, his looks so arresting. She heard his impassioned, driven voice as he spoke to Penny. It moved her to listen to him talk about the mechanical man and hear his zeal and his intelligence. It bound him to her heart and memories, but he belonged to Penny now.

Penny sat at her desk, scribbling furiously in the journals. Carrick paced beside her. With the tiniest tick of her head, she looked up. A stolen glance of longing at the man she was just beginning to have feelings for.

Penrose ached to see them from a closer vantage point. The workshop was bright and hopeful and both of them full of ideas, right on the cusp of discovering each other. The realization hurt. Keat was lost to her forever. But Carrick was fresh and new to Penny. Even if they had a brief amount of time together, Carrick and Penny deserved every moment of happiness they could grab. She crept closer until she was just outside the door. Suddenly, she remembered that night. The blonde woman at the door. How had she forgotten?

She had to get away. Turning to run, she tripped and fell to the ground loudly. Immediately, she realized her error. Events began to unfold exactly as she remembered them; it was as if she played a part in one of Keat's movies. A part that she was powerless to step out of.

She said to herself, "Now the door will open, and I'll see Carrick." A moment later it did. He stood there, the light streaming from behind him. She froze, half-bent over the bell, her blond hair covering her face. Petrified to look up yet unable to stop herself, her gaze rose and their eyes met. Time ceased to matter.

Her emotions came roaring back—the hope, the intense longing for him, even the simple joy of being beside him. The feelings swarmed her and, standing right there, her heart broke into two pieces. One piece would always be at the Arundell Manor she knew and loved. The other piece would forever be with Keat, and nothing in the world could be done about it. It was a pain she would live with forever.

Penny stepped into the doorway just then. Her face ashen, her eyes wide as saucers, she looked like a child. Her fear was palpable as she stared at Penrose.

And Penrose hated to see her so afraid. She wanted to comfort Penny, to tell her it would be okay, even if it wasn't exactly the truth. The need to reassure Penny was so strong that Penrose couldn't fight it. Lifting her hand, she was about to speak when she remembered Mrs. Capshaw's stern warning. She walked a razor's edge. So, Penrose stepped back into the darkness and fled, knowing that Carrick would chase her.

Racing as fast as she could, she didn't dare look behind her. The trees flew by as she ran, and the ground blurred beneath her feet. It had been a mistake to come, and now she was afraid.

Perhaps Carrick wouldn't catch her. It was a foolish

wish. She already knew the end result, just not what happened between them.

She came around to the front of the house but before she reached the road, someone came from behind and tackled her. Down she went, hard and fast. A boot was lowered onto her spine and it held her against the ground. She twisted around and saw Carrick looming above her with the moon beside him, illuminating his harsh expression.

"Who are you?" he asked in a voice edged with anger as he looked at her. He peered closer. "And why are you familiar to me?"

She could barely breathe. "I'm... I'm," she began to say, but there was no way to explain who she was. "I'm no one," she finally said, giving up and letting her head drop to the ground again. "No one you know, Carrick."

"Then how do you know my name?"

"Does it matter?"

"Seeing as how you're under my boot, it matters very much."

The last thing she ever thought she'd feel with Carrick again was fear. But as his boot held her to the ground fear sizzled inside of her.

"Spit it out," he said. "How do you know her? Why did you wave at her?" He bent over her, leaned so close that their noses almost touched and said, "How do you know my name?"

Her hands clawed the air as she struggled to rise. "Let me up," she huffed. "Let me up and I'll explain."

There was a hand at her back, and, with a rustle of skirts she was standing. Disoriented, she smoothed her hair. The strange sensation of dreaming swept over. Everything seemed unreal. Vivid, but not real.

He stood a few feet away from her, scowling, his hands clenched at his sides. "You have three seconds to start talking," he said, taking one menacing step forward. His voice was familiar and yet threatening.

But even more familiar was the odd compulsion to move events along. She risked everything in these moments. Everything. The words found her, not the other way around. It was easy. She began to speak. "Penny stole something from me! She stole my job. My future. You!" she said, and paused.

"What the hell are you talking about?" he asked.

She took a deep breath. "Carrick, you once told me that we have only the briefest chance at happiness."

"I once told you? I just met you. Are you mad?"

How tired of that question she'd become. A bitter laugh escaped her. "It would be easier if I were mad. I'll just say it plainly. I'm caught in a time loop. I am her. Lost to time now. I am Penny."

"No, you are not. You are insane."

"You're just like someone else I know with that accusation. Set that thought aside and just listen." Her voice turned strong and certain. She began to talk, her words coming fast. "I know the painting where your mother had you colored in brown hair with a smile on your face, and I know the configuration of all the gears in your mechanical man. I know all of these things."

He crossed the space between her instantly and grabbed her arms hard. "I'll say it again. What the hell is going on?"

She cried out at his touch and spun away. "No, no, no," she said quickly. "Don't come any closer… I'm warning you. I walk a razor's edge." His grip made her uneasy. This was so very dangerous. She was a fool to have come. One wrong word...

He laughed. "Even you, crazy as you are, won't let me touch you."

"Wrong!" she said. "From the moment I saw you I thought you were beautiful. You have a wild, otherworldly look. And I am her! Penny feels those things for you." He must know that. If only one good thing would come of this disaster, let it be that their love could bloom and Penny could stay with him.

"This is insanity. Utter insanity. Then why don't you just tell me the future?"

"No. I cannot do that," she whispered, remembering the admonition to save herself and no one else. But couldn't she save the budding love and attraction between Penny and Carrick? It was worth a chance. "Already, I've told you too much. I can only say she wants you and desires you."

"My God." He was shaking his head, his brows drawn together. "You suffer from lunacy."

"Just hear me out. Then I'll leave."

"Speak then."

"I cannot say much. Only this. I'm left..." She wrung her hands together. "I'm a scavenger, left to follow along in destiny's shadow, seeking whatever shelter I can. And you want to talk to me about your misfortune. How the whole world hates you. Well, at least you have a world."

Everything came together inside of her. Fear and rage and more fear. "And besides," she said, hating that her emotions turned her voice shrill, but she couldn't stop it. "You have happiness waiting inside for you right now. Penny sits there thinking only of you."

He snorted. "Her? She wants nothing to do with me."

Her white-blond hair flew around her face as she shook her head. "You are blinder than I ever knew! She longs for you and thinks about you constantly." Her eyes met his, and with her soul she implored him. "If you trust only one thing I tell you, trust this—you may have only one little sliver to be with her. The briefest heaven. Carrick, grab it. Grab your happiness, your piece of heaven, while you can. Believe me. Your world could come apart at any moment. Nothing matters except those brief moments of love and happiness."

"Happiness. Love. What big words. Words I don't know the meaning of. Never did. And she is you? You are the same?"

"Yes!" She was wild, her hair blowing about her face. "I cared for you. I desired you. And now I'm lost to you. There's no hope for me here. I know my words sound foolish, but you of all people understand that unexplainable things can and do happen. At least do this—feel her lips on yours and then make your decision."

"If you desired me once and she desires me now, then prove it. Kiss me." He sneered at her, and she saw the pain, the challenge in his twisted features. "Prove your words. Because I know you won't even touch me. And she never will. Ever."

It all came down to this. She grabbed his hands, pressed them against her waist. "I can still remember the feel of your hands on my body. You were my lover. For a short time. But there's hope. You can have her forever if you listen to me. So listen."

"Speak." His voice had shifted.

"You may not believe that I traveled through time, and you don't have to. You only have to know that Penny wants you." She reached out and gripped his forearms. "So, yes, I will prove it to you."

A sneer pulled his lip tight. "Go ahead," he spit out.

"Gladly," she said, leaning up, her lips touching his. With that one kiss, she hoped to save all of their futures.

He stood still, not moving at all. But he did not pull away or stop her. She deepened the kiss, remembering the sweet times she'd had with him.

Suddenly, he boomed a response, smashed his hands through her hair, clutched her and drew her in with raw need.

She kissed him with a lifetime of anguish. Pouring into him everything she still yearned for with Keat but would never have again. He was gone to her. She could scream in anger of it. But she had Carrick. If only for a moment, she could remember, take shelter in it.

He overwhelmed her, yanking her tight against him.

She knew him at that moment. The real him. Emotion unchecked by fear. By rejection. She knew him to his soul for a quick instant. But she remembered, and it was a gift. A goodbye present. Because it didn't belong to her anymore. It belonged to Penny.

It all became so clear. One brief nirvana. It was all she had left with him, and she melted into him. Longing, pain, love, heartbreak all flooded her, and she spoke to him of these things with her lips. He responded in kind, passionate and wild. And then she shuddered, a heaving sigh that came from somewhere deep inside of her.

She pulled away, the hardest thing she'd ever done. "That. Look for that."

"What?" he asked in a husky voice.

"Look for that shudder, that response to you, and you'll know she wants you. Badly, too."

"I have to go," she said, pulling away from him. "Time is wasting." She was aware that this might be the last time they ever touched, the last time she felt his warm skin on hers. She backed away.

"Forgive me," she said. Was she speaking to him? Or to Keat? She didn't know.

"Wait!" he called out as she ran away.

She stopped running, reluctant to turn around. She looked up at the black velvet sky and the silvery moon. That was how they used to be. Penrose black as night, Carrick bright as the moon. Now they were two pale stars locked into distant positions, destined never to meet again. Without turning around, she said, "Please, Carrick, heed my words." Then she turned and ran away.

"Wait!" he called out after her.

But she couldn't look back. She moved through the thick air, pulling on the branches as she passed by, needing the feel of things to reassure her that everything was real. With her white hair and gown and her quick gait, she resembled a ghost slipping along the gravel path.

It was a long walk back to The Winding Stair. It seemed as though she walked beneath the rustling trees forever. Finally, she emerged from the forest and Charleston lay just ahead. Now that she wasn't beneath the canopy anymore, the milky-blue moonlight blinded her, and when her eyes adjusted, she saw a man sitting right in front of her on the side of the road. He sat defeated, head in hands, like a king reflecting after a great loss on the battlefield. Even seated, she recognized his body posture, tall, with straight shoulders. The familiar Arundell frame.

"Carrick?" she whispered, unable to believe that he had somehow moved so quickly that he could be ahead of her on the path.

"Keat," he replied raggedly. And then she noticed what her moon-blinded eyes had missed—his hair was jet-black. Just like that, her legs gave out.

Keat shot up to catch her, reaching her just in time. His arms encircled her, grasping her around the back and scooping her up. He folded her into his arms and embraced her. "Penrose," he said, breathing her in, winding his hands farther around her torso and grasping her even closer, as if he were afraid to let go.

It was impossible. But those arms felt like bands of truth supporting her. It was him. "Keat," she said in a breathless voice. "How did you—"

"The tunnel," he whispered, his head buried in her hair. "I followed you."

"What if something had happened? What if I lost you forever or you died?"

"I'd rather die than not know where you were. Than to be without you, Penrose." His grip tightened around her so hard that she gasped. "Penrose," he said. "I'm sorry that I never believed you." His voice was thick with regret. "You were right all along."

"I forgive you." Her words were given simply, freely.

"God, you were right. Until I experienced it, I couldn't fathom it. And look at me now. I have my whole life in order, but I'm helpless as a babe here. I've been wandering, trying to make sense of it all. I may have gone back in time, but I don't even know how to get from one place to another. Life is no simpler."

She knew exactly what he meant. "Oh, Keat, I'm in this century trying my hardest to return to you," she said. "Because I couldn't bear it, either. And now, you're here." She laughed, almost giddy, looking up at him and raining small, happy kisses on his cheeks.

His lips found hers and demanded more. Finally, he broke away and said, "When I came out of the tunnel, a little boy with pale hair chased me from the house, yelling and screaming at me."

"That was C.J.!" she exclaimed.

"I know. He shouted the most awful things at me. I ran like hell, Penrose." He sighed. "There's something I never told you. When I was a boy, I saw him—C.J.—he came to my room in the middle of the night. I thought he was a ghost. But he wasn't…he wasn't."

"I saw him in your house, too. I followed him into the tunnel. Do you know what that means?" she said in a rising voice. "It means that he can travel back and forth, and if he can, we can! It means we can, as well." She hugged him. "We can go back," she said, gripping him even tighter. Even though she was filled with hope, it was a long time until she felt whole again. Pulling away from him, she said, "Come on," and tugged at him. "Let's go. Mrs. Capshaw will be so glad to meet you! Let's go to The Winding Stair."

Penrose was dead wrong. Mrs. Capshaw was not glad in the slightest to meet Keat. "Penrose Heatherton, what have you done?" she hissed as she stood in her doorway eyeing Keat up and down. Curling away from him, she looked in his direction as if he were cursed.

"He followed me to our time," she replied. "I didn't bring him here."

Mrs. Capshaw sighed, a sound dangerously close to a growl. "The potential for a disaster just became a likelihood." Shaking her head, she took two steps back, allowing them to enter the pub. "Take him upstairs. Don't let him out and, whatever you do, keep him in your sights at all times."

The seriousness of her demeanor surprised Penrose. Keat took a step. "I think I can help," he offered.

"Help?" croaked Mrs. Capshaw. Holding up her hand, she pinched her fingers together. "You're this close to disaster, and the scales might have just tipped in the wrong direction. Everything is at risk right now. Every single thing. You risk the future merely by talking to me. You must hide, and only at the last moment can you come out."

She swung around, her heavy skirts swirling in the air. "Take him upstairs. Right now. And, for God's sakes, Penrose, keep him there."

Control had always been something Keat took for granted. He had an excess of it. But now he had none, and it scared him. From the second the tunnel swallowed him up, he'd been careening, unsure of everything. It was a nightmarish feeling, but it opened his eyes to the suffering Penrose went through.

He considered himself a man of science, but he had to set all of that aside to believe what he was seeing. He had to focus on feeling instead of thinking. It was a tough transition for him to make, but there was no other option.

If Penrose hadn't found him when she did, he would've been a doomed man. Though, he supposed, he would return to Arundell and lurk around the edges, needing to be near the one thing that was familiar. Just as Penrose had done. When she'd told him she would never leave the manor, he thought that remark strange, but now he knew what she meant.

Penrose explained the plans for returning and, for a man who was used to being in control, he felt very dependent on a thousand different variables, none of which he had any control over. It was the most vulnerable he'd ever felt in his entire life.

They slept and made love for days. If one good thing could be pulled from the experience, Keat reasoned, it was that their last days of certainty were filled with passion and love. After that, they would enter that door, and it was up to fate.

Chapter 24

Just like that, two weeks slid by, and on the day of the earthquake, Penrose woke at dawn with an unsettled feeling. She tossed and turned, unable to fall back asleep. Keat lay beside her all tangled in the sheets, sleeping like a baby. She sat up and ran her hands through her blond hair. A thousand small problems could pop up and prevent them from even getting to Arundell Manor. And, worse, once they arrived at the manor and the earthquake hit, anything could happen.

The variables swirled in her head, all the possibilities waiting to happen or—worse—go wrong. But the big unknown, the very scariest part of all, was the little door to the tunnel. What would greet them on the other side of the door?

She nudged him and he opened his eyes. "Keat," she said, "what if—"

"Stop." He said in a sleepy voice, cutting her off. "Don't torture yourself again. We've gone over this for days. Fate doesn't like to be second-guessed. Penrose, you need to have faith."

She laughed harshly. "Faith is not something to have. It's something to get rid of."

"Come here," he said, and pulled her down into the covers. "Do you think fate would bring us together from one hundred thirty years of distance—not once but twice—just to turn its back on you?" He ran a hand through his tousled hair. "No. No. Scratch that. Don't think. Feel. And if you can't feel it, just look at me. I have no worries. I'm with the woman I love. I fear nothing. Whatever fate hands us, she hands it to both of us, and we face it together."

His hand trailed along her spine, bumping along the little ridges of her backbone. "Come here and let me show you what faith is, how to let things progress without worrying about the outcome." His smile was lazy and wicked, as he drew her close to him. "Endings will happen naturally. Just follow along."

And he was right.

At four o'clock that evening, Penrose waited for Keat at the door of The Winding Stair. Mrs. Capshaw stood beside her, her jeweled hands interlinked with Penrose's.

"Take care, my dear," she said. "And I hope I don't see you again. And you know I mean that with the utmost sincerity."

"I know," replied Penrose, hugging her.

Keat and Mrs. Capshaw shook hands. "Be careful," she said.

"Always. And thank you," he said.

The sun still shone, though softly, when they began

their walk to Arundell. Gold fingerlings of light stretched between the trees and fell on the ground in bright circles. They walked along the dappled road, holding hands. Keat showed no nervousness; he was easy and free with his gait.

She thought of their home, the Arundell of the future. "Do you think we'll make it back to our home?" she asked.

"I'm hopeful we'll make it somewhere," he said. "But I'm certain that wherever we end up, we'll be together because I won't let go of your hand. And that's a promise."

They reached Arundell and passed through the gates as the moon began to rise in the sky. The tree-lined road stretched in front of them, and they strolled slowly under the canopy until the manor came into view.

Keat stopped walking. "What a sight to see."

And it *was* a sight to see. The white stone of Arundell glistened like a pearl. "It takes my breath away. In a way, I hate to leave it."

"I can certainly understand."

They went and stood behind the ancient oak tree that kept watch by the pond. It was fully dark by then, and they were well hidden in the shadows. "Now we wait," she said, and try as she might, she still couldn't quiet the grim apprehension she felt. But there were hints that something was amiss.

She noticed unusual happenings that she hadn't before. Small things like the curious absence of mosquitoes, and large things like the pungent smell of the marsh grass, stronger than she'd ever smelled before. She felt the earth readying itself, hunkering down before it let loose. The colors of the night were even richer.

The moon had never been so silver, the sky so black. The breeze slipped over her skin as if it were memorizing her. These things comforted her.

She said to Keat, remembering the first earthquake, "There will be a large sound, like an out-of-control train."

"I'm ready for it."

There came a tugging on her skirt and she turned to see C.J. standing beside her. "C.J.!" she exclaimed, gathering the boy in her arms. He went willingly and returned the hug fiercely. Then she remembered. He shouldn't know her. But it seemed as if he did. She thought of Mrs. Capshaw's warning. *The razor's edge.* She pulled away and stood up. "I can't hug you. I'm sorry."

"Penny," said C.J. He looked up at her, his expression grave. "It's all right. I know everything. I know about the two houses. You know the other Arundell? The scary one."

She wasn't surprised. She'd seen him, after all. So had Keat. She said, "I know the scary Arundell. Only it's not so scary once you get to know it." She ruffled his hair. For the first time, he seemed like a child, afraid and innocent, and not the angry boy with the genius intelligence she'd first met. "But I'm curious, how do you know?"

"I've known...forever." He gave her a wan smile. "At least it seems like forever. My life before. This is going to sound mighty wild to you—"

"Trust me. It won't." Keat came and stood beside her, watching the boy intently.

"Well, you see, I was born in 1850."

"It's 1886," she said gently, a strange foreboding coming over her.

A touch of the old C.J. slipped out. "I know. Of course I know!" He looked away with a pained expression. "I live with my parents. I have two brothers. The war hasn't started yet. I race to the walls and hide in them when anyone comes over."

"Oh, my God," she said. "You're Carrick, just like I'm Penny?"

He nodded fiercely. "I knew you were just like me!" he said. "When it first happened—there was a blue light, you see—"

"Of course," she said, nodding.

"And I ran toward it. It was so pretty, but when I went into the hole, I ended up here. And I hated it. It was so scary. I hated him." He wiped his eyes with the back of his hand. "I hid. I watched him. I listened. And one day when he caught me out of the tunnel, I made up a story that I knew he couldn't argue with. I kept trying to go back to my own time. Even that would have been better. Less scary, you know?"

She nodded.

"But every time I saw the blue light and went in the tunnel, it took me to the scary place. But I had to keep trying. I had to."

"It's all right now," she said, hugging C.J., the razor's edge be damned. She knew firsthand how frightening it was, and she was an adult—far better equipped to cope than a child.

"But I don't hate him so much anymore," he whispered in her ear. He pulled back and looked at her. "Because when you came everything changed. He changed. Life got so much better. I wasn't near as scared as before. I want Penny to stay," he said. "But I know what's going to happen. I remember the first earthquake. It was so strange that night, wasn't it?"

"It was."

"And when I saw the blue light, I had to take my chance. And you followed me. But when I came out of the tunnel it was different again. Not like before."

"How?" She was almost afraid to ask, but she had to know.

"It was like time went backward in the same place. That never happened. I always switched houses. It always sent me to the other house. And when I crawled out of the tunnel, you were walking up the path. On your first day of work. I watched you from the window." He made a hitched sound, and his lips curled down as he began to cry. "And I don't want her to go in the tunnel. I don't want Penny to disappear. I saw in the scary house, and you looked so familiar. But your hair was weird. I don't like it like that. All white," he said with an apologetic glance. "Then I saw him—" he jerked his head toward Keat, his voice wavering "—coming out of the tunnel. And now you're here. I knew something was brewing, so I took a chance and talked to you. But I'm scared."

"Don't be scared," she said, realizing that she had more faith than she thought she did. "And don't worry. We're going to do our best to make sure Penny stays with you. You see, I love her, too, and I want her to stay with Carrick. Forever."

His whole face lit up. "Really?"

"Really. But I need your help. When the earthquake comes, I need you to stay far, far away from the tunnel door. Can you do that for me?"

He nodded. Almost as if fate were listening, a far-off rumble began. Low and constant, the sound built upon itself as it drew closer. "Here we go," she said. The noise of the rattling earth muffled her words, but C.J. nodded. He understood.

Keat stepped up and held out a hand. Penrose saw unshed tears filling his eyes. "Young man," he said when the boy took his hand, "it's an honor to meet you."

C.J. looked up at him with a mixture of awe and confusion right as the ground beneath their feet trembled slightly and then stilled. The earth went completely silent. Not a cricket to be heard.

Their eyes met, each of them looking for reassurance. And then the earth let loose. A rumble coursed through the ground and it sank away from beneath them. They tumbled and fell. Keat shot up and pulled C.J. and then Penrose to standing, and they began to stagger toward the house.

The next minute—for it was no more than a minute—stretched out longer than a lifetime. The ground undulated like rippling water. Crunching, gnawing noises filled the air, and a smell, dank and loamy, like rotting secrets, swirled around them.

Penrose trained her eyes on the front door, fighting with all her might as the ground shifted in each direction. The front door broke free of its hinges and swung open, revealing the bright light of the crystal chandelier. The lights became a beacon, calling her forward, and she followed Keat, who was struggling to help C.J. up the front stairs.

She reached the landing. There was only a brief second to exchange glances before Keat reached out and clamped down on her hand, hard as steel, dragging her into the house. C.J. raced ahead, and she felt a swift rush of relief when he ran toward Penny at the end of the hall.

Penny. She looked confused standing there, not knowing that at that moment her future was being tacked down and made certain. She could stay with Carrick and help him become whole. She could keep falling in love with him. Penrose lifted her free hand, the quickest wave, before turning to the tunnel.

The door slapped open and shut and the blue light flashed onto the floor. "Are you ready?" asked Keat.

She nodded, realizing that she didn't have to grab her future. She could let it guide her because just then her future stood beside her, his hand firmly holding hers as he pulled her closer to the door.

Keat reached the door, sliding on his knees and expertly holding it open as he pushed Penrose through the opening. He never let go of her hand, and as the door shut behind them, she smiled, unafraid. Wherever fate led them, they would arrive together.

* * * * *

MILLS & BOON®

nocturne™

AN EXHILARATING UNDERWORLD OF DARK DESIRES

A sneak peek at next month's titles...

In stores from 14th January 2016:

- **Night Quest** – Krinard, Susan
- **Enchanted Warrior** – Sharon Ashwood

Just can't wait?
Buy our books online a month before they hit the shops!
visit www.millsandboon.co.uk

These books are also available in eBook format!

MILLS & BOON®

Man of the Year

Our winning cover star will be revealed next month!

**Don't miss out on your copy
– order from millsandboon.co.uk**

Read more about Man of the Year 2016 at

www.millsandboon.co.uk/moty2016

**Have you been following our
Man of the Year 2016 campaign?**
🐦 **#MOTY2016**